SHADOWS WITHIN

THE SHADOWLESS: BOOK ONE

Copyright ©2017 by J.P. Cane

Interior design by Pamela Morrell

ISBN: 978-0-9991598-0-4 (Hardcover Edition)
ISBN: 978-0-9991598-1-1 (Paperback Edition)
ISBN: 978-0-9991598-2-8 (e-Book Edition)

AUTHOR
PARTNERS

Dedication

For Sweet
You are my sunshine.

Prelude: Straw by Straw

A field of scarecrows. A murder of crows.

In the field where he hangs like a sacrifice to the birds, Reed's gaze drags over the desolation before him. Pinned to the abandoned crosses, tatters of cloth flap in the breeze. Remnants, perhaps, of those who escaped or were carried away on the shrill wind. Elsewhere in the lifeless field, hay-filled burlap figures remain fixed to skeletal posts.

In his straw-stuffed body, where chaff may have woven itself into something heart-shaped, pangs of loss and guilt dwell. Wasting away here, listening to the scratching of wind through thistles of his chest, he submits. This is what he deserves: to be gutted by grief and reduced to a mere shell of a man because he didn't do enough to save the woman he loves.

He pictures her smiling face only to see it marred by screams. He writhes on his cross, recounting those last moments when the monsters seized her out of his life.

Caw!

Startled, Reed feels a weight upon his head, talons prickling through the brimmed hat stitched to his scalp. The crow utters another low cry as its weight shifts, then ultimately flaps off for a more stable perch. Frigid air cuts through the flannel clothing, blown by the flapping wings. Several black feathers catch on his shirt.

The crow peers at Reed with an avian jitter. Claws scratch at the cross-beam as it sidles closer and inspects Reed's shoulder. Sensing something sinister in those ebony wings, Reed shrugs his shoulders to nudge the bird away. It hops aside only to return, flapping those shadowy wings that stir up soul-chilling air.

More squawking crows gather on the limbs of the empty frames ahead of him. Each one gazes at him with something more than curiosity. Their heads turn left and turn right, their deep, black eyes blinking and fixing on him with something more than passing interest. All together they fall under stern silence. Reed swallows dryly upon seeing this grave line-up—jurors about to deliver their verdict.

The first bird by his shoulder plucks a thatch of straw from Reed as the others look on. Reed shouts, screwing his eyes shut in fright, but there is no pain. Instead, a seeping numbness blots out sensation.

The birds before him bob and gabble to one another with something in their eyes. A hunger. Somehow he understands that with each snatched piece of straw, a memory is removed; a piece of Reed obliterated. What has he lost? Blowing out candles on his fourth birthday, surrounded by friends wearing paper hats from the local pizzeria. His mother's face with its permanent rosy blush, light eyes, and the expression of a veteran unfazed by the young Reed's mischief and injuries. Those precedents were already set by his three older brothers.

His eyes widen as the crows' wings spread. Arching shadows lengthen toward him, coalescing into a single reaching hand. All at once he understands his approaching fate and the fate of the other scarecrows. Not the wind. Not escape. But picked apart. Straw by straw.

The crows launch off their crosses and swoop toward him, beaks poised to strike, their hand-shaped shadow ready to grasp. Reed yanks his straw arms, but they're held fast to the wood. The sky fills with the blizzard of black plumes that threaten to smother Reed if he doesn't free himself. The first bird continues to filch straw from his shoulder. He tugs again with an adrenaline rush. A loud rip of fabric as the rusted nail gashes a sleeve, but an arm is free!

The crows are upon him now. All he can see beyond a protective arm is a flurry of feathers. Darting beaks perforate his faded shirt. Bits of straw poke through like worms from the ground and are snatched up in beaks. The cancer of absence spreads. An epic snowball fight after record snowfall left drifts higher than the parked cars—gone. Granddad's funeral where he felt ashamed for not crying, then faked it for the family's sake—gone. His first kiss, an impulsive lip-lock with braces-wearing Leslie McGrady between classes—gone!

Reed cries aloud at the idea of what will become of him, the fright of having his very soul torn apart. His arm flails in vain to deter the birds. He wrenches his other arm free, losing some more straw in the process, and hops to the ground. In a blind run, he screams through the field.

A game of kickball with schoolyard friends caught in the wind; the name of his high school science teacher snagged by stalks of wheat; how to tie his shoes blown south.

On he runs, coming apart, shedding straw. Clipping through the field stalks, fumbling over earthen ruts, tumbling down knolls, he leaves tracks of himself. Afraid to look back, Reed tries to hold onto memories of his bride. Their awkward initial dates; the gasp at the unexpected diamond ring; her words, "I do"; Paris in the afternoon.

With each vivid moment, he has the sensation of experiencing them again for the first time, as though he has found a doorway into each memory. Lily is beside him in the left ventricle of the walk-through Giant Heart exhibit inside the Franklin Institute. She sits atop his shoulders above the waves by the Atlantic City shore. She faces him at the altar under a veil inside St. Joseph's. They embrace atop the Eiffel Tower.

But they are only moments, their relief fleeting. The shadow-hand reaches for his heart. The crows hunger for the rest of him.

part
I

one

Joie de Vivre

R eed and Lily Williams hurtle along the boulevards of Paris in what he mistook for a taxi, but is more likely a stunt car. Or soon, a hearse. Any moment now, Reed expects a steep ramp to appear to take them over a moat, or tanker trucks, or Belgium.

Lily loosely laces her fingers in his, casual about their pending fiery crash. For his part, Reed checks his seat belt a fourth time, plants his feet under the seat before him, and grips the door's handhold.

When the cab whips onto the cross street, the force of the turn pressing his body against the door, an emergency vehicle zooms past. Its bleating passive-aggressive siren catches the attention of the firefighter in Reed.

On another street, Lily argues in French with the driver.

"Lily, don't distract the man."

"He's deliberately taking a longer route," she says.

"We're not in a hurry. Tell him we're not in a hurry."

When the whole car seizes up, coming to a sudden halt, Reed realizes they've arrived at their destination. Lily pops the door, while he checks that his balls haven't been sucked into his body.

He thought the cabbie on their first outing was reckless, but it turns out the whole city is full of drivers who think they're in a *French Connection* car chase. How the traffic circles aren't heaps of smashed cars instead of the majestic spouting fountains is a miracle. He will never complain about Philly cabbies again.

"God d—" he begins to say, but catches himself. To Lily he says, "Sorry. I meant to say, thank God we didn't die."

She kisses his cheek. "You worry too much."

After he pays Evel Knievel the fare, Lily leads him into the *pâtisserie* she has been raving about.

"Wait till you try them," Lily says while in line, her arm in his. He has never had crepes. They look like pancakes that slept in, too lazy to rise.

Lily expertly orders for them both in French. Just a guess, but Reed thinks they pass for natives as long as he doesn't speak, which suits him fine as he's not a conversationalist. Happy to have her do the talking, he loves the sound of those tempting French words dancing off Lily's tongue as though they showed some leg before dashing behind a curtain.

Ooh-la-la.

"What?" Lily asks, appearing self-conscious.

"Don't you mean, *que?*" Reed teases.

She pats around her mouth. "*Qu'est-ce que c'est*, actually."

He says, "Like I said."

"Are you going to tell me?" She counters his grinning with her fake annoyance. With the real thing, she'd fold her arms across her chest, tighten her mouth, and peer at him like he was one of her students caught eating paste again. Instead her eyes go wide and she holds up her hands as though ready to catch a throw.

He says, "You. You've got this sexy superpower."

He has known that she can speak French—her father's side, the Martins, settled in Philadelphia after fleeing revolutionary France, bringing along and passing down their language and traditions—and she treated him to some choice phrases while they dated. Now seeing her in full command of the language, the culture, and the streets, fills him with admiration.

And yes, God, does it light his fire.

Comfortable and confident, Lily blends in with the citizenry like a chameleon. He loves experiencing Paris with her, his private tour guide, who knows all the ins-and-outs and best places for live music or scenic spots as though she has a key to the city.

"I promise to use my power only for good," she says with a wink.

"I hope not. It's damn sexy," he waggles his eyebrows.

"*Vraiment, mon bonheur?*" she says drawing the words out.

He grunts. "Lingerie is French, right?"

She nods, listing other words that may be in her boudoir like negligee, camisole, brassiere, lace, and satin.

Reed says, "We'll have to add those to our shopping list."

"And what will you be wearing?" she says in a what's-in-it-for-me tone.

"My bunker pants," he says, meaning part of the firefighter gear he had worn when they met, although she was semi-conscious at the time. Later he would joke she passed out from his brawny good looks rather than the smoke.

"You didn't pack that."

He laughs, "Exactly."

When the food arrives smelling warm and tempting, Reed pictures cartoon steam curling off the plates like beckoning fingers. Eager to comply, Reed devours half the fruit-oozing crepes before Lily takes her first forkful. She encourages him to slow down enough to actually taste it. He's used to chowing fast, but he does his best to pace himself now. After all, he will not get to experience a two-week honeymoon again, so best to soak up every minute.

The hot chocolate, so off-the-charts delicious, takes the breakfast to a new level. Into the ceramic cup goes whole milk, then melted chocolate, accompanied by a cloud of whipped cream and a slit vanilla pod for garnish.

He sips. Savors. And gives Lily a look of contentment with a dollop of cream on the end of his nose.

***

Sleeping, eating, shopping, worshiping, touring, Lily had planned it all over the months leading up to the honeymoon. Reed had not more than glanced at the itinerary Lily drafted, revised, scratched out, reworked, and embellished with the kind of stickers she put on her students' homework. He did put in for the City Museum of Science and Industry, when he learned of it.

At the time Lily said, amused, "You do know it's for children."

"Children of all ages," Reed said. "It's like the Franklin Institute. We had a good time there, right?" Growing up, Reed returned again and again to the Institute for its hands-on learning exhibits.

Lily said, "Yes, well it was a lot of fun when I only had to worry about one big kid running around, instead of many little ones."

Reed grinned, "I was well behaved after my nap."

Lily laughed, "We can fit the museum in here," she pointed to her schedule, "but we'll have to keep it to an hour as it's a little far afield."

Now with time in mind, Reed makes the most of their visit to Cité des Sciences. Crossing the moat that rings the building and paying their way past the toll-taker, Reed leads Lily through its floors and halls, while dodging dashing kids. Their first stop is the wing dedicated to mathematics.

As they wait their turn at the 3-D tic-tac-toe game, Reed says, "In school, I wasn't too bad at geometry. I had a little kit for my compass, protractor, and mini-ruler."

Lily says, "Ooh, a math geek." She drapes a hand over his shoulder.

"I was not a math geek."

Lily appears unconvinced, reminding him of the do-it-yourself and engineering shows he's hooked on. "And you keep one of your father's slide rules in its own leather sleeve. You are a math geek."

"It's not like a joined a club. I just picked it up from all the home projects my dad and I worked on. Measuring this, calibrating that. All the fractions you need in a socket wrench set."

After mathematics, they moved on to acoustics. Using parabolic dishes, they whispered to one another many yards apart. Then on a floor piano, which produced human notes, they played Chopsticks. Lily finished the visit with a minute of "Frère Jacques."

*****

Lily stuffed a church crawl into their itinerary. Each day they'd attend Mass and today's choice is the Church of La Madeleine. On its steps, Reed lags behind to take in the neoclassical exterior, which appears more like a Roman temple than a Catholic church. The Corinthian columns dwarf him as they uphold the triangular pediment and its grand frieze depicting *The Last Judgment*.

Inside, La Madeleine takes his breath while he takes his time absorbing it all. The Catholic service begins before he reaches Lily seated in a pew. While reciting the prayers he has learned, his eyes wander over the barrel-vaulted ceiling. Sunlight shines through each dome's oculus like spotlights from Heaven, enhancing the beauty below. At the center of it all is the magnificent sculpture of Mary Magdalene. She serenely gazes down at one of the angels circling her.

The angel wings remind Reed of the gargoyles he saw in a pictorial book back at the hotel. A common fixture of many churches, some of the sculptures were ghastly. He imagined the devil ones awakening at midnight, spreading their stone wings, and swooping down on unsuspecting peasants.

Lily takes his larger hand in hers, gently tethering his drifting thoughts to the ground, the here and now. He squeezes to reassure he's with her. Together they pray.

But over the length of the service, his thoughts drift once more. He thinks on the nameless men who had built all that he sees. No power tools, just their own strength and skill. Those men weren't just worthy of the name craftsmen, they were the template, the very mold. How many of them lived to see this place completed? How many even lived to return to their families each night? Did the men's spirits haunt the place? He wonders if there are ghost stories here.

"We should visit the city catacombs," Reed says after services.

Lily puts up a hand as if to ward off the very idea. "You're on your own with that one."

"Have you seen them already?"

She shakes her head, "I don't want to go. Creepy. Dark. Confined." She rubs her shoulder as though suddenly chilled, "They should let the dead rest. I think there's something unseemly about it being a place for tourists to gape at their remains and poke at their bones. Those were real people who had real lives."

Exactly what Reed has been thinking.

"Go if you want. We'll make room. Perhaps tomorrow?"

"Maybe," he says, already dropping the idea.

***

Their suite at Hotel Le Hervey in the 8th *arrondissement* affords Reed the opportunity to see a sunrise in a new land. He savors a cup of coffee and the kick-ass view beyond the flower boxes. It's as though their hotel's concierge took their order for perfect weather. A bright orange sun paired with a cloudless vivid blue blaze. Crisp October air, but not so chilly that Lily will have to bundle up.

Lily had been right. His attitude warmed after his earlier grudging acceptance of their destination. In truth, he never believed he'd be here. All those months, the wedding and this honeymoon seemed far off, like a mirage that tempted, but didn't really exist.

He had wanted to get married. Hell, once he proposed, he was more than ready to just grab Lily up in his arms and elope. She'd have none of that. Her dream wedding was already set in her mind. But she promised him that their having a proper engagement and wedding would be worth his waiting. And she was right, of course.

At the altar, before family, friends, Reed's engine company in their dress uniforms, and a hell of a lot of strangers, Lily's veil was lifted away and Reed saw her lips quiver in a smile, her eyes shiny with tears, her face reflecting his love of her. The vision rewrote his definition of happy.

Now, part of him still can't accept it. That any moment now, he'll wake from the best dream of his entire life. Their honeymoon a brilliant illusion, Lily, just a vivid fantasy, and he'd snap back to another day of wait-and-hurry-up in the firehouse.

In the distance, the Eiffel Tower looks real enough. Solid, rising above the buildings nearer in, it's a rocket ready to launch. All he has ever seen of it has been in movies or brochures. Now with the real thing in sight, Reed realizes Lily has expanded his world yet again.

The sight amazes. Tier by tier, the rising sun's rays send the shadows scuttling off. Reed thinks to take a picture and swaps the coffee for his phone. As he squares up the iconic tower in the display he frowns over the poor imitation there. The phone reduces the moment before his eyes. Heeding their earlier discussion about savoring the moment, he returns the phone to his pocket. He tries to chisel into memory the sun's steady rise and the brilliant colors seeping in to the sky.

He knows Lily has underlined, circled, and highlighted the Eiffel Tower on their itinerary. Now he's revved to go too. To hold her on that deck, looking out onto bright days ahead.

Yep. She was right. He likes it here.

He takes another sip of coffee and sets the cup down on its saucer, vibrating, not with caffeine, but eagerness to tackle the day.

Below, Rue du Faubourg wakens. Cars dash past Parisians opening their businesses with customers on their heels under French signage. This is a more upscale neighborhood. On their walks past high-fashion boutiques, fancy art galleries, and luxury goods shops, Reed hears his travel wallet whimper.

He tries not think on that. Already money has caused him to start their honeymoon on the wrong foot. He won't let it happen again.

"Enjoying the view?" Lily asks, approaching him from the main room of the suite.

Reed turns to see her showered and dressed as he has already done.

He gives an approving whistle.

She wears a navy top and an off-white skirt, a nice shade of lipstick, and of course the new gold band on her finger that matches the one on his. Both are inscribed with their initials followed by the wedding date.

Lily had banned jeans and tees for the trip—too touristy and too common for fashionable Paris. So, he bought a second pair of khakis and brought some slacks and button-down shirts that weren't stained. He liked blue, but she preferred red on him. He opted for a wine-colored shirt with the cuffs rolled up a bit. On his wrist ticks a silver Cartier—an engagement gift from his in-laws.

Without a word, Reed guides her by her shoulders, positioning her out on the balcony. He steps back, squints, then moves her a touch to the left. He steps back again, smiling. There. Her and the Tower. "Now that's a view."

But instead of reaching back into his pocket, his hand reaches out for hers. When she takes it, he pulls her in and smells the vanilla in her perfume on her neck.

She laughs in surprise, as he leads her in a slow dance. At six even, he's half a foot taller, but compared to her in rhythm and style, he comes up short. Ballroom dance lessons for their wedding have improved his steps, and it feels good to put those moves to use now.

"We don't have any music," Lily says.

He gets out the phone after all. In moments it's playing Bruce Springsteen's, "If I Should Fall Behind," from their wedding playlist.

At the reception, before their first dance as husband and wife, Reed had expected to feel awkward with so many eyes on him, but it wasn't like that. He only thought about her, and how amazing she made him feel. Just as she does now.

Reed hums by her ear.

On the small balcony, they continue to move in a tight circle, the Eiffel Tower coming into view and going out again and again. He wants to suspend this moment or slow it down till their hearts beat together in time.

She looks up at him.

He whispers, "You were right."

***

Each day they spend a collective couple of hours grazing among trays, turnstiles, and buckets of trinkets to find the perfect souvenirs for family members and friends, oh, and themselves too.

While in a shop packed with tourist merchandise, Reed considers a miniature Eiffel Tower in his hand. "How about right here and now we start a tradition? Every town we visit together we get a memento. The same kind. When we get home we put them all on a shelf."

"What would we get?"

Their fingers browse magnets, mugs, key chains, pins, shot glasses, bottle openers, and postcards.

Reed says, "I had a friend who took street signs. Before sunrise tomorrow, we'll get one. You distract anyone who might come by. I'll get a ladder and some tools."

They decide on snow globes.

Lily puts her sunglasses atop her head and hunts for the right brooch for a friend, while Reed idly looks over a display of Santa Clauses and nutcrackers. It's not even Halloween yet. He wonders if this stuff is out all the time, or like back home, Christmas season starts earlier and earlier each year.

He holds up a porcelain sugar plum fairy that has exaggerated willowy limbs, ballerina outfit, and delicate butterfly wings. More art than toy. He nearly drops it when Lily pops up behind him.

"Can you reach for me?" She points to a higher shelf, wanting a particular doll. It is of a girl wearing an old-fashioned sailor suit.

As he reaches for it, his eye catches sight of a scarecrow doll. Bundles of straw form bristly limbs and torso, all wrapped in rough fabric. Rude black stitches hold the pieces of its face together and its wide-open eyes are as creepy as they are life-like. He turns the doll around to face the wall.

"Here," he says, pushing the girl doll into her hands as he heads to the exit.

***

While they stroll in the darkening evening, Reed notices Lily stealing glances of him.

"It suits you," she finally says.

"What's that?"

She traces his lips with her finger. "Your smile."

To think he has been playing it cool all this time. No denying it now.

"Well, you put it there," he says, his smile spreading.

After a few yards, she asks, "What are you thinking about?"

He shrugs, "Nothing, really."

She nudges, "Come on." Then with her bright brown eyes at full power, she says, "When we get back to the room, I'll wear some of those French words we talked about."

"Damn straight, you will," he says, goosing her hip. "Fine." He rakes a hand through his short brown hair, putting his thoughts together. "Being here…"

"Yes?"

"Just…" he laughs, "I'm happy. More than I can remember ever being. More than I thought I would be over here. Now, hold on." That didn't come out right. "I mean it's Paris—it's cliché—like it's every sappy romance movie rolled into one. But it delivers. Maybe they spike the wine or pump some love drug into the air in the Metro, whatever it is, I'm feeling it. It amazes me, like you amaze me."

She leans into him, listening rather than cutting off his loosening mouth.

"And I've been thinking about earlier today when we were up in the Tower. I know it meant a lot to you. You dreamed of it, and you planned for it. To be honest, I didn't get it before. To me, it was just a monument. But when we were up there," he tugs her close, "I got it. I realized that you chose to share that moment with me."

She laughs, "Yes, I did. Why does that surprise you?"

He shrugs, though knowing why.

Money. Firefighting and moonlighting pay the bills and his financial discipline banks the leftovers, but he's a beggar compared to the Martins. He's still unused to her family having so much of it. His friend Chuck is openly jealous, as though Reed found a winning lottery ticket. Hard to argue that, but at the same time Reed sees the deep quarry between what Lily deserves and what he can afford. The engagement ring, a whole glittering chunk, gouged his savings.

"Well…" he eases into answering her. "When I first saw the hotel room, I know I didn't exactly handle it well." Storming from the room to cool off, more like it. The suite was like a mini palace. It was too nice. And even though they were not footing the bill, all he could see were price tags on each item. "But it wasn't really the suite. Who doesn't like one million thread cotton sheets, fresh flowers, real marble, and a balcony with a great view? But it's been overwhelming. I'm just not used to it. You are."

He holds off before he says something stupid.

After a period of quiet, Lily says, "Do you know, the moment that I had realized you were my man was when you said, 'No' to me in the fire station? Turned me down flat."

"I was more polite than that. I didn't want to date a mummy."

She playfully shoves him. "I had one bandage," she says, while lifting her right arm.

He remembers that forearm wrapped in beige tape. Since the burn healed, she never cared to cover the scar that remained. He sees it now, a brand of their first encounter.

She says, "You knew about me and my family. For many, that might have mattered, but not you. You impressed me by not trying to. You're the same great guy with everyone. And for anyone, you have a hand out to shake, or to help, or to hold. The money didn't matter then; it shouldn't matter to you now."

She runs her hands down his arms, "I have everything I could ever want right here."

He nods accepting the way she puts it.

"Though fresh flowers would be nice every once in a while."

He grins, "Deal." That hadn't been so bad.

"*Très bien, mon bonheur.*" She throws her arms around him and kisses him.

Relieved to be cut off, he kisses back.

Music plays. Really. He hears accordions and other instruments.

"Do you hear that?" he asks.

They turn and sure enough, there's a bunch of guys strutting down the sidewalk. They're arrayed with accordions, a guitar, and even bongos.

Lily claps in time as they approach while he gets out his phone, putting it in video mode to capture the spontaneous concert.

Ah, Paris. Life is damn good and he has the best bride a man could ever want. He did win the lottery, Chuck, thank you very much.

The players circle them, singing something in French. Are they drunk? After a few revolutions, they continue on their way. He and Lily cheer them on.

A moment later, a crack of pain jars Reed. Someone has slammed into his back. Staggering a half step forward, he loses his phone and all sense. What the hell? Has some drunk tripped into him—no—the asshole grabs onto Reed from behind. Then Reed hears the most awful sound in his life. It sends Reed's heartbeat into full gallop. A fright he never knew before— Lily wailing in terror.

Hands clamp over both their mouths. Enveloped in arms, he's lifted off the ground. A woman says something in French. At his ear, a male British voice whispers, "You won't believe it now…" The man squeezes, grinding Reed's arms into his sides, hurting him. "But before long, we're going be best mates."

two

Waking Up Wrong

F or a moment, Reed Williams believes he is still in their hotel suite, a newly-married man blissfully embraced by the new Mrs. Lily Martin Williams. They could get up, shower, and check off their Parisian itinerary. Or better yet, lie here all day, the entirety of their world this sham-heaped bed fitted with Egyptian cotton.

They would eat buttery almond croissants. He would prepare coffee while she read *Le Monde* aloud, adoring her lilting French, though not understanding a word of it.

But as the imagined coffee would brew, little inconsistencies percolate. He can't hear either of them breathing. The body holding him is cold. There is lavender under his nose, the sheets are silk, and a strange oily taste coats his tongue.

He is not himself. A wrongness seeps into his awareness. Back in high school he had dislocated his elbow during a wrestling match and though it healed, the joint never felt the same. Now his whole self feels dislocated.

His chest feels very warm, as though someone slathered on muscle rub. And worse still is this eerie sense of ravens flapping in his head. He can hear their wings stir the air and their cries cause him to panic. The black birds chase him into wakefulness.

Cradled in another's arms, Reed feels soft flesh pressed to his lips as he nurses as a newborn. Coldness fills his mouth and oozes down his throat. Like nothing he has ever tasted before, he gives up on trying to identify it, finding it just simply satisfying, finding it just perfectly right.

In the drink, voices, faces, feelings all rapidly pass through his mind, gone before he realizes they are there. Again and again an attractive brunette woman appears. He knows her name: Marie de Telfour.

She is stroking his hair, soothing him with French lullabies.

Pulling away, Reed opens his eyes. Marie is before him… and under him. She's got on delicate lingerie. And her smooth body is cold, maybe because she's thin. Pretty, for sure. At least until he looks up. Her eyes flash with an unsettling hunger and her smile chills. He feels like a mouse being toyed with by a cat.

Unreal, unnerving, the disgust chases away his desire for more of whatever he just drank. He tries to escape her grasp, but she holds firmly.

"*Tu es éveillé,*" she says.

A white candle's flame lights the bedroom. The room is small, the way most things in Europe feel smaller. Together they take up an intimate canopy bed. The old wood grain doesn't match the other furniture pieces pushed against papered walls. These gleam with lacquer finishes and shudder with shadows so deep, he might slip into them, just fall away into the floor.

What isn't black is pewter or chrome or china—the knobs and hardware, the upholstery rivets, the paneled ceiling. Simply contrasts of light and dark. Squinting, it occurs to Reed that he may be colorblind. The colors of his life are gone.

Sitting up, he feels as though he been cracked apart and put back together wrong. His chest burns. From the drink? It isn't alcohol. Thicker—like Pepto-Bismol.

In Marie's unyielding grip, he is coaxed closer to her lavender-scented flesh.

"Get away from me! Where is Lily?" he struggles. Then he realizes he's bare-ass naked. "Where the fuck are my clothes?"

Marie gives a flirty smile, "*Oui. Tu es beau.*" Her hand searches beneath the silk covers. Reed jumps out of the bed at her grasping, glaring at her. "*Magnifique,*" she adds slyly with a lewd eye on him. Then after a moment she relents, waving a hand.

At the dresser, Reed finds folded clothes. They aren't his, but feeling too exposed to care, he snaps up the dark boxers and swallows several times, prompted by the metallic aftertaste left by the drink, drug, poison? Hand to his chest, the warmth there is feverish.

He catches sight of her, partially screened by a drape of gauzy white. She licks the inside of her wrist where there is a dark wet streak. He wonders if she's lapping the same liquid she just fed him.

Seemingly unaware of him staring, Marie adjusts herself on the bed by propping the pillows behind her. Quite animated, she gabs in French while he grabs clothes to jump into. She ticks some list off her fingers.

Even if he could understand what she is saying, he is not listening. Only one thing interests him now. Bracing for the answer, he asks, "Where is she?"

The question brings the woman, Marie, to a halt. Her face clouds over with dismay and she says something in French to herself.

"Where's my wife?!" He points to his ring, but it isn't there. His wedding ring isn't on his finger. "What did you do with it?" Cinching the belt on the size-too-large pants, he moves toward her. Only days ago, Lily had put that ring on his finger. He vowed to protect her. And now what? This woman took it? And his clothes? What kind of sick game was this? Reed considers dragging Marie out of that bed and shaking the answers out of her.

Marie doesn't cower, but reacts as if stung, as if she doesn't expect the man whose life she's ruined to be pissed at her. Pissed being the least of it.

"In English! Tell me. *Now.*"

"Asleep at the bottom of the Seine, *mon cher*," she says in chapped English. "Forget her. You have me now."

The words knock him numb. He had sensed it before he woke up. He had feared it last night. Now the ten-ton weight of reality has dropped on his heart. The room shrinks to nothing, and the floor rolls under his unsteady feet. As he sinks to his knees, visions of last night flash in his mind, but play as though he is outside his own body. They are Marie's memories. Somehow, he knows this. Her memories in his own head. How can this be? Where are his?

From Marie's jumbled perspective, Reed sees himself struggle in the grip of a British man with stringy oiled hair. Marie coolly gave orders. Yards ahead of them, two men and a woman pushed and pawed and tugged at Lily. "Let her go!" His arms pinned, Reed felt like he was fighting in a straight-jacket. They mocked Lily's pleas. She was farther away now. Adrenaline flooded Reed, and his muscles burned. Someone groped Lily's breast. Reed tried twisting away, but the Brit was like a slab of marble with arms. Lily's sobs knifed Reed's heart—deep and mortal. Reed was straining out of his own skin, willing to break his own arms to get free. But he couldn't. He couldn't help his crying wife. "Take me—not her! Take me—not her!"

Now, thinking on the horror causes his empty gut to lurch up into his throat. The three had taken her to God-knows-where and did God-knows-what to her, till she ended up in the river.

Why did Marie kill Lily and take him alive? It doesn't make sense. He doesn't speak French or know anything of French culture besides what he picked up from guidebooks and what Lily taught him. He doesn't have money or power. He's a thirty-three-year-old firefighter from Philly. For God's sake, if not for Lily, he couldn't have afforded their first-class flight to Paris. This was supposed to be the start of their lives together.

He puts a hand to his temple, eyes closed, thinking on Lily's final moments. He can't imagine worse. He can't believe it. She's dead. Killed. Murdered.

With rising anger, he growls, "You bitch. Why? Why? Why?!" He leaps to his feet. He scans the room for something to pick up and throw. If he had his softball bat, he'd smash every damn thing in this room.

Returning to the bed, he boils, "You fucked up. She had the money, not me. I've got nothing." He tears away the bed's curtain. "God help you…"

Unperturbed, Marie replies, "We *are* gods, *mon cher*. We do as we please. Soon you will learn this."

He looms over the bed.

Lily's terror and screams replay in his head. His anger builds into rage, choking off his words. He raises his arm and tightens his fist to strike. And Marie lounges there in dark silk and lace without a care. As though this hellish ordeal is a minor nuisance she can fix with soothing words. She took his wife—his life—away.

Raw as he is, deserving as she is, a moral safety he's had since childhood holds him back. He won't follow through. But how he so very much wants to.

He's not violent. He protects. Instead, he'll haul her out of that bed, drag her to the nearest phone, make her call the police and confess. And to do just that, he reaches for her small wrists, but in that moment, Marie says simply, "Stop."

The word pulls him up short, the power cut from his body. In a breath, the impulse leaves him. His now purposeless arms drop to his sides. How had she done that? The taste still on his tongue and the heat of his chest remind him of the drug.

Marie continues, working out the English words slowly, "We have both been wronged. Hold your anger for later."

She quits the bed. With soft steps, she goes to a jewelry box atop the dresser. There's a brief rattle of metal as her fingers stir inside it. She gets something. Then she draws beside him as if to lend some twisted kind of comfort, kissing his face. A halo of pale blue shimmers around her like an apparition—color superimposed on the black and white of the room.

"What have you done to me?" he whispers.

She puts his wedding band into his hand. "I hoped you would not remember. And soon, you will not." She attempts to soothe him with touches of her cold hands. "*Mon cher*, Reed, you have many questions, and we will have many nights to answer them." She fingers his solid chest. "You are quite warm," she gasps. Then a deep smile forms. "You have a noble heart. And it is brave and fierce like a lion. Just as I said, you are powerful."

Reed wonders if this woman is psychotic in addition to being sadistic.

Her fingers walk across his shoulders, "Tonight you meet our friends."

Reed recoils, having the sudden sense of a raven hopping across his arm. It passes in a second, but he felt the bird's slight weight and its clawed feet prickling his shirt. He stabs Marie with a sharp glare. "Don't fucking touch me!"

Marie pulls her hands back. She regards him like a mother who is patient to wait out a child's tantrum. Stepping away, she draws open the heavy drapes. The day has passed, relieved by a grey October mist of evening. Over the panes, unseen branches wave shadows, eerie as a black-and-white monster movie.

He slept the whole day? A whole day at this woman's mercy. A day without Lily. Her body is out there alone. He wants to gag.

As if to make a peace offering, Marie says, "We will shop for a new wardrobe. Anything you like. And I promise you that you will not know pain or fear anymore."

He seeks his personal items. Marie had taken his ring from a jeweled box atop the bureau, so he goes there to open it. Inside are some British coins, a ticking Cartier watch, photographs, a wax pencil, charcoal sticks, a necklace with a claw, and more. Nothing that appears to be his. Where is his wallet?

"God damn it," he shouts, then hurls the box, its contents spray out onto the floor. Not satisfied, he thumps his palms on the bureau and looks about himself for something else to get a hold of. In the middle of the room, he grabs up an ottoman and scowls at Marie, daring her to say something. She smiles indulgently. He yells when he flings it into a free-standing barrel-shaped cabinet. Its doors spring open before falling over, its insides running out.

While Reed stalks for something else to throw, the bedroom door opens, and a man peeks inside as though checking on rough-housing kids. Reed recognizes the man's pasty face, greasy hair, and the mad eyes that appear as crazy as Marie's. Marie waves him inside and greets him with a kiss on both cheeks and turns to Reed, "Remember Eddie?"

Yes, he does. He remembers Eddie very well. He's the Brit who held him as easily as if Reed were a teacup dog, keeping him from Lily and her attackers. Told Reed they'd be "best mates."

"Everything all right?" Eddie asks Marie.

Reed's fist connects with Eddie's face. The man slams backward into the armoire, and the whole thing embosses the plaster wall. Unlike Marie, Eddie doesn't have a hold on his actions, at least not yet, and Reed doesn't hesitate in beating him bloody while he can. Bent over him, Reed hammers Eddie again.

"*Non!*" Marie puts herself between the men.

Behind her, Eddie rubs his cheek. With swollen words he says, "I understand, mate. Would have done the same in your place." He observes Reed's wreckage. "Not to worry. It's not our shit."

Reed grimaces, holding his sore right hand. Eddie is flesh over concrete.

Marie places her hands on Reed's chest. "Enough." The words cool Reed a bit, robbing him once more of retribution. "Finish dressing and wash your face." She moistens several of her fingers with her tongue and musses with his hair.

As Eddie gets to his feet, Marie smiles with excitement, speaking in rapid French.

"He better be the last. It's dangerous already," Eddie replies. After a look at Reed, he notes, "You're sure about this?"

"*Oui.*"

Eddie gingerly touches his cheek, "He remembers last night. That's a problem."

Marie says more to reassure him. Eddie looks unconvinced, but says nothing more.

Reed notices his travel wallet has fallen out of the wreckage. He bends to one knee as if to tie his shoe. After tucking the wallet away, Reed becomes knotted in thought when trying to tie the laces. He holds the ends, unsure how to proceed, as though he had never done such a thing in all his life.

"*Mon petit lion*, what troubles you?"

"There was a rhyme I knew from when I was a kid. I can't remember it."

"Do not be troubled." Bending down, she gently takes the laces from him and laces up his shoes.

They aren't his shoes as they pinch a bit at the toes and over the arch. Not his style either—these are made of hideous alligator leather. "Everything is wrong," Reed says.

***

Reed takes refuge in a small bathroom. A momentary sanctuary till he figures out how to get away from Eddie and Marie. That is, if he can't kill the smug assholes. The little Brit is unbelievably strong and the psycho witch put some weird spell on Reed. Whatever she has fed him must have given her some control over him, like he's hypnotized. Maybe while he slept, she planted commands into his subconscious. Creepy as hell.

Their whispers beyond the door are probably about him and how to torture him further. Good luck with that; nothing can be worse than this.

After he turns on the tap, Reed leans against the sink, his hands gripping the bright porcelain as if it is a rock in a swift current. Too much swirls around him now: the surreal moment of waking in a strange woman's bed; the fathomless grief of learning his wife is dead; the vulnerability and rage Marie caused.

His shoulders hitch nearly to his ears as his breath quickens. Confusion, pain, grief churn inside him, stoking his internal inferno.

Lily is gone. Dead, murdered, thrown away like garbage.

He screams and his arms fly out, both fists cracking through and disappearing into the wall before him. He yanks fistfuls of the gypsum plaster out, leaving numerous gouges in the wall.

Lily needed him, and he couldn't do a damned thing to help. Those bastards.

Searching for something to grab, he finds the towel rod near the toilet. The flower embroidered hand towels go flying after he tears the rod from the wall. Picturing Marie, he swings it down, down, and down again on the lip of the sink, till the rod becomes pieces.

His fury undiminished, he finds all that remains is a small cabinet fixed to the wall. Reed wrenches it free and smashes it against the wall, adding more holes, and sending framed pictures crashing to the floor. When that's used up, he kicks the wall till, finally, he collapses.

Shuddering with unanswered anger, he pulls out his stolen passport wallet and slips out a square of plastic tucked behind the bill-fold. A photograph, the kind snipped from a photo booth strip, shows Lily with her arm hooked around Reed's neck. He's laughing at the camera while she is in profile with a smile she only wears for him. The day he proposed.

He presses his trembling lips to the photo and tries to recall the moments over the weeks and months of their relationship that had led to that day. Too many of them are tenuous in his mind. He does remember Lily said the word, "love," first. He said it back, because, well, what else could he have said in that moment? If he loved her, what would that mean? Their future was not one he spent much time thinking on. He had enjoyed what they had then—dinner dates, Phillies games, museum tours, making out. Well, sort of. They hadn't gone all the way to home plate yet. Lily had made it clear early on that she was not one for casual encounters. If he wanted to be waved in, he'd need to prove his worth. He'd need a ring.

And a ring was serious. It would put him on a path with a certain outcome. Up ahead was an engagement party, wedding plans, the wedding, a house, kids. *Responsibility.* And what if they were wrong for each other? Could he ever be sure? Right at that moment, nothing was broken, so there was nothing to fix.

Lily was anxious during their ride to the home of one of Reed's older brothers. The occasion of a third birthday party seemed as good as any for Lily to meet more of his family.

Reed tried to reassure her, "You were a hit with my parents. Hard part's over." She seemed unconvinced, so he added, "Lil, they will love you. You're fail-proof."

Lily re-straightened the bow atop the small wrapped box in her lap. "I hope she likes it. You were no help." Her tone let him know that she wasn't exactly pleased to have to guess what to get his niece. She had wanted him to ask his brother what his daughter would like. Reed hadn't asked, and he insisted that she needn't bother getting anything. He had it covered.

He said, "She's three. Inside five minutes, she's going to break, lose, or ignore whatever we get her."

Lily asks, "What did you bring?"

"I got a sticker book and extra stickers. The glittery kind."

"At a pharmacy, no doubt. There's no thought in that at all."

"What are you saying? I got construction paper too. What? Look at it this way: since you did bring something, yours will look great in comparison to mine. Right?"

The party had gone as Reed expected. With one exception. His brothers, sister, their spouses, and their kids were eager to meet the woman whom Reed had rescued, and whom stalked him till he agreed to a date. They embraced her as already a member of the family.

And while Reed chatted with a family friend over some longnecks, the moment happened. He saw Lily holding one of the drooling crawlers in her arms. The tyke's fingers were pink and green with frosting that now smeared Lily's cheek. She burst into laughter. A laugh that was so open and carefree. A laugh that should be bottled and sold to treat depression. A laugh that shook off all of Reed's hangups. He saw Lily, saw himself beside her as she held their own child.

He was in love with her. Deeply. No more doubts. He wanted her forever, to have babies with her, to have a house, a small lawn, and neighbors and family dinners. He was hooked on Lily. In that moment, his heart yearned to get that ring.

With a sharp bird cry, the fond memory becomes a haunting landscape. A now-familiar hallucination seizes Reed and puts his body in that abandoned field. His weathered burlap skin is sunken in places where straw is lacking, his form a half-stuffed pillow.

The wind kicks up and the sky darkens as clouds scud by. Reed chances to look. Not clouds, but birds, smaller crows and larger ravens, hang in the air. Each has a black eye on him. One or two at a time, the birds dive for him and Reed runs for his very life.

The grip of the hallucination loosens, leaving Reed as broken as the bathroom.

What has he become? His hands, chalked with plaster, don't have a scratch. What weird shit is he on? Cigarettes and beer have been his hardest vices, so he has no frame of reference.

While gasping on the tile floor, he manages to sit up and survey the damage.

Not to worry. It's not our shit.

Curious, Reed slumps to one side to reach for a black frame amongst the debris and shakes loose the glass fragments. In the photograph, two hikers smile atop a crop of grey boulders. Behind them, a narrow waterfall spills down rising cliffs. The hikers are not Marie and Eddie, nor anyone

Reed recognizes. About to leave the frame on the floor, his eye catches on the man's necklace. Dangling from the simple thong is a long claw. Like the one in the jewelry box.

Reed wishes he hadn't looked. Doesn't want to know what happened to them and if any of this shit is theirs.

Who are those people out in the hall, and what is he up against? There must be clues. Reed's attempts to assemble the events of last evening prove frustrating. As he grasps a piece, the perspective shifts to Marie. Her thoughts are taking up residence in his mind and kicking out memory tenants, throwing their belongings out the window. One moment he was gazing at Lily as they took an evening stroll. From the day's shopping, she wore the new fall coat with lots of buttons. But wasn't this a different night? Didn't she wear his leather jacket for the sudden chill?

He clamps his hands to the sides of his head trying to hold onto his own version of the events, but it simply isn't there.

From Marie's viewpoint Lily and Reed were approaching her, just off to Marie's left. He realizes this wasn't last night. He's sure this was the previous night. Lily did have the button coat, and they weren't in a park, they were walking back to the hotel from a concert at the plaza. Why was Marie there? They weren't assaulted then.

Marie watched them go by as if she were invisible. Surely Reed would have noticed Marie as they passed. Lily faded from her notice as Marie's attention narrowed on him. It was as if Marie was leering at him. She marked his brown eyes and short hair, muscular build, calloused work-man's hands, then his ass as he passed.

Marie followed just steps behind them. Neither he nor Lily noticed.

And then... Marie's view turned black and white just as Reed's is now. The band of blue shimmered about his memory-self. At the center of him were vibrant red and orange colors. They had the vague shape of a wild animal stamping about and practically roaring. What did Marie say in the bedroom? He has a lion's heart.

Marie's eyes dropped to their hand-holding. Their inseparableness— she admired it. Or envied it. And something else. A sadness. No, deeper: a grief conjured by these memories and linked to a faceless, nameless man.

She watched Reed and Lily go into their hotel.

Marie had stalked them. The attack wasn't a random mugging or tragic run-in with a local gang. They were targeted. Or, *he* was targeted. Lily was collateral damage.

Why? Why did any of this happen?

The water from the faucet circles the drain. Tentatively, a shaky hand reaches for the grey soap bar and passes it under the stream. After rinsing his foamy hands, he lathers up again and dips his head toward the basin.

Marie's slimy touch hasn't come off. Reed doubts that even pumice soap could remove the experience of sharing Marie's bed while unconscious, unclothed, and vulnerable. How long had she fed him that drug? Has he overdosed? Bending himself over, he puts two fingers deep into his mouth to tickle his throat, trying to induce vomiting. He hopes to hurl up that black shit out of his stomach.

Nothing comes up.

While in seclusion here, he has avoided the mirror hanging above the sink. What will he see? With a deep breath, he looks directly at the glass. His twin looks back with the same dread. In this near-colorless world, he appears paler. As with Marie and Eddie, a sluggish blue halo wavers around his form. He staggers back when he stares into own eyes. They're the eyes Marie, Eddie, and the others possessed last night: black pits where demons swam.

God damn. He presses the palms of his hands over his eyes, rubbing for a long moment. But those freaky eyes remain and he squirms as though a hairy tarantula has crawled down the back of his neck and into his shirt.

He turns away and tries to reassure himself. They all had those eyes last night. They must have taken the same drug he's on now. It'll pass.

He needs to get out of here.

He needs to focus. Years of training and experience have taught him to deal with a rapidly changing situation using a level head. Do not panic. Keep breathing. Concentrate. However, a burning building is one thing. This is some category of devastation unto itself.

Know your exits. He had told Lily this when she wanted to hear about his firefighting training. When something goes wrong, go to your safe place. Don't think. Just go.

The bathroom has no other door or windows. Nothing at hand for a weapon either now that Reed has broken everything. If Reed can't overpower Marie and Eddie, then he'll have to get away from them somehow. He can run to the authorities or back to Philly. Then what?

A soft rap on the door. Reed doesn't respond. A firmer rap is followed by Marie cooing, "Come, Reed."

And so his body obeys.

three

On the Run

I n the speeding Fiat, Reed sits rigid in the rear seat with Marie while Eddie drives. She has her arm entwined with his, and an uncomfortable silence breeds between them. On their right, the Seine flows with them. Even with the sunglasses Marie gave him to conceal his eyes, Reed can make out the rippling river remarkably well. Points of light wink on the dark surface. And somewhere in its depths lies his treasured wife.

Whenever Lily had popped by at his apartment, she would bring Philly pretzels, thick loops of dough, like yeasty links of an anchor chain. And at the firehouse, she'd bring a deep ceramic bowl of chicken, pasta, and fresh herbs. Enough to share. The guys appreciated the delicious break from the usual grub, giving an exaggerated, "Thank you, Ms. Martin," as though they were her schoolkids. Then after she left, they'd whistle approvingly at her beauty. The lieutenant would say to Reed, "If you die in a blaze, what's the acceptable waiting period before I can ask her out?"

Reed bites down his anger and grief. "Why didn't you kill me, too?" His hand tries the door lock. He'll jump out of this speeding car. If he tumbles correctly, he may survive. He'd run to the river and dive in, no matter how cold. He'd swim its every square mile till he finds her.

With Eddie interpreting, Marie answers, "I should be thanked for this life I gave you. I could not let someone so brave and handsome as you slip away."

"Door's shut tight, mate. For safety," Eddie assures Reed who finds the handle useless. "Settle in."

She pats his hand while Eddie says, "I am excited to see what we will do together."

With mounting gloom, Reed watches the lights captured in the glass of the window. He had assumed he awoke in a house somewhere in the city, but it was in the suburbs. After about a half hour of Marie trying to engage him, they reach the city limits. Parks, museums, and historical buildings that have seen countless revolutions, upheavals, and strife pass by him.

"*Mon lion*, Reed, what do you think of Paris? Is it not more grand and beautiful than you had imagined? Tell me."

Paris is grand. Reed had admitted this to himself when he and Lily first stepped out of their hotel to experience the city. Though he had been eager to travel any place not along the Interstate 95 corridor, Reed did not have Paris on his list of world destinations. When in a cynical frame of mind, he viewed the city as overrated, like a celebrity who was famous for being famous and not for some natural talent; one whose self-importance outsized her significance and ability. It had a famous television antenna, snooty waiters, and art he could yawn at online.

But Lily had set him straight, painting a captivating picture of her time in Paris and France generally. So it came as no surprise to him where the honeymoon would be. The city turned out to be as charming and beautiful as Lily said, as Lily was. It was easy to see why she gushed about it all the weeks leading up to their wedding. His preconceptions of a stuffy tourist trap were dispelled by his interactions with real Parisians who were like people he would find anywhere.

Now the City of Lights is a grim, dark place. Marie and Eddie have seen to that.

Without looking at her, he says, "We are *not* having a conversation." Her voice, her touch, her smell all make his skin want to crawl off his body. He feels wretched. Marie's memories are crowding out his own, and the black birds steal more. He knows how Marie had felt about him for the past two nights. Her lust and desire are like slimy tendrils coiled in his head. He feels like putting a drill to his temple to bore into the infected portion of his brain. He wants to escape the car, the city, the continent.

From her purse, Marie takes out a cellphone. Her dark eyes continue to inspect and admire Reed as she speaks into the phone. He feels uncomfortably warm under her gaze like an ant under a magnifying glass in direct sunlight.

Unable to follow the French conversation, Reed can only wonder whether it concerns him. What does she want from him? Where is she taking him? He stares through the window at the waterfront. People of every sort stroll, play, sightsee, kiss. He remembers being that carefree with Lily on some stretch of the bank.

After zipping her purse, Marie smiles at Reed, and he finds himself smiling in return. It was an inadvertent one, a reaction, but a smile nonetheless. Alarmed, Reed turns on Marie, clenches his jaw, demanding, "What are you doing to me? You're in my head. Get out. Get out!"

Marie flinches at Reed's outburst.

Reed tries to stoke his anger, believing that it may give him the edge he needs to get control. He must think of Lily and the brutal violation of her. Her murder. Chucked her body away. She didn't deserve that. Not waiting for Eddie to interpret his words, Reed lunges between the front car seats and grabs the steering wheel. If he can't escape himself, he'll take these monsters to Hell with him. He yanks the leather-wrapped wheel sharply right toward the river.

Eddie's shouts join the retorts of car horns and screeches of tires. He seizes the wheel as the car careens over the next lane and sweeps off the road all together. Pedestrians scream and leap out of the way. A formidable elm tree remains on the car's course. With a quick elbow to Reed's throat, Eddie is able to straighten the wheel and stomp on the brakes.

Clutching his gagging throat, Reed slumps into his seat briefly before he and Marie slam bodily into the backs of the forward seats. Before either can recover, Eddie reaches for Reed, grabs a fistful of Reed's brown hair, and shakes violently.

"You stupid git! What do you think you're doing?" He shoves Reed back into his seat.

"Eddie!" Marie admonishes. She takes Reed's side, gently examining him and straightening his hair and whispering French.

Undeterred, Eddie says, "Mother Marie or not, you try that again, I'll make you my personal hand puppet!" He finishes with muttered expletives and puts the Fiat back on the road.

Reed recovers from Eddie's assault but remains annoyed by Marie's caresses. She's nearly atop him as though they never left her bed. He pushes her away, more forcefully than he intended. She doesn't appear to mind.

Eddie growls something in French to Marie.

Whatever it is, Marie doesn't agree, and Eddie doesn't appear to like it. He says, "Then keep him on a leash till he does."

A disturbing thought crosses his mind. "We didn't fuck, did we?" Naked and unconscious the whole day, who knows what might have happened.

Eddie laughs. Whether because he thought the idea ridiculous, or because that's exactly what had happened, Reed can't tell.

Marie pesters Eddie to resume interpreting, then says, "Nothing so crude." Settling nothing, she goes elsewhere, "Did you know I was a fashion model?"

"I know I don't care." He has no trouble seeing it. She looks like a runway beauty. Dark styled hair, thin body, and long legs that put her a couple of inches taller than Lily.

"I know you work with your hands. You are a craftsman, an artisan. You like knowing how things work, taking them apart, putting them together again. You care for your tools, and you dream of having a workshop of your own. A place to be by yourself with sawdust and oil."

"How do you know that?"

"A mother knows her son."

"You are not my mother."

"In this life, I am."

Reed can't picture his mother. He knows her hugs and her Sunday dresses, but he can't see her, as if she's been smudged out.

She says, "I am in you as you are in me. Linked." She gestures between her heart and his. "You are a hero. You help those who need it."

"I am not. I do what anyone would do. I just have training."

"You will help us when the time is right."

He removes the shades for emphasis. "If you need a fire put out, I'll be there with kerosene."

The point made, the car is quiet for the remainder of the ride.

***

Marie announces that they have reached the Latin Quarter, and soon the car turns into the district's heart where the arteries quickly constrict. After numerous traffic lights, the car dips into an underground parking garage.

Marie exits by Reed's door when Eddie comes around to open it, then helps him out. She speaks to the pair in a bouncy tone while guiding them to the stairwell.

"She says you'll be meeting our brothers and sister. They can't wait to see you, again." Eddie's tone softens, looking conciliatory, "Look—it gets better, OK? Just don't be a tosser, and we'll all get along."

Reed taps his head, "What the hell did she give me? I'm losing my memories."

Eddie smiles, but in a way that chills Reed. "Got the visions, do ya? Consider it a good ol' cleansing."

He notices Eddie's face hasn't bruised. It's not even lumpy. Reed's jabs weren't love taps and should have left their mark.

"Best shit in the world." Eddie slaps Reed on the back, "Embrace it. Things will go easier that way."

At the end of the stairs the three enter the rear of a café. The place is three-quarters full of young men and women. College students, Reed guesses. Books and papers spill out on their tables while they read and chat, sip coffee, or smoke.

The scene strikes Reed as strange. That he's observing it rather than being in it. Removed from the people here and their cares, as though he's behind a one-way mirror. Writing term papers, or arguing political points, or gushing over pictures, or whatever else they're doing, it seems all so petty. Like he's watching little kids squabble in their sandbox.

The smell of tobacco twitches his system. Oh, how he would love a Camel cigarette right now. He can almost taste the toasted tobacco of the French brands here. For Lily's sake, he quit months ago. *Damn.*

Reed zeroes in on a patron waving a cigarette during his conversation with another. The smoky sweet smell is as reassuring as a friend in this unfamiliar city. The man must have one to spare. Clearly in his line of sight, Reed looks at the man expectantly, but is ignored. The blue around the smoker has more snap than that of the dying flickers that are Marie and Eddie's own. Wishing he spoke French, Reed would say, "If I told you the night I'm having, you wouldn't believe me. And it's not going to get better, but I could really, really use one of those." Instead Reed mimes to no avail.

About to cause a scene, not so much for the nicotine fix, but for being ignored, Reed is ushered away. Eddie propels him towards Marie who stands near a window booth. Seated in the booth is a dark-haired woman with a nose ring who drapes herself over a man, obstructing Reed's view of him. Another joins the group from the café entrance. This man carries a large sketch pad under his arm and barely acknowledges Marie on his way to sit across from the affectionate pair.

Reed recognizes the trio seated in the booth. From Marie's memories of last night, he knows their names. Jean-Paul, Clarice, and Ron. His eyes flick to Ron, the one with the sketch pad. Reed can hear Lily shriek when Ron had put his hands all over her body.

Reed's whole body tenses. Scenarios of violence play out in his head, each more gruesome than the last. He knows it's unlike him. Marie had been right that he helps others. Growing up, he was watchful of his younger sister, stared down schoolyard bullies, took first-aid and CPR courses. He considered becoming a first-responder—cop, EMT, firefighter. After witnessing firefighters rescue his good friend and their neighbors, that clinched the track he wanted to take.

Before tonight he can't recall such personal hate for any single person, much less wanting to kill them. Now he knows of five such very deserving people.

Eddie draws Reed closer to them as Marie leans over the table, lecturing the three about something. Soon he'll be mere paces away. He considers taking Eddie's forward momentum to throw him into Marie, then leap on Ron. Smashing faces would be satisfying, but in seconds numbers would overtake him. If he couldn't handle two of them before, he wouldn't be able to handle all five now. Then no doubt, Marie would use her voodoo, short-circuiting his revenge. When would he ever get a chance again?

Out of options and out of time, he swallows his anger and pride, pushing them down, down, stomping on Eddie's foot, then elbowing his chest.

Reed is through the rear exit before anyone else notices.

***

This is my life. This is really happening.

Reed dashes down the stairs. He reaches the bottom in incredible time. His head snaps right and left. Left. He runs through the concrete lot, past numerous European, American, and Japanese cars. Behind him, he can hear the steel door bang open, followed by loud footfalls. Eddie's coming. Reed ducks between two cars, listening. At the end of this row and to the left is the ramp that leads back to the street. Reed crab-crawls to the next pair of cars, trying to remain quiet.

"Come out, you wanker!" Eddie bellows, causing Reed to cover his ears. The echo is tremendous. Reed puts his ear to the ground to look beneath the cars, but he doesn't see any feet.

Eddie continues to shout, but the echo makes it difficult for Reed to gauge distance and direction. Marie and the others will soon notice Eddie and he are missing, and they'll begin searching for him. They might already be at the garage's exit, waiting to take him back. Back to what? Why did they kill Lily? The kindest, most generous woman he had ever known; beautiful head to toe and down to her soul.

His chest brightens again with the flash of heat he experienced earlier tonight. It radiates through him, causing his muscular arms and hands to flex. With a fist, he decides he will have to move—now. Either he will be caught and perhaps killed or he'll escape and perhaps live without his wife. Instinct nudges him toward escape.

Reed makes a dash across the next aisle, bent over for a low profile. By the next pair of cars, all is still clear. Eddie doesn't seem to be near. Nor is he shouting anymore. Where is he? Reed didn't expect the Brit would give up. The ramp up to the exit is at the end of this aisle of cars. He crouches near the end of a dark Opel. No sign of Eddie. The fire within him pains his upper body. Peering over the trunk he makes one last survey and then heads toward the ramp.

Before Reed reaches full stride, a cinder block collides with the side of his face, knocking him into the hood of a VW Beetle.

"You're bloody stupid," Eddie says.

Holding his jarred jaw, Reed wobbles on his feet and sees Eddie come out from where he had hidden behind a support column. Eddie's on top of him before he can assess anything more. Another solid, powerful blow connects with him, this time in his stomach. Reed crumples at Eddie's feet, surprised his intestines haven't popped out like snakes from a can. He holds his middle as though that will ease the pain.

"I don't know what she sees in you," Eddie sighs.

Reed wonders if he may also mean Lily. He huffs out some curses, but can barely hear them over his wheezing pain.

"She's getting sloppier with each one." Eddie drops a heavy hand on Reed's head, like it was an iron bar. "And I'm getting tired of cleaning up her shit." Eddie takes Reed by the hair, roughly pulling his head up to look at him, like a puppet on strings.

Reed blinks several times, seeing three Eddies get in his face.

"Ron told me that bird of yours screamed real good before she died. Begged for her life," Eddie cackles.

Reed isn't going to hear more of his wife spoken that way. Lava courses in his veins. The fire has intensified, bringing focus once more. He channels the pain and takes Eddie's crotch in a swift motion. Eddie loses his voice when Reed squeezes in that most tender area. "Finally shut up, huh, asshole?" Reed gains his feet and lifts Eddie over his head and pitches him backward.

Reed spares a glance to see the Brit fly over one aisle of cars before crashing onto the roof of a Mercedes in the next aisle. He charges up the ramp before Eddie even moves a hair.

***

Upon reaching the cobblestone alley, Reed lets instinct guide him away from the carpark. He runs down the sidewalk and then round the block, weaving through Parisians and tourists enjoying the cool autumn evening. Blocks of boutiques, tourist shops, and pharmacies fly by.

His aimless route returns him to Quai de la Tournelle with the Seine just on the opposite side. Traffic brings him to a stop. Reed takes the moments until the crossing signal changes to check for pursuers. Not spotting anyone provides some relief. How far did he run? The confusion of traffic disguises the answer, though he's certain it has to have been at least a half-dozen city blocks.

Wired and alert, Reed feels like he's a top athlete at the peak of his career. He's not the least bit fatigued. Or even huffing.

Or even breathing.

The green light beckons people to the other side of the street and Reed decides to try an experiment. Expelling his breath and sealing his lips, Reed crosses Tournelle to find his way to the river. Only when he has descended the stone steps to the wall that rims the river does he open his mouth. And only because anguish breaks his composure. His body hasn't rebelled, threatening loss of consciousness or death unless he inhales precious oxygen. He no longer cares.

On his knees, he trembles while he gazes into the rushing water. Maybe he should shift his center of gravity so that he simply falls over into the river to join Lily down there. But if he doesn't breathe, can he drown?

Instead he confesses his regrets, repeating, "I'm so sorry," and "I love you."

He hears screeching tires, but it's not until he hears shouts that Reed senses he's been found. He's on his feet and looks up. The sound of footfalls on the stone surface above urges him to leave. He runs, choosing to pass the next two staircases and take the third.

Once on the street, he waves for a taxi. Three pass him by.

He can feel a tugging inside his head. Marie again. She's in there somehow. Each tug urges him to turn back the way he came.

"Never!" He tries to think on something else. Someone else. He focuses on Lily. He follows her puffs of breath in the chill air and her ponytail bouncing with each step on their morning jogs. He doesn't care for running or jogging, but he'd chase Lily anywhere.

Unwilling to stay and be caught by his pursuers, he hurries across the street, ducks into an alleyway connecting him to the opposite side of the block. Keeping an eye out, he tries to get transportation again. More taxis pass. The last one stops for another pedestrian, laden with paper shopping bags. He bolts, getting there just as the door opens. He apologizes when he shoves himself in and latches the door.

"Go! Go! Go!" He chances glances through the rear window, expecting to see Eddie over the wheel of the Fiat, sneering mad.

***

Inside the police station, Reed seeks out the nearest uniformed officer. In hurried breath, he tries to explain all that has happened. Words came out on top of one another and, even to his own ears, sound not the least bit sensible. Yet the officer pays him no attention until Reed is well into the telling, and only when he gets in the officer's face. The officer's expression shows no concern, only annoyance and incomprehension.

"There's got to be someone who knows English!" Reed says.

The officer jabs Reed with a clipboard of paperwork before turning away from him. Reed feels like snapping it in two and throwing it back. A second officer, tagged in by the first, comes over, and asks in English, with only the mildest interest, what seems to be the problem.

Reed repeats himself, hardly any clearer than before. He distills it down to drug gang, kidnapping, and murder. "They killed my wife, and they're after me." Only when he mentions the name, Marie de Telfour, does the officer show true interest. He directs Reed to a chair at an unoc-cupied desk. "Wait here, *s'il vous plaît*."

Left alone, Reed taps the desk, needing a cigarette more than ever. He feels mad with anger, grief, and fear. He's going to break soon, and he can't help but feel something is wrong here. What if they think he killed Lily? Suspicion always falls on the husband. What proof does he have? He can't believe it himself. Who can help him? Who can he call? His par-ents could only commiserate. And how can he tell Lily's parents? He has suspected they never liked him and probably thought Reed was after the family fortune.

He feels trapped and panicky. Marie's tugging adds to his para-noia. At times, it's stronger and at other times weaker. Nearer, farther. Warmer, colder.

The black and white room is half filled with people ringed in rip-pling blue. By an office door all the way down the floor, the second officer talks to someone in a suit, their eyes cutting Reed's way now and again. Something in Reed's gut is telling him to go. Not safe here. He tells him-self that he's over-thinking things. But the suit's body language is throwing red flags. Then Reed notes something. The blue around the suit is more sluggish and paler than everyone else, reminding Reed of what he saw around Marie and Eddie—and himself in the mirror.

The tugging turns stronger.

In a moment when their attention is elsewhere, Reed slips out of the station.

This is wrong; this is wrong. Though Reed is unsure what is right any-more. Everything is inverted. An ordered world turned inside out.

"God, tell me what to do," Reed cries out.

As before, he has difficulty getting a cab. He's seems only to be able to get the attention of the wrong people. When he finally does get into one, he dithers on where to go. Every direction seems bad. His thoughts run from one blind alley to the next. He has faced many fires and a tight spot or two, but he has never felt fear like this before. It pinches his vision, as though he is looking through his firefighter mask in a smoky room. There's no one left to save but himself. In which case, he would go to safety. Safety is home.

"Airport."

God help me.

four

Straw

I nside Charles de Gaulle airport, Reed hurries to get a ticket, only to be waylaid by a serpentine line. When persuasion to slip ahead of those before him fails, he resigns himself to stand at the line's end. Though the sensation of Marie tugging at his thoughts has weakened, Reed's still tense and frayed. He keeps his shaded eyes on alert for her or Eddie. At each whisk of the automatic doors, he expects Marie to stride inside. She would spot him and call out, "*Mon lion,*" that pet name he finds so obnoxious and patronizing, and then…

He freezes. Marie appears. Three people stand between him and the ticket counter. He attempts to appear inconspicuous while continuing to watch her. She is not looking his way. He hopes that she will walk off in another direction. But she turns her head. Reed flinches, then sighs in relief. It is not Marie—a different face.

At the counter, with trembling hands Reed shares his passport and credit card. He feels like a criminal caught in a conspiracy. His eyes continue to scan for anyone who might try to wrestle him out of the airport and back to Marie's house. The ticket agent tells him of a flight boarding in minutes that he just might catch, otherwise he will have to wait until

morning. His fingers drum on the counter as the clerk proceeds to punch
in his information. No, he doesn't have any baggage to check. Coach
class. Any seat is fine. His fingers clench into a fist. He will never make
it at this rate.

Reed hurries through the terminal and its security gauntlet. Upon
reaching the gate, he spies one last passenger disappear past the door. He
shows his boarding pass to the gatekeeper. Minutes later he collapses in
his seat, shaky hand to his brow. The airline seat is welcome relief. No one
knows him here. There is no chance of Marie appearing through the curtains or Eddie revealing himself from behind a newspaper.

The physical distance hasn't removed Marie from his mind, however.
Her memories persist. She said that they were linked. Did this mean he
would have no relief from her? Would she continue to buzz like tinnitus,
driving him mad?

Passengers are still finding their seats and stowing their carry-ons.
Each shimmers blue. This strange vision reminds him of thermal-vision
goggles, where people are white silhouettes. He hopes the drug wears off
soon. What if it doesn't? Can he be treated?

The heartburn hasn't gone away either, and he rubs absently over his
shirt. This is going to be a long flight.

Marie's memories strut through his mind, teasing him with visions,
some beautiful, some ghoulish. Pervasive is a deep sense of loss like a flood
has come and submerged something or someone precious.

Reed tightens his jaw and squints behind his shades, trying to banish
her. He won't commiserate.

"Get out of my head, you bitch!" he says. Passengers around him look
up from their Sudoku puzzles, paperbacks, and tablets.

He focuses on Lily, trying to have her outsize Marie. A pang of guilt
drops through him. He blames himself. He had known he wasn't right
for her, unworthy of her—and now she's dead. Then he catches himself,
parrying away these thoughts and counter-striking. She chose him. She
loved him.

He remembers their third date. That's when he began to realize that
Lily was different and that he didn't want this date to be the last. For the
first time, he had worried about ruining things in a spectacular fashion.

"Third date's key," his friend Mina told him. "Make-or-break time:
end a casual acquaintance or begin a real relationship."

"I thought she was just being grateful. You know, polite," Reed said.

"I don't think the etiquette is that you have to offer yourself as thanks for being rescued. She could have gotten you a gift card or something," said Chuck, Mina's husband and Reed's friend since they were recruits.

"She asked you out, right? She likes you. Go have fun," Mina said.

"You're so lucky. I wish a girl asked me out," Chuck said.

Mina slugged his arm.

"Hey! I meant before I met you, of course."

"What if I say the wrong thing?" Reed said.

"Just be yourself instead of this pathetic wretch before us," Mina concluded.

And Marie and her gang murdered Lily.

The plane reaches cruising altitude and at thirty-five thousand feet he doesn't feel any closer to Lily. She must be in Heaven and looking down at him. She had believed in guardian angels—God-sent protectors who stood between their wards and mortal danger. She knew Reed was hers. Now, would she be his?

What would you do in Heaven all day? What do you do with forever?

Reed wonders if there truly is an afterlife—a place for the Good, another for the Bad. It had been one of the innumerable big questions that seldom occupied his thoughts. Then he met Lily who spoke of Heaven as though she had summered there as she had in France. She reasoned, "If there is a good God, there must be a good place waiting for us."

He had asked her, "What is it like? What is Heaven to you?"

"Like coming home," she said. "You are away so long—on the road, cold maybe, tired, then you come to a door, you open it, and on the other side is this—light—bright but not the kind to make you squint. Warm and cozy like being in your favorite fuzzy pajamas. And there's grandfather, who carried me everywhere and made me feel so good about myself, and grandmother who taught me about forgiveness. It's love forever. Your faith rewarded. You belong."

He wishes he had her firm faith. It provided her such strength and comfort, while he had always been soft. He had believed in God, though in an absent-father way. Lily was not put off by this and in fact she had warmed him to attending church services with her. Far from absent, Lily believed God and His only Son were always near. By the time of the wedding, he had officially been baptized and confirmed.

They haven't consolidated their living situation though. The plan had been to move in together before the wedding, but finding the right place, at the right price, in the right area, took longer than expected. They got the keys to the new apartment about a week before the wedding. So for now, it collects their wedding gifts.

To get to the aisle, Reed brushes past the passenger beside him without waiting for him to move, unconcerned with excusing himself, leaving a wake of surprise and indignation.

Stretching his legs, he moves in a circuit down and across the aisles. NO SMOKING signs taunt him. Not that he has a cigarette to light up. His chest could probably serve as a lighter. The fire there is unrelenting.

This touches off a memory of a fire. The smoke was clearing, and what wasn't burnt was soaked. The whole scene was suffused with a reddish glow. The mask over his face limited his peripheral vision and the respirator caused him to sound like Darth Vader.

To his partner, he confirmed another room was clear. But some distinct feeling—God, Lily believed—compelled him to return to the adjacent room. This time he saw movement and soon heard a labored cough. He rushed to the woman's side and called for his partner. She was still now, on her side. He gently rolled her onto her back, and with his partner leading the way through the smoke, dragged her out.

When they emerged from the building, Reed lifted her. Around him, men from his crew and other stations continued battling the blaze. It wasn't until he released her to the paramedics that he realized her hand had been gripping his coat.

Just then a bird squawks as though someone's pet got loose on the plane. It startles Reed, who cries out. He can see the raven before his eyes, half-in, half-out of this world. It's on his shoulder then flits off. The ghostly shadow flaps away with straws in its beak.

Then the bird is gone.

Did he imagine it? What was he just thinking about? He can't be sure. He lost the thread. Something about their third date, then the trail goes cold.

Some of the passengers stare at him, curious and concerned about what had caused him to shout.

"Never mind."

***

The plane rumbles when its landing gear strikes the runway, bringing Reed to wakefulness and Philadelphia. The unshuttered portholes show it is still night. Those around him are on their feet, opening overhead bins and checking under the seats for their belongings. Reed remains slumped holding his head in his hands, feeling disoriented and pained with the worst heartburn. He has managed to put an entire ocean between himself and Marie, so certainly he can finish this last leg of the journey. Summoning the reserves of his will, he pulls himself up, staggers down the aisle, and files out to the jetway.

After customs, Reed leaves the terminal and goes to the taxi stand. At his turn he rolls inside, sinks into the seat, and informs the cabbie of his destination. His groans fill the back of the cab as it bumps along some pot-holed roads that lead off the expressway into Fishtown. The fire within him since waking this evening has never abated. While occupied with running for his life in Paris, he was able to channel it constructively. Actually, he believes it may have given him the strength and speed he had needed to escape his pursuers. And now in the cab it's impossible to ignore. He feels as though his heart is a blast furnace, giving off waves of heat throughout his body.

He just needs to hold on till he gets back to his apartment, where he can pass out on his own bed and let the drug run out of his system. If he should ever wake in the morning, he's going to have to tell Lily's parents. He'll have to steel himself for that unbearable moment. He'll have to do it face-to-face. Look Richard and Anne in their eyes and tell them what happened to their daughter.

To the rearview mirror, the cabbie says, "Hey friend—you like, I take you to hospital? You look like you have my wife's chicken *tikka*."

At the stop light, the cabbie turns in his seat for a better look. Whatever the man says, Reed doesn't hear it. He pops open the door, heaves himself out, then collapses. He crawls across the asphalt. By now, the cabbie has come around the taxi and attempts to help Reed to his feet by pulling him up by Reed's arm. The cabbie shouts in pain and blows on his hands. Unbalanced now, Reed staggers toward the sidewalk, trips over the curb and scatters aluminum trash cans, making a noise loud enough to wake those in the lower floors of the apartment building.

Now on his knees again, his vision dims, and he is ready to pop. He can smell plastic melting and hears the cabbie give another shout. He crawls across the concrete walk till he bumps a pine tree. Using it for support, he gets to his feet.

All at once, it is considerably darker, and Reed tussles with a man stronger than himself. Eddie? How had the Brit found him? Fear chills him for a moment. Only a moment. The man is not Eddie.

Water sloshes around his and the stranger's ankles.

Now in the steel manacles that are the man's hands, Reed looks up and up at his face. He is exquisitely handsome. Long black hair, smooth cheeks, pencil mustache, and eyes so deep they arrest Reed's struggles. Those eyes fill Reed's vision. Tranquil, beckoning, causing Reed to forget himself. Before he knows it, he is in the strange man's embrace.

"Marie de Telfour," the man whispers like a French silk handkerchief drawn over his ears. "*Vous appartenez à moi.*" The tone carries the familiarity of a friend from the past returning when he needs him the most.

But Reed doesn't know this man. Reed knows this is wrong. He can feel the chill water lap at his knees. He shuts his eyes and throws a fist, then another, and another. The man, the hallucination, is gone. Reed has been punching the tree. Bloodless gashes split the skin of his knuckles.

Marie's memories have fooled him again. He blinks rapidly and tries to get a grip on himself.

Someone says, "Careful."

"This is the guy?" says another. "Looks like Blade gave as good as he got."

"Not entirely. Recognize him?"

"No."

Reality is touch and go. More strange men? He can feel them grab at him.

"Ow! Damn!" one says.

"Get gloves on."

In a moment, the two men hold him on either side and walk Reed to a parked car. He's guided in and when the door shuts, he tips over and out.

part
II

five

Salvage

Kyle Dowd wakes with unease. In company with his usual dismay of being alive, an unidentifiable feeling clings to him as he moves through his desolate house. In the shower, under the chill water, he can't scrub the unease away. The feeling has some association with last night. While he shaves he considers meeting up with his friend Michael whose buoyancy often lifts Kyle's mood. But Michael is more fool than confidante. Donning his taupe suit pants, herringbone-patterned dress shirt, and muted silk tie, Kyle decides to take refuge in the basement to sound out what bothers him.

Carrying one of his mice, he descends wooden steps, snapping the pull-chain lights overhead as he goes. Having a mouse or two for company convinces Kyle a rodent audience is less weird than talking alone. His habit of monologue developed after he was initiated into this new life.

Leaving the mouse at one end of the long plywood table, Kyle pulls a stool at the other end. He had carefully packed away the previous set and now is undertaking an alpine landscape that will resemble a Swiss town when completed. One by one, he examines the contents of the new kits that had arrived. Nothing is missing; however, a piece of track is cracked. Instead of discarding unserviceable pieces into the waste bin, Kyle created a scrapyard in an unused area of the table. Inside and amongst the rolling stock, busted trestles, and discarded landscape, he hides cubes of cheese, payment for the earful of Kyle's chatter.

Kyle places a burgundy-roofed chalet near the plunge of a waterfall and positions cows out to graze in the pastureland. From the corner of his eye, he can see the white mouse exploring. Its pink nose probes overturned freight cars and pewter pedestrians, like a nuclear-age-B-movie monster, immense with fallout, on its way to the cheddar.

The basement is unfinished, just a brick and stone room. Drop lights provide ambient illumination, and gooseneck lamps clamped around the plywood brighten the tableau. Everything casts a soft shadow. Except Kyle, who has none at all.

He and the mice reside in a pocket enclave along the east bank of the Schuykill River. Rowhouses, restaurants, and taprooms edge an industrial area. The market at the end of his block is where he gets cheese for the mice. Of the wider working-class neighborhood, his underworld reputation keeps his person, his home, and his luxury car unmolested. Farther beyond and years gone, Kyle had attended boxing bouts. Then the ring shut down, with little to mark that it had existed at all.

He has the body of a man in his early forties, though he is two decades older. The more the decades pile up, the faster time passes, the more human connections wither, the more his experiences blur together into a chronological smear. Months are days, years are weeks, and his mice are dead in a wink.

Thus he doesn't bother naming them. And for the same reason he doesn't keep perishables; the few items on the kitchen counters and inside the fridge are plastic replicas. For some time, he has intended to replace the baroque vinyl wallpaper with antique white paint and repair the crown molding. Maybe even fix the static on the Zenith console television.

Down here in the basement, the miniature world takes shape in Kyle's hands. The uneasy feeling persists. While he whittles, paints, and snaps, he lets his voice take him back to the previous night.

***

For Kyle Dowd, Camden, New Jersey, was haunted. From its alleyways to its rooftops, specters of his past fogged the cityscape. Their wailing was nearly audible. And to this gloom, Kyle returned again and again to make amends.

Last night, crossing from Philadelphia over the Ben Franklin Bridge, Kyle followed Route 695 to where it elbowed south. His black Audi, nearly invisible but for its headlamps at this dark hour, soon exited. Not wishing to draw attention, he drove slowly. All the wrong elements were out past midnight. Some of them knew Kyle by name.

The residential area between the highway and the Cooper River went back to the 1950s, and the subsequent years had not been kind. Along the way he passed fenced-in lots weeded over, boarded-up businesses, and graffiti on top of graffiti like bright decay.

Parking the Audi under an oak, Kyle killed the engine. In the passenger seat was an open shoebox half filled with white envelopes. A gloved hand took one from the stack and pocketed it in his wool overcoat. With reluctance, his hand on the door latch for a long moment, Kyle got out from the car and locked it. He checked his russet hair in the sideview mirror. He wouldn't be seeing anyone; this fastidiousness was borne of habit.

He parked five blocks from his destination so the noise and lights wouldn't alert light sleepers. Though eager to get through his mail drop quickly, he restrained his pace and thought about getting back to Philly and working on his model trains—a way to unthink about the world. Tomorrow, he'll catch up with his friends Malcolm and Michael. They're an odd pair, but they're the only ones Kyle knows who weren't involved in his past. Malcolm didn't ask questions, and Michael just wanted to have a good time. Everyone else wanted something from him.

Kyle focused on the task at hand. The narrow three-story homes on Bartlett Street appeared like book spines fused together. Footsteps clipped on the concrete as he passed, shadowless, under streetlamps.

Arriving at the address, he withdrew the envelope from inside his coat, then opened the outer door. He bent to stand the narrow end on the metal threshold and let it lean on the steel door so that when the owner left for work, the packet would fall inside. Written across the front in black Sharpie marker was the name, "Whittaker." Inside were twelve iron-crisp Benjamin Franklins.

Stanley Whittaker had been a money-launderer and a skillful accountant who thought he could shift some numbers his way with the Blue Syndicate none the wiser. He was right. For a time.

Then one bright morning, Kyle's shadow had fallen on Mr. Whittaker's door. He rapped with his gloved hand. He knew that Mr. Whittaker was at home and alone—the wife and kids left for work and school. He heard Mr. Whittaker grumble his way to the door and open it wide enough to glower at Kyle.

"Whatever it is, I'm not interested," he said while buttoning the upturned collar of his silk shirt.

"I'm here on behalf of Donovan Blue. You know Mr. Blue, correct?" Kyle said, catching Mr. Whittaker's eyes with his own.

The pop in Mr. Whittaker's bluster answered for him. His undone necktie slipped through his now slack fingers down his front and landed between his feet. Kyle had brought a tie of his own; the tie was neatly bundled in a leather bag he carried.

"You look ready to mess your fine navy trousers," Kyle observed, keeping his gaze. "I'm not here to kill you, Mr. Whittaker. Put on a pot of coffee and let's talk."

Kyle set the bag on the kitchen table while Mr. Whittaker filled a copper kettle with tap water. Kyle asked, "Do you have a piece of paper?"

Mr. Whittaker nodded and put the kettle on the lit stove. Kyle watched him slink about his own kitchen as though he were the intruder.

Kyle knew how this would go down. Holstered under his suit jacket, Kyle's Colt would go unused. Mr. Whittaker was no hero and would do as Kyle instructed as long as he thought he could talk his way out of it.

Mr. Whittaker took a memo pad and pencil from a drawer under the laminate counter and set them on the table.

"Pen, please," Kyle said.

"Sorry. Here." He replaced the pencil with an executive pen engraved with someone else's name. "How do you want your coffee?"

"The coffee is for you. You can Irish it up if you need something stronger to settle your nerves." Kyle believed his calmness only made Mr. Whittaker more agitated.

Mr. Whittaker shook his head and sat across the kitchen table. His right leg was restless, as though it, at least, might get away. Before he could say something, Kyle headed off any questions the man might ask. "We'll wait on the coffee."

Kyle was in no hurry. He glanced around casually while Mr. Whittaker focused on a spot on the floor. Kyle noted the refrigerator plastered with kids' drawings and family photos.

Unmarried and childless himself, Kyle wondered why a family man would risk the life he built. By all accounts, the Whittakers were a typical loving family. Love wasn't enough? Mr. Whittaker needed something more. Respect? Status? Prestige? Seemed a foolish gamble to Kyle. But then again, foolish gambles were what kept him employed.

When the kettle spouted steam, Mr. Whittaker got up and poured himself a cup over instant coffee granules and sugar. The mug shook in his hand as he returned to the table with it. The coffee nearly spilled onto him before he could get a sip.

"I'll pay it all back," Mr. Whittaker blurted.

"You have the money now?" Kyle asked. He wasn't surprised that Mr. Whittaker didn't first deny his wrongdoing. Some part of him must have felt superior for the years of putting something over on the Blue Syndicate.

"I can get it. Soon. All of it," Mr. Whittaker said, finally looking at Kyle.

"Are you going to skim it from some other trusting clients?" Kyle's tone was mild. It wasn't his money that was stolen. He was curious if Mr. Whittaker had some plan B, should he get caught. "Or do you in fact have it? In a suitcase in the attic, or wrapped in plastic bundles in the vents?"

"Who are you? I know most of Mr. Blue's guys."

"Because you haven't been spending all that you took." Kyle lifted his gloved hands to encompass the house. "Not on this dump of a place, that's for sure."

"No. No," Mr. Whittaker agreed. His eyes pleaded, "Please. Tell Mr. Blue that I'll make it right."

"New suits. A car that's one model nicer than what you had before. Family vacations. Nothing that would raise suspicion." Kyle watched Mr. Whittaker evenly. "But I've been told, somewhere along the way, you bragged to the wrong ears."

"You're the Gentleman," Mr. Whittaker realized.

Kyle had heard that name, among others. Who dubbed him that, he didn't know, but it had stuck. Criminals loved nicknames.

"Right? Well dressed; all calm and cool; the red hair." Mr Whittaker's voice trembled, "A freelance gun."

Kyle didn't answer, but Mr. Whittaker was correct in that Kyle was independent of any organization, allowing him to be dispassionate in accomplishing his assignments. And yes, he dressed well; he was a professional, after all.

"You said you wouldn't kill me."

"I won't have to. You will. After you write a note." Kyle pushed the memo pad and pen, past the leather bag with rope coiled inside it, toward

Mr. Whittaker. "And bring me that suitcase, or bundles, or whatever bag you stashed the bills."

"No. I won't do that," Mr. Whittaker said, finding some defiance at last.

Unconcerned, Kyle said, "You will. You can salvage what's left of your life. Take some good out of this."

"What?"

"You will," Kyle said a third time and held up one finger, "because when your wife returns home from work, you don't want me to be here." A second finger goes up, "And the Blue Syndicate won't ever come for her or your daughters." The third finger was meant to appeal to Mr. Whittaker's vanity. "And by making this easy for me, you get to have an open casket, instead of a closed one."

When Kyle had successfully completed that assignment, he never expected to return to the house on Bartlett Street.

Yet, here he is. Again.

Kyle closed the screen door and backed away, looking up at the curtained windows. The lights were out, and the whole block was quiet. He surmised that the widow, Mrs. Whittaker, and her daughters were sound asleep. In the morning, she would discover another of his installments, though Kyle suspected she would return all the money if it would bring her husband back. Did she wonder who her benefactor was? Or why he left a lotto winning at the door? Kyle would never enlighten her or any of the others. He left no correspondence. Nothing to trace the envelope or its contents back to him.

His Italian shoes scratched the cement as he turned in place to leave. Several paces later, he heard a door open, then the squeak of a screen door.

"Wait!" a woman shouted from behind him.

Kyle instantly froze and slowly turned his head. Mrs. Whittaker leaned out of the doorway, looking directly at him. He gaped, unbelieving.

"Wait! Please. Don't leave."

She wore a frazzled bathrobe. Every sleepless night drooped under her eyes. One hand was on the inside handle of the screen door and the other held the envelope out.

How? He delivered his payments many months apart, intentionally staggering the frequency to avoid such a scenario as this. How could she know what night to expect him? She couldn't possibly stay up this late every night on the chance he'd come by. Astonishing. There was no stopping a woman so determined, so bereaved.

Pinned in place, he pivoted so he faced the house. He hoped she wouldn't invite him in.

"Is this about Stanley? Did you know him? You did, didn't you? Who are you?"

While he collected his thoughts he clicked his teeth together. Sandwiched between the two doors, her questing gaze fixed on him. He hadn't ever considered needing to answer such questions. Obviously, she had had time to think of what questions she would ask.

The clutched envelope shakes in the air, "Why?"

"I'm sorry for your loss," he answered, then winces at how rote and unfeeling that must have sounded.

"You were in the business—like he was? You know about that, right? You understand what I'm asking?"

Kyle wasn't certain what Mr. Whittaker revealed to his wife. He hedged, "We didn't work together. Not exactly." He turned again, intending to leave it at that.

Mrs. Whittaker shouted, partly in anger and partly in desperation, "What is this for?! Why do you come out here like a God damned shoemaker's elf, leaving these envelopes?"

This got Kyle's attention. Chastened, he returned.

She offered the envelope, "Take it. I want straight answers."

Kyle made no movement to take it but did approach so neither would need to raise their voice. From the other side of the screen, Kyle allowed his eyes to wander. He discovered something attached to the upper door jamb—a commercially available sensor. It should have a mate attached to the screen door. When they come apart, an alarm would go off inside the house. So that's how she knew to come down. Clever woman.

"I just about fell asleep when I heard the door," she said, following his thoughts. "Why are you skulking around at this hour?"

"To avoid questions."

"I haven't spent any of it."

"That covers a lot of expenses."

"I didn't know where it was coming from. I assumed the obvious, that it had to do with Stanley's death. I thought it was dirty."

"It's taken from dirty people."

She nodded, her face lightening a shade, grateful for a direct, honest answer. "Was it really suicide?"

"Yes." So much for honesty. Killing the truth is uncomfortably easy. Is it for his sake or hers?

"Then why are you leaving us money?"

Kyle confessed through the screen, "The payments aren't for you or your husband's sake. They're for mine. He wasn't a bad man, but I was. I still am."

He had put an end to a lot of lifetimes. He was good at the job. A mechanical process that he performed well and took satisfaction in doing it clean. Not for fun, only for knowing he did it well. He once thought he would do it forever. No longer. Now there was only one lifetime to end, but it would have to wait. "It's a small part of what I owe."

She responded, "He left me a note. He tried to explain that he was involved with some financial scheme and he did things he was ashamed of. He didn't want us to find out but knew we would, and he couldn't live with it. What did he mean?"

"Your husband did a wrong and it ate him up. Some powerful men asked him for a favor many years ago. It was a simple thing with little risk. Then they'd come back and ask for another favor. A little more risky, a little less simple. And soon, he was in deep."

Tears sprang up in Mrs. Whittaker's eyes, and the white envelope crumpled in her hand. "Why did he keep it a secret from me? Why didn't he tell me?"

Kyle tried to explain, "Bad men don't lose sleep on funds going into the wrong account. Your husband did. But he never knew how to make it right. They threatened him to keep quiet."

She shuddered, perhaps with this realization of the double life her husband had led. Kyle's account still didn't reveal the whole truth, but he wanted to spare her from knowing that Mr. Whittaker didn't need arm-twisting. He helped willingly. Up to a point, he enjoyed his cut and feeling important to important people. He wasn't so innocent.

"How are you getting by?"

"It's hard. The girls miss him. And I'm worn out. I've hardly slept, and I had to take a second job to make ends meet."

"Then use the money."

"I hate him all over again." Already crying, Mrs. Whittaker started laughing between sniffles.

Rummaging through his pockets, Kyle found a handkerchief and bent his arm around the open door to hand it to her.

Thanking him, she wiped her eyes then her nose.

"I hated him after he died. Then I've hated myself for hating him. He didn't tell me about any of this until he killed himself. You know how the body was found? Our youngest daughter found him." Her breath caught when she related this. "He couldn't have known. She had gotten ill at school—it turned out to be stomach flu. So a neighbor-friend took her home early. She found him."

Kyle looked away.

"I was supposed to find him. I had to be called at work—she was hysterical. I found the note. Once I read it, I knew not to show the police. He was dead, and there'd be no point in extending our daughters' misery with questions and investigations.

"But since it was a suicide, the insurance company wouldn't pay. The family helped out with what they could, but they wanted to know why he did this. Was he depressed or sick? I didn't know what to tell them. I didn't know what to think. Then these envelopes started showing up. I had to make sense of it. They seemed to come at random, so I didn't know which mornings to expect them. Then I saw on TV a commercial for these things that you can stick on windows to go off if a burglar opens them."

"Very resourceful."

"I suppose." Mrs. Whittaker fell silent, squeezing the handkerchief in her hand that is tucked under her chin. Then as quickly she started again, drawing in a fresh breath, a renewed vigor. "It wasn't fair that he did this to us. He could have told me. Even if he was convicted, his daughters would still have a father to write to in prison. I could have visited him."

"What are their names?"

"Hillary and Gloria."

"Before you know it, they'll be ready for college. Put the money toward that. That way you aren't spending the money, not yet. You're just putting it under the mattress. See how you feel when the time comes."

"My youngest is a senior at Rutgers on scholarship," she said.

This was another stunner. For Kyle, they were still the girls in the pictures stuck to the refrigerator. Now all grown up and moved on. More than can be said of him.

He said, "Then pay off the loans or give it away. But I'm still leaving envelopes."

"Till when? You can't continue this forever."

"Don't worry about that. Try to get some sleep."

"Why don't you come inside? It's cold. You can have a drink before you leave."

Kyle started, about to reach for the edge of the screen door and step inside the house. For a moment, he forgot dreading this very situation.

Why couldn't he? He wanted that human connection. It's been so long. Over the decades such bonds had fallen away; people grew old, died; time kept speeding up. It's been work all this time. Endless work. He had thought immortality would be a hell of a lot of fun.

So what now? Enter and join Mrs. Whittaker at her kitchen table? Swap stories, gossip like neighbors? Bond?

"I have cocoa I can heat up," she said.

Kyle withdrew his hand and raised his green eyes to hers that are puffy from the tears. She looked beautiful. Whatever Mr. Whittaker saw in her all those years ago when they had met was still there in those eyes. Maybe Kyle helped tonight. She knew more about the circumstances of her husband's death. Maybe she could get unstuck, no longer stay up all hours of the night, use the money, find someone to love again.

Her expression filled with understanding, and she let Kyle step away. He needn't explain, but he wanted to. He tried to, but all that came out were unfinished thoughts.

"You never told me your name."

"Dowd. Kyle Dowd. Like you said, it's cold. You should get some sleep. He loved you, and he would want you to live your life, to be happy. Will you do that?"

"I will, Mr. Dowd. I hope you learn to do the same."

***

"Do you think I made a mistake?" he asks the mouse.

The mouse does not reply.

"No. It was the right thing to do. I couldn't have gone in. What would I have said to her?" What does he ever say to anyone? Nothing. And that, Kyle realizes, is what has bothered him since waking tonight. For decades now, he has not shared his regrets, this human failing, with anyone.

From the kitchen, the rotary wall phone rings.

"It was the right thing to do," he says. The words are truer than Kyle realizes. The feeling is more solid. He makes a connection. He helped a woman. And just a bit, he helped himself. He allows himself to consider this bright spot.

Kyle scoops the mouse up before taking the flight of stairs up to the main floor. On his way to answer the phone, he returns his pet to its pals in the cage. Then the brightness is forgotten.

chapter
six

Deja vu

R eed runs. The field darkens. The wheat shrivels. The ravens' shadow hand pursues.

Quills of straw break from Reed's huffing form, trailing in the furrows of the earth. They glimmer and wink like diamonds against the coal of shadow—memories whose brightness fades.

The ravens swoop, talon tips just missing stitches. Stumbling, arms out wild, Reed presses on in hurried aimless routes. Rocks stub his feet, cut his boots, bring him to his knees. A spray of straw fans out. Gloved hands scoop up the straw and a single white petal, urgently stuffing his chest before he's strafed once more…

***

Reed flails awake, falling out of bed and landing on a parquet floor. His banged elbow confirms he isn't dead yet. Reuniting with Lily will have to wait.

Pulling himself to a seated position, back against the mattress-topped steel cot, Reed looks about the darkened room. A slender triangle of fluorescent light escapes the half-open bathroom door.

59

Mon cher, Reed.

The voice in his head gives him a start. Did Marie whisper just now? He can almost feel her arm draped over his shoulder, touching her head to his. He wriggles his shoulders to shoo away his phantom tag-along.

Reed! His dead wife screams.

"Lily!" His shout echoes in the empty room. How could he have left Paris without her? Why didn't he just pitch himself into the Seine? Who is he anymore? Reed feels like a coward, and he hates it.

His hands move along his bare chest. The scorching pain of last night has diminished some. He feels the heat confined deep in his heart, like a pilot light, where he hopes it will remain.

Anxious in his new surroundings, Reed gets to his feet and moves forward, nearly tripping. The bedsheet has wound around his leg. Annoyed, he kicks himself free and feels his way toward a wall, then for a light switch. Finding one, he turns the light fixture on. The efficiency apartment, maybe four- or five-hundred-square feet in size, appears spacious without furnishings. He remembers such deception after he had moved into his first apartment, how that space shrunk to such a degree that Reed had considered rigging his twin bed to fold up, Murphy-style.

The blare of a phone startles Reed, who mistakes it for a bell in the firehouse. Following the ringing into the kitchen area he answers a rotary wall phone.

Before he can say a word, the caller speaks. The baritone voice, male and unfamiliar, says, "Mr. Williams, we ask that you be patient. We'll be along soon. In the meantime, you can use the shower and get dressed." The call ends.

"Who are you?" He hangs up on the dead line.

Whoever brought him here had removed his shirt, leaving his slacks and socks on. It occurs to him the shoes are brown, the slacks are khaki, and the shirt is dark green. The footlocker has gold clasps. Colors. Filled with relief and almost joy, Reed wants to embrace every hue.

Prompted by curiosity, Reed goes into the bathroom, which has the pale odor of bleach. The blue towel folded over the bar and the tan shower curtain drawn back tempt Reed to twist the knob for hot water and slough off the past few nights, like crusts of dirt.

But he doesn't know this place or the man on the line, increasing Reed's urgency to get home where he can stand under the high-pressure showerhead, wear his own clothing, and have some semblance of his old self again.

Above, the fluorescent tubes hum as he looks in the mirror. As he had suspected, his brown eyes are back. Leaning in, he inspects each, pulling down the lower lids to look for any trace that the blackness might have pooled into their corners. Clear. He rubs them, then draws his hands down over cheeks and jaw. His face, no rougher than the other night, has perhaps a touch more color.

Had he imagined it? The drug and its effects were real, and the hallucinations were so convincing. Searching his body, Reed can't believe it, but he remembers having punched a tree last night. His hands show no sign of having done so. In fact, he appears entirely fit. No. Still no pulse. Two fingers at the wrist and again along the neck fail to detect even a minimal twitch.

Reed returns to the foot locker and finishes dressing quickly. He strides to the exit, loose laces jumping along with him. The steel knob refuses to turn in his hand. He twists firmly. Shaking it makes a soft rattle.

Why can't even the smallest things be easy, straightforward? He's thwarted at every turn, as though he's in a maze with only dead ends.

"God damn it!"

Lily would admonish him for taking the Lord's name in vain. He repeats the blasphemy in some hope that it might conjure Lily beside him. *Lecture me day and night for a month, just be here.* But she is not here. And Reed wonders where God was when Lily really needed Him.

He hammers the door with his fist. Why didn't You take me instead? Reed hopes Lily is getting answers where she is now.

He chides himself for being a coward. Not only had he failed to save her, he couldn't even avenge her. Ran like a rabbit instead of standing his ground like—well—like a lion, to quote Marie. At least if he had fought, maybe he could have killed one of them. Punching Eddie had felt good, even though Reed was worse for it. Maybe he should have held onto the thug when he had him by his balls, then squeeze them into a sack of spackling paste. Would have shut the asshole up real quick. Instead, Reed ran; ran to the police; ran from the police; ran home.

Now what?

How can Reed face anyone? What could he say to his in-laws, if they're still his in-laws now that their daughter is dead.

He'd have to work up to it. First check with his friend, Chuck, whom he has trusted with his life, and gauge how he reacts and hope to God that he believes him. Chuck would say go to the police.

Before any of that, he will need to get out of here.

Looking around, Reed sees heavy drapes near the cot. He moves himself between the cot and the wall, parting the drapes to reveal the window. Venetian blinds are lowered to the sill and twisted closed the wrong way, so the aluminum slats' undersides are showing. Reed pulls the cord, lifting the blinds.

Evening. Again. He had slept the whole day. Again.

Darkness—it's becoming something almost tangible, pressing itself against every window he looks through, looking back. Like black eyes. Maybe he and Lily both died, but he went the wrong way. Or maybe he's in Purgatory waiting for the End. He snaps his fingers on that thought. This is some afterlife hazing ritual meant to purge him of his sins.

One story below, vehicles with the blue, white, and gold colors of Pennsylvania license plates, flow. Finally something is going right for Reed. He is home, and this knowledge renews him. Shading his eyes, he scans for landmarks, but his range is reduced by crowded buildings and dark between and above. He'll have to get his bearings outside.

Reed tries to undo the latch on the window, but it won't slide. Not a bit. *This is crazy.* He'll have to smash the glass. He turns in place and tosses off the mattress so that he can use the cot's metal frame. Across the room, he hears the steel knob turn smoothly and the door opens inward. Still holding the cot over his head, Reed pauses to see two business-suited men enter wearing unreadable expressions.

"Set the cot down, Mr. Williams," suggests the first, perhaps amused. "Good. Now, take your seat." He has pale skin and thin brown hair. The second is a black man with a patch of white on his mustache and white sideburns. The door behind him clicks shut.

"I'm Alcott Ashton, and this is Leonard Webb," the man continues. The sound of their dress shoes clipping the floor is loud in the spartan room. He pulls the foot locker before the cot, using it as a bench to sit opposite Reed. Their knees nearly touch, and Reed feels uncomfortable with him being so close and the other one standing over him.

"We have urgent matters to attend to elsewhere; and I am certain that you are eager to get home. Therefore, the more cooperative you are the sooner that will happen. Agreed?"

Unsettled, Reed nods once, rubbing his palms across his thighs. Mr. Ashton's voice isn't the one he had spoken with a few minutes ago, which could mean the other, Mr. Webb, was the caller.

From his jacket pocket, Mr. Webb removes a smartphone. After some taps on the screen, Mr. Webb reads, "Reed Williams, resident of Stapleton

Tower, apartment 721..." In his smooth voice, Mr. Webb reviews his date of birth, social security number, marital status, schools attended, and other personal information.

"How?" Reed asks.

Mr. Ashton brings Reed's attention back to himself. "Answering our questions will do for now." Mr. Ashton speaks with a fading English accent, more cultured than Eddie's. "A murder transpired last night and you were a suspect, but in light of certain facts, you no longer are one. Still, you are a waif and that presents its own problems."

"Are you detectives?" He isn't sure what the man is talking about.

Mr. Ashton gestures, holding off Reed's question with his hand. "What is your connection to Troy Dawson, also known as Blade?"

"I don't know anyone named Troy or Blade." None that Reed recalls. Has he forgotten some crucial information?

"How about a woman named Roxy Marchetti?"

"No."

"Are you certain? She is quite unforgettable."

"I've been forgetting a lot. I don't remember knowing a Roxy Marchetti."

"Prior to us finding you, where were you about last night?"

Marie coos inside his head. Reed grimaces. "I was returning home from Paris."

Mr. Ashton's eyes note the wedding band. "Where is your wife?"

Reed's pilot light flickers brighter. Irritated, he asks, "Who are you guys? Am I under arrest or something?"

Have the French police contacted the Philly P.D. and told them Reed's story? Faxed over a sketch with WANTED typed above his head in bold letters, and FOR MURDER beneath his shoulders?

Mr. Ashton asks, "Who are *you*? *What* are you? Do you know?"

"I don't." He holds up his hands—guilty. "OK? I'm in some serious shit right now. You wouldn't believe it. I'm this scarecrow running for my life." Across his chest, he tugs several times at the fabric of his shirt. "I'm coming apart."

Mr. Ashton says nothing and instead gives a questioning glance to Mr. Webb.

Mr. Webb says, "No word, yet."

Back to Reed, Mr. Ashton says, "Something occurred in Paris. I have speculated on what that occurrence was. It exonerates you from the murder, but it places you in an even more precarious position."

As Mr. Ashton's words bring relief, Reed is already nodding his head, breaking in, "Yes. She was murdered." Reed jumps to his feet, "But not by me." He glances to Mr. Webb then back to Mr. Ashton, "I tried to tell them last night. But, one of them glowed—I was on some kind of drug—" Reed cuts himself off when he realizes he's not helping his case with this honesty.

Coolly, Mr. Ashton looks up at Reed, "Remember your seat, Mr. Williams."

Mr. Webb doesn't lift his eyes from his device.

More firmly, Mr. Ashton says, "Sit. Now. I will leave that to the French authorities. One murder is quite enough."

Reed sits on the steel bed once more. His hands rub each other. He itches for a cigarette.

"As I have said, this confirms what we already suspected. You still possessed your boarding pass in your pocket along with your passport and driver's license. And with the ring, it was a trifle to put things together and run down public records. Simple Pinkerton work."

At this, Reed catches a brief smile on Mr. Webb's face. He wonders what else the man knows.

"You tripped some wards at the airport." Then as an aside to Mr. Webb, "I am surprised they still work—they are fairly worn out."

Mr. Webb declares to his phone, "Lovelace, set a reminder: reapply airport wards."

A prim female voice responds, "Reminder set: reapply airport wards."

Back to Reed, Mr. Ashton says, "When we found you, you were quite out of sorts. In fine fettle, by the by?"

Reed nods again, wary.

"Normal vision restored." He picks and offers the sunglasses to Reed. "Hold onto them. You will undoubtedly need them later."

Reed takes it and is about to ask why that is, but Mr. Ashton moves on with his questions. His hands clench. They're holding back—they know something.

"Who is your sire? Is he presently in Paris?"

On his feet as fast as before, Reed snaps his eyes on Mr. Ashton, "Shut up for a damn minute." His lump of a heart grows hot. "I haven't understood anything you've been saying since you came in here. The past two nights I've been through some serious shit that I understand even less. My wife was murdered. Out of nowhere, this gang, drugged up to their freaky eyes, grabbed us. They threw her in the river and threw me into a car. Made me take that drug shit too.

"And I ran. I saw an opportunity to get away, so I ran. Like a coward, I ran. And since then I've been sick with myself and I'm not sure I know who I am anymore. Like maybe the drug changed me. Can that happen? I can't remember important things. And I can't feel my pulse."

In front of the two men, he holds out his arms, "Feel for yourself. Tell me I'm crazy."

Neither act surprised, and neither move to test him.

"And as I've been sitting here, while you're asking your questions, I thought that none of this would make sense to you, that you wouldn't believe me. But now I'm thinking you aren't surprised. You know more than you're telling me. If you're going to arrest me, then do it. But I'm not answering any more questions till you start doing the same."

When Mr. Ashton begins to speak, his body language unchanged, Reed mule-kicks the cot away. "Tell me to sit—one more time."

"Perceptive, Mr. Williams," Mr. Ashton says, not the least bit sympathetic. "You are in an excitable mood. Understandable. However, that will not do. Gather yourself before you do something rash. My questions were intended to establish a baseline of your knowledge of pertinent facts. Evidently, you know few."

A beep catches their attention. Then the phone's electronic voice says, "Message from Tamerlane."

Mr. Webb looks up from the screen and reports to his partner, "All-hands meeting in thirty."

On his feet, Mr. Ashton says, "Right. Inform them that we are on our way. And get Kyle. Wait. No, I will phone Kyle from the car." He motions for Reed to follow, "Let us get you on your way, Mr. Williams. Accompany us out."

Mr. Webb moves ahead, tucking the phone into his jacket. Effortlessly, he turns the same steel knob that Reed hadn't been able to budge earlier before. He opens the door for Mr. Ashton who looks down at Reed's feet on his way through. "Your laces are undone."

***

As his shoes scrape the cement steps of the apartment building, Reed eyes the cars and people on their way home. Time for him to do the same. Given his experience with cabs last night, he decides he will walk there. The gabled spires of the Liberty Place buildings point the way; he'll aim there then continue northeasterly into the Fishtown section and home. About three miles.

As though guessing Reed's thoughts, Mr. Ashton says, "Home holds no answers for you."

"Neither do you," Reed challenges, at his limit with the man's game of asking questions and only hinting at having any answers.

Mr. Ashton remains cool as ever, casually stepping over to a woman who appears to be waiting for someone. Stretching her neck and glancing about, she takes no notice of the pasty man's approach. As in the cafe last night, Reed has the sense of being an observer looking at the woman through a telescope.

Speaking above a whisper, which focuses Reed's attention, Mr. Ashton says, "Do you think by going home, you will return to your routine? You will sleep through your shifts because your alarm clock fails to rouse you each morning. Ask yourself: when did you last eat?"

Reed hasn't thought of food. Between the stretches of sleep and peaks of adrenaline, eating never occurred to him. His last bite must have been dinner with Lily.

"You will hunger, but not as before. Some evening soon you will feel it, not in your stomach, but in your head. And if you are not wise to what will satisfy this need, how to satiate it, then it will grow more insistent, clawing away any rationality you still possess. And that is when you end up killing people. People like her. See the ring on her finger? Do you want someone else to lose their wife because of you?"

"No," he says, startled as though Mr. Ashton has smacked his face. Has he become a dangerous man? Does he really think he can go home and return to a normal life? What is he now? What life is there for him without Lily? Or his heart?

Mr. Ashton says, "A reassuring answer." He leaves the woman and guides Reed. They join Mr. Webb waiting by a Lincoln sedan with a custom paint job: grey body and orange accents. "Answers are inside. But you won't like them."

Mr. Webb gets behind the wheel, docking his smartphone in the center console, while Reed sinks into the passenger seat behind Mr. Ashton. "Welcome, Mr. Webb," says the same electronic voice Reed had heard in the apartment. "Select destination?"

Mr. Webb declines the assistance, and further declines to hear pending reminders and messages while Mr. Ashton takes out a flip-style cell phone. He says, "Good evening, Mr. Dowd. Yes. Not a small matter has come up. You will be needed at Tamerlane. Attend promptly in one hour. Good evening."

In a few blocks, Reed begins to recognize his whereabouts. South to Lombard, then cut west, perhaps heading toward highway 76. Reed asks, "Where are we going?"

"An estate named Tamerlane. Heard of it? It's located in Fairmount Park and is the residence of Lord Devlin."

"Master Devlin," Mr. Webb says with an acid tone that sounds more like, "massa."

"Who's that?"

Distracted, Mr. Ashton says, "Every society has its hierarchy, Mr. Williams. Here in Philadelphia, he is at the top of ours. You will need to meet him. Formality and all."

He hears the click and snap of the glove box opening and closing. The next moment Reed flinches, pressing back into the leather. Mr. Ashton has turned to face Reed, loosely holding in his lowered hand a large revolver.

"Concentrates the mind, does it not? I only have this ride to begin to explain to you what you need to understand. What you should have learned from your sponsor. So pardon my dramatic lesson, but we need to pull our oars together."

Mr. Webb continues driving, apparently not disturbed by this turn in the conversation.

As blunt as the gun itself, Mr. Ashton says, "You died, Mr. Williams. Through will and desperation you came back. But not as the man you once were."

Has the gun gone off, Reed wonders, because he feels Mr. Ashton's words shred through him, confirming his fear. A bullet of fatal truth. *You died.* His body jolts against the seat as he absorbs the impact. *My God, I knew it.* He can hear the cries of the crows—that nightmare landscape, has it been real this whole time? A Purgatory that follows him wherever he goes? He thinks on all the impossible experiences like the black eyes, the blue rings, the fire in his chest, that feeling of being apart from everyone else. Is he a ghost?

"… no breath or heartbeat…"

Mr. Ashton's still speaking.

Reed's thoughts have talked over the man. "What?"

"I said you are no longer human. Perhaps even now, sloshing around in your head, are experiences of another person, as real as your own. The same person who likely, however tenuously, manipulated you, like a marionette." Mr. Ashton wags the fingers of his free hand.

With the other hand, he raises the revolver.

Reed's eyes snap to the barrel and back to the man.

"Would I shoot you, you would not die again. Even with a pair of neat holes in your heart. Painful, certainly, but in no time, you would be right as rain."

Mr. Webb spares a glance to his partner, "You're paying for the new upholstery."

"For now, take it on faith that my assertion is true." With his thumb, Mr. Ashton draws the hammer back and the cylinder rotates. "Or do I need to demonstrate?"

It is a lot to take on faith. But how could Mr. Ashton know what is in his head and what he has seen? He did have Marie's memories "sloshing" around. Before he lost consciousness last night so close to his home, he experienced Marie again. She had been in some danger. A man held her—she was frightened—but then there was serenity. Then darkness.

Now that Reed thinks on it, that memory was Marie's final night. He could feel her heart clanging on her ribcage. She had been human, and now she is not. And neither is he.

Reed could feel her heart as his own when Eddie had held him down the night he died. While Marie shushed at him, he struggled for his life, for Lily's life. He screamed for help as he was too weak—pathetically weak—to get Eddie off him. But when Marie opened her mouth, he gasped. Her teeth were sharp. She bit him, drawing blood. He had never been squeamish about blood, even his own—years of handling hammers, saws, razors, drills, and heavy equipment cured that. But the wet, slick feeling of his own blood wetting his neck, soaking into the collar of his shirt, running away with his life, revolts Reed, violates him. He feels it all over again. He was murdered, and the fact shakes him to his core.

Reed gasps, coming up from the vivid memory as though it had arms that held him underwater.

Mr. Ashton says, "I need to hear you say it, Mr. Williams."

"I'm not human." Saying the words tighten his throat like a shot of whiskey. The truth burns. As much as he cannot believe it, he can believe nothing else. This is what has itched at Reed since he woke in Marie's bed—a feeling of otherness, somehow wrong in his skin. He lost something. His humanity. His soul?

"Neither am I. Mr. Webb is. For now." He lowers the gun, letting his thumb ease off the hammer. "Excellent. We are making progress. The one who turned your world inside out was your sponsor or sire. What is his name?"

"Marie de Telfour." *Mon lion.*

"I gather she ruined your honeymoon and killed your wife?"

"Yes."

"If it is any consolation, in our society, what this Marie de Telfour had committed was a violation. Such things are not tolerated on this side of the pond. This existence is a gift for the few worthy of it. To force it upon those unwilling is against our code. Alas, the benighted ones of the Old World still hold to the fashion of tyrants and slaves."

"If we're not human, then what the hell are we?"

"We are rarefied men. Ageless, exalted, powerful."

We are gods, Marie had said. A blasphemy that Lily would take Marie to task for.

Reed tries to follow, "So the drug Marie gave me brought me back from the dead?" Reed recalls nursing from Marie.

"Not a drug. Her blood. Ichor as it's commonly called. You and I—we no longer have the red stuff.

"It's typical for the sponsor to continue feeding the initiate their own ichor for a time. This strengthens the bond already between them. Think of it as a safety feature, granting the donor the ability to command their initiate's actions should they become overwhelmed by the hunger I had mentioned and thereby harm others. Had Marie de Telfour continued to feed you her ichor, over time, she would effectively leash your will to hers. Fortunate that you escaped as soon as you had."

He returns the revolver to the glove box.

Mr. Webb cruises northerly on the highway with the Schuylkill flowing on the passenger side.

"It is remarkable that your ignorance has not been a fatal condition. Without knowing what you are, what you are capable of, what your body requires, you have managed to slip out of her grasp and returned home before sunup.

"So let us not tempt fate any longer. Ignorance can be remedied. Tonight and the nights to follow, you will pay strict attention, in order that you will not harm yourself or those around you."

Reed says, "So I'm a monster. There's got to be some way to undo it."

"Certainly not," Mr. Ashton says, settling nothing.

"And what about my wife? What about Lily? What about justice for her? Marie and Eddie and the rest of them—they murdered her and they get away with it? Fuck that."

"What would you propose to do about it, Mr. Williams?"

"You're the guy with the answers. There has to be something. What about this Devlin guy? You said he's the boss here. Who's in charge over there? We contact him, fill him in. Wouldn't he want to know? If Marie did this to us, then she'll probably do it again to other people."

"Undoubtedly. However, we have no formal relations with... well, whomever is in charge. My understanding is there is a bit of tumult in Paris and many other territories besides. It's a bit of an ongoing sport on the Continent. And as I have told you, their ways are not ours.

"Tragic as it certainly is, your wife's death is not my concern. There is nothing you can do tonight. Your vengeance will have to wait."

"I don't have time to wait," Reed says. "I told you I'm losing my memories. These crows are stealing them. It's like I'm made of straw, and they're picking me apart."

Mr. Ashton says, "I honestly don't know how to respond to that."

"Will I lose them all? What will happen to me?"

"I cannot say I've heard of that before. But do not worry. I've already collected a sample of your ichor after we put you in the apartment last night. We'll get to the bottom of that soon enough."

"I can't just sit here and not do anything. I've screwed it all up. God, I loved her."

Mr. Ashton looks out his window.

Off the highway, the Lincoln follows the winding tree-lined road through the Park. As the mileage goes by, fewer cars are seen.

Mr. Ashton shakes his head and sighs as though out of patience with Reed's stupidity. "You still haven't grasped the whole situation. As I said, there is much to cover. Such is the reason we do not grab strangers off the street and initiate them. There is a process. Like a courtship. You meet, you become acquainted, you learn if you share the same interests, dreams, et cetera. Then if everyone's agreeable, you take the plunge. It is not for everybody.

"Your own life hangs by a very fine thread. Since you fled, that makes you a waif, one without sponsorship, which, in turn, makes you a danger to everyone. We punish the sire for disregarding the code and we kill their fledgling out of self-preservation."

"Then why not kill me? Can you?"

"There are methods. Was Marie warm to the touch? Like you?"

Marie's icy fingers linger on Reed's skin. He shakes his head. "She was very cold."

"Fascinating. You're still alive, because you may have value. Lord Devlin will decide that. Do you believe she will pursue you here?"

"She's insane. I have no idea what she'll do."

To Mr. Webb, he says, "We'll need to expect that she does."

Mr. Webb says, "Lovelace make a note: monitor the airport." The console in the Lincoln's dash and the smartphone inside his jacket beep in acknowledgment.

Reed sinks in his seat feeling absolutely lost. His hand grasps for Lily's to squeeze but does not find it. What would she make of all this? Would it challenge her faith or confirm it? If she had been sitting here with him this entire time, listening to Mr. Ashton, believing him as Reed does, however crazy the man sounds, what would she think of her husband now? Would she see a monster? Would she run in horror?

He grimaces and balls up his hands. *No.* She wouldn't, and he's ashamed of even thinking it. She's love. And she's forgiveness. She wouldn't abandon him like he did her.

Looking up at Mr. Ashton, he says, "I don't want to go back."

"One night at a time, Mr. Williams. We shall see what Lord Devlin decrees."

The road changes from asphalt to dirt, from four lanes to two, then one. The trees crowd each other, arching over the Lincoln with colorful boughs. The wedge, indicating the car on the G.P.S. screen, turns in a blank field. They're off the system's records.

"Here we are: Tamerlane."

chapter
seven

Babel

Professor Malcolm Gold had been confounded by Grace's detachment in his class this evening. She didn't move except for her steady breathing and a finger that caressed a creased paper held in her hands. It was as though a doll of her likeness was deposited in her place. Worse—she didn't raise questions or answer his. Only in the absence of her voice had he realized the light it brought to his lectures.

Normally animated, Grace sparkles in the lecture hall or here in the coffee shop, where they meet after the evening class. Her words paint delicate worlds before his eyes and sing in his ears, lifting him from monotony. She will come tonight, won't she? He checks the entrance, but sees only a student wave and take a seat on an overstuffed couch as his friends scoot aside.

Malcolm sits here after his evening lectures, reading peer studies, grading papers, and allaying students' concerns. The Blue Cup is a favorite in the University City area of Philadelphia. Students from the surrounding campuses can be found here from fresh-baked-muffin mornings till stale-coffee closings, gabbing with friends or cramming for exams. Malcolm considers this his office more than the one on campus. The informal atmosphere makes him accessible to his students.

Turning to his work once more, Malcolm slouches in his seat, the cuffs of his black slacks not reaching his ankles, revealing white socks in comfy loafers. His lips move while he reads a university textbook. His voracious mind speeds through the academic volume; left eye on the left page, right eye on the right page, each zipping top to bottom. His hands keep pace; one jotting notes in tight cursive across a legal pad, the other turning the pages.

In his youth, Malcolm had absorbed stories of people with extraordinary mental prowess—those who could memorize shelves of books or learn languages in days or solve computations in their heads. Inspired, Malcolm trained his mind with cerebral calisthenics, treating neurons as flexors, stretching and strengthening his mental acuity. Now he has reached a point where he can give complete concentration on two separate tasks simultaneously.

Delicate brown hands emerge from the edge of his peripheral vision. Unmistakable, their fine structure and long fingers that articulate a delightful language all their own belong to only one of his students. Malcolm looks up from his work. Grace Situ seats herself across their table, the one they have spent countless hours chatting over.

He wears his uniform, his lecture clothes: a paisley tie knotted around a starched white collar. A blue mug of coffee sits beside his pad, partially obscuring someone's phone number tattooed in the wood. The *Philadelphia Inquirer* lies neatly folded beside his glazed cup.

He catches her hand pass over her mouth as though to stifle a yawn to discreetly pop in a mint tablet.

"Good evening again, Miss Situ." Attempting to rise, his coat catches under the chair leg, impeding him. Awkwardly, Malcolm extricates himself. But she has already taken her seat. At the inept greeting, he inwardly chides his uncoordinated body. Where his intellect is nimble, his body fumbles in social interactions. His movements are tentative like a child still learning etiquette—more imitative than natural. He fares better with her, though. His prize pupil.

Social interactions have always been difficult. His intellect sets him above, drifting in the clouds of ideas, so that when he touches ground, he wobbles, unused to the gravid world everyone else occupies. But with Grace, he feels more, he speaks faster, the air electrifies, his skin pulses.

"Good evening, professor," she replies with a distinct South African accent revealing her Xhosa heritage. "I didn't mean to interrupt. I will wait till you are finished."

Though not his suggestion, he had been delighted when she informed him that she decided to refocus her graduate studies of anthropology to incorporate linguistics. Though in their second semester together, this ritual kaffeeklatsch had beguan only recently.

Malcolm dog-ears the page, closes the book, and puts on a pair of eyeglasses. Half-frames hold rectangle lenses in front of his brown eyes. They add some years to his apparent mid-thirties. Much older still, a fact he cannot share with Grace. There is time for that later when he has her trust.

Grace is one of his few international students. To be so far from home for so long takes a certain kind of person. Though foreign students often do well despite the difficulty of the courses, it comes as no surprise to Malcolm that several seek him out for extra tutelage. In her case, he feels as though he has become her confidant as much as her teacher.

His next utterance is spoken in Afrikaans, one of her native tongues. "You were conspicuously silent in class tonight. We were all poorer for it."

She laughs. "Excellent. You are learning quickly." She has been teaching him the fundamentals of the language. In exchange, he helps her with Latin.

Malcolm tilts his head, expecting her to answer his earlier remark.

"My apologies, professor. I have been distracted all day." She responds in Dutch, one of several languages in which they are conversant. And the game begins. A contest rather than a conversation. A linguistic dance to see who will misstep first. The scope of their *lingua franca* includes Afrikaans, Dutch, French, and English.

"Distracted describes a woman partially aware of her surroundings. You were absent. While your body was seated in the third row, ninth in from my left, your mind was entirely elsewhere. You even let pass my assertion of Twain's Paradox."

He is more verbally agile, nimbly switching from one language to the next—even in the same sentence, like pidgin. This is the typical endgame flourish. Apparently undeterred, Grace enjoys the wordplay in the ruins of Babel.

"That is in your favor then. I would have derailed your class with my objections."

"Just so. It was raised as a device to elicit a reaction from you. The dialogue would have been stimulating." Conversations with Grace are like uncorking a vintage wine, to be savored together by the fire. She is a fine lingual companion, one who enjoys the warm tones, subtle accents, and rhythmic cadences of speech as much as he does.

He would be pleased to listen all night. Her words unspool like a silken ribbon, perfuming the air. Not only in her musical enunciation and engaging tone that anyone could recognize, but in qualities Malcolm uniquely appreciates. For him, words, written or spoken, have always been vivid, nearly tangible. Each letter has its own color. An "A" is lime green and a cantaloupe orange "O" turns pale lilac when a tail is added to form a "Q."

"You are kind. You have always been kind." Her brown eyes glimpse his own.

"Clearly for naught," he continues past her. "For rather than taking a bite of the controversy, you continued to chew on a nut of private consternation. Tell me this perplexing pith had been a quandary for the sages and not a quotidian trifle." He infers from her silence and downcast eyes that the matter is not trivial. "Your reticence permitted Miss Torenz to contribute tonight."

"Are you saying I monopolize the class time?"

"I am observing that your progress in this course has surpassed that of your peers. They recognize this and are hesitant to be heard, lest they appear foolish. I have been trying to appeal to the competitiveness of Miss Torenz and others to encourage more participation on their part."

"Thank you, but I owe you for that."

Soon after the semester started a month ago, Grace approached Malcolm, already overwhelmed with the course material. He invited her to sit. She did. She fretted to him that perhaps she made a mistake in choosing this track of study. Actually gasping, she apologized for wasting his time and would withdraw from the course.

Malcolm had lent her his handkerchief to dry her eyes, and said in a patient voice, "You are more than you know."

Her confidence thence buoyed, they worked on matters that gave her the most difficulty. And though her grasp tightened, she continued seeing him.

Presently, he demurs, "I have not done anything but present the class with facts. It is for the students to interpret them and apply them skillfully. You do both exceedingly well. So well that I would have no reservations in having you lead my undergraduate lecture next semester should some unforeseeable event require my absence."

Grace's eyes widen. "Does this mean our after-class sessions are over?" She stretches her long ebony fingers across the plain of conversation to reach the pale tips of his. But his fingers leap away like startled gazelles. His hand smacks his mug and sloshed cold coffee drinks up his paperwork.

Malcolm makes a noise, annoyed. He is less disturbed by the ruin of his notes and more frustrated again by his body's betrayal.

Emptying the napkin dispenser, Grace wipes the table with a deep frown.

The waitress supplies more napkins and tells Malcolm she'll bring him a refill.

"That will not be necessary," he counters.

"I'll have a cup of green tea." Grace cleans her fingers while adding almond biscotti to her order.

Feeling that he has bungled the evening, Malcolm turns in his seat, so he is in full profile to Grace. His profession places him as an authority figure to impressionable minds, if not passionate hearts. For this, he has been careful to keep his students at bay. He's never informal with them. Never intimate. His desire is kept in check.

And yet she weakens these defenses with her earnestness, ingenuity, and proficiencies. She springs upon the challenges of the material, sometimes clumsily, but with verve. There is joy here. There is freshness. He wants to cultivate her, as his protege; to tone up her confidence, to harness her insights, and shape her talents. Such promise he has not seen in many years. Perhaps not even once.

Malcolm's thoughts fumble off course from the academic to the romantic. Her warm character, her melodious voice, her sweet lips worthy of a sonnet. Which he has written. Several, in fact, are on loose-leaf paper folded away in an inner pocket of his long coat.

Would it be terrible to indulge one time? He is sorely tempted to break his personal protocol. Just a nip of the crimson trickle of her warm wine. His tongue slides between his teeth. Then aware of it, he sucks it back in.

No. Why would he jeopardize that with a less-than-professional relationship? Not now. This flower must bloom before he plucks it.

He says quietly, looking at the next table or beyond it, "Miss Situ, listen closely for the following words are not ones I dole out to any A student. *You are gifted.* We have a great deal of time ahead of us to work together. Once you've completed your current studies, you should consider doctoral work right here with me. There is no better university to exercise your talents. You will merit the greatest acclaim, I assure you."

He falls silent again when the waitress steps to their table holding a tray with her order. Grace smiles a touch as the blue mug and matching saucer are placed before her. Curls of steam carrying off the tea's scent. Her fingers take hold of an end of the biscotti, tapping off the loose crumbs.

Malcolm folds his hands in his lap.

Grace just holds the almond biscuit, her eyes looking somewhere else in contemplation. Now he has done it. He must have said something wrong. He possesses perfect recall, but cannot pinpoint his *faux pas*.

Finally, she says, "Have you ever loved someone?"

Confused by this turn in the conversation, he doesn't answer immediately. His eyes almost return to her. "I believe I have. A long time past."

"No one now?"

"Ms. Situ, these are peculiar questions."

"Not even one date?"

He shifts in his seat as if suddenly overcome with a rash. "Why do you wish to know such personal matters?"

"To know you better. To you know you at all. Does it always have to be about schoolwork? I've never been to your apartment or wherever you live. I've never seen you outside the classroom or the Blue Cup. Do you have pets? Do you have a favorite movie? Or food?"

"Those aren't relevant—"

She clips in, "Why do you continue meeting with me? You know I don't need tutoring anymore. Why do you see me?"

He holds up his hand—a pleading gesture. "Ms. Situ. I'm your professor, and my preoccupation is to provide the foundation for you to achieve great things. That is why I agree to see you here." He turns to face her to bargain, "We will have all the time we need for these questions after you earn your degree. Then I will no longer be your professor, but your peer, your colleague."

"Only colleagues? Is everyone either a colleague or student to you? Can we ever be more?"

"Ms. Situ—"

"*Grace,*" she says, snapping the biscuit in two. Her fingers curl as she leans low over the table, challenging, "Can you say, *Grace,* Malcolm?"

"Ms. Situ, if you will be patient," he begs, his usual distant tone bludgeoned.

"Hey, professor," says a young woman with a canvas satchel over her shoulder. "Almost didn't see you there."

Malcolm retrieves his wool overcoat that had slid to the floor after the young woman had bumped his chair. Looking up he recognizes one of his students, then asks, "Eager for the results of your essay?" His hand passes over the stack of scored blue books. Each shade of grade is represented.

The student instantly shakes her head. Then, "Hi, Grace. How are you?" With some impatience, she says, "Good. Thank you."

"You look so pretty. Love the hair. Are you going out or something?" Grace looks at Malcolm for a long moment. "No. No reason."

Accepting this, the woman nods and waves goodbye.

In light of this exchange, Malcolm now notices Grace's appearance. Normally tied up, her unbound hair is elegantly styled. She is wearing a scarf, a silk turquoise blouse, and light, but pleasing, color on her lips and over her eyes. Nearly flawless except for the discontented look on her face.

"What is really troubling you? Something happened before class tonight. What is it?"

In answer, Grace unfolds a delicate origami bird of carmine hue. He can see hand-written letters loop over the paper.

She reads aloud, in part, in Afrikaans:

"O bird that soars with my heart. Grace, I have accepted the fellowship after careful thought over one glass of Sauvignon Blanc we picked up at Bouchard. I am to begin next semester. How I wish you were with me now. To have opened that post with me and to sit beside me as I telephoned Mr. Mketo. I want you here now. To be my wife..."

Grace's voice dries up while staring at the letter gripped in her hands.

Malcolm is dumbstruck too. She had scarcely ever spoken about her boyfriend all these months. He had been anonymous, off-stage—an innocuous detail. Now he is at their table on bended knee, holding open a velvet box containing a sparkling promise.

He removes his handkerchief from his coat pocket and snaps it open several times, as if to wave away the suitor. Then he hands it to her.

"Thank you." She daubs the corners of her eyes, "What do I do?"

Her query just now had been plaintive, the words wilting over the table. The sensation fades, but for a long moment he says nothing.

Is this rhetorical? Can he advise her, truly? She respects him and his words would have consequence. He could decide for her. He could decide for himself. He could be self-interested and persuade her to remain here. She is too young for marriage and to settle for domesticity. He could offer her a different ring. A promise of honors, prestige, *immortality*. The near infinite doors of opportunity would all slam shut if she were to leave now. She is so close.

If he would be honest with himself, he would recognize the wall of professionalism he constructed imprisons more than it protects what lies on the other side—a heart that is not entirely dead. It may beat for her if he lets it.

"Miss Situ... Grace—"

He is too late.

She puts the handkerchief back into his hand, then squeezes with a genuine, wise smile. "I will miss this."

eight

Tamerlane

The Lincoln passes through a wrought-iron gate set in a low stone wall. Headlight beams coast over the gravel road, parting the darkness. Interspersed among the centuries-old oaks, maples, and hickories, are small fallen-in structures overtaken by foliage and rot. Farther up the road a couple of cottages still stand, and the stables gleam with fresh white paint.

Solar-powered lampposts illuminate the manor, which appears like a giant red brick. Rectangular, simple, and solid, the Georgian two-story house has a peaked roof and slender, shuttered windows. Smoke from two chimneys puff signs of life inside.

When the car gently rolls to a stop, Mr. Webb shifts it into park and idles in his seat.

Ready to get out, Reed wonders why they are still sitting here. Mr. Webb's large hands remain fixed on the wheel as he stares straight ahead.

Mr. Ashton prompts his partner, "Let's go."

"I'm not seeing that cracker."

Leaning in, Mr. Ashton says, "Just keep Mr. Williams company while I brief them. Should Mr. Dowd arrive in that time, make introductions."

Mr. Webb holds firm.

Reed sees a faint smile on Mr. Ashton before he says, "I'll lend you Mason and Ridge on Friday."

Surprised, Mr. Webb turns to gauge Mr. Ashton's sincerity, "Both?"

"Both."

Mr. Webb huffs out of the car, "Let's get this over with, damn quick."

***

The formal and symmetrical style of Georgian homes such as this one reminds Reed of Pennsbury Manor. He had toured William Penn's home with his elementary class. He was riveted by the reenactors demonstrating how everything was done by hand; the materials, animals, produce, and water raised and drawn from the estate grounds, then made into tools, furniture, clothes, and supper.

The school trips had laid a foundation in him so that when he turned thirty, he wanted to build on that and learn about architectural history. In the library, he flipped through magazines and checked out books to read in the station break room.

With newfound appreciation for the technical stuff, he revisited some of those places, such as the Masonic Temple, loaded with questions for the tour guide. What tools were used; where did the materials came from, and how they were transported; how many men and how many years did the projects take?

His plans had been to quit the side jobs and begin working for himself by creating original furnishings and the like.

So much for that.

Inside, the tick and gong of the grandfather clock, the crackle and woodsy smell from the fireplace, and the sound of distant violins greet them.

Mr. Ashton shows them to the sitting room and disappears down the central hall, lit by gas-fed sconces, to one of the rear rooms. His footfalls recede. A door clicks open, music swells, and closes.

Reed asks, "Before we came in, what was that about back in the car?"

"Just business that's none of yours," Mr. Webb says in a tone that's perhaps sharper than he had meant, because his expression then turns apologetic. He leans in close, "I don't like it here."

"Me neither," Reed says. Something is wrong here.

The room feels a bit crowded with painted figures watching them. Above the chair rails, set in gold frames, oil paintings spread across the four walls. Mostly men, mostly wigged, the subjects are dressed in the fashion of an earlier era. Some are full-length portraits of officers in dress uniforms, others are men partially represented with books in hand, and a few are just heads and shoulders looking like nobles of Tamerlane. The fire enlivens each of their faces to a haunting effect.

One portrait draws Reed's attention. It depicts a woman on a settee with an improbably tall wig and peacock feathers, wearing a sunny yellow dress. Her face is pale, her cheeks are pink, and her dark eyes gaze past his right shoulder.

"That's Miss Catherine. She's more beautiful in person. And kind."

Reed opens his mouth to ask Mr. Webb a question, only to close it. A moment later he again fails to get words out. What should he ask? This is out of his realm. It's like… It's like… Nothing. It is so out of his experience that he can't grasp one edge of it. He isn't human any longer. What do you do with that?

Reed steps closer to the portrait. "She's here?"

"In the new house across the square." Mr. Webb continues in a subdued tone that conveys sympathy, "I'm sorry about your wife."

This startles Reed. Mr. Webb is the first anyone has spoken of Lily as though she mattered. This kindness causes Reed to wonder if it is a coincidence that it comes from someone human. Has decency died with the others?

Blinking several times, Reed manages a quiet, "Thank you." In a moment, he has his travel wallet in hand and slides the picture of him and Lily out from behind his driver's license.

"That's a fine-looking woman," Mr. Webb admires. "Taken on the boardwalk. Atlantic City?"

"How did you know?"

"You're all in beach clothes. The backdrop behind you. She's got that new accessory on her finger. Did you just propose? Atlantic City would just fit."

"I must have." His eyes linger on the picture before putting it away with a trembling hand. "Excuse me," he says and steps over to the mantle, holding onto it. A sensation of sourness soaks him. With his memories failing him, pictures are all he may have left of Lily. He faces away from Mr. Webb as he shudders. He can't believe she's gone.

His eyes feel hot, and he takes deep breaths. He's losing more of her. He rubs his face.

"Reed…" Mr. Webb says.

"What?" Can't he have a fucking moment? Reed turns to see Mr. Webb look pointedly at the hearth. "Shit!" He leaps back from the flames that nearly singe his slacks through the screen.

"Steady. You all right?"

"What do you think?" Reed says, regarding the fire as a hound ready to bite again.

From a drawer of a small leggy table, Mr. Webb takes a square of note paper and a golf pencil. "Now I need a description of Marie and anyone else involved." Registering Reed's surprise of the man's use of analog note-taking, Mr. Webb says, "Dead-zone here. There's a landline in the other house."

Reed looks around himself, noting the lack of electrical and ventilation systems. "All of this is original?"

He shrugs. "Tamerlane is outdated in more ways than one. Tell me how to spell Marie's last name."

Reed describes the dark-haired woman in her thirties. White. About five foot nine with no visible tattoos or scars. Thin, nice skin like a model. Either in his imagination or from a memory of hers, he can see flash bulbs popping around Marie as she smiles and poses. "A British guy named Eddie hangs around her. He's stocky, has greasy hair, and about two or three inches shorter than she. There were three others with them: Ron, Clarice, and Jean-Paul. They're the ones who took Lily."

Tucking away his notes, Mr. Webb explains that when he gets back to the car, he will send out the information and a dragnet will be set up, but it may take some time. "When you get in there, you'll be with Mr. Ashton and three others. You got Lord Devlin, Mr. Milos—he's the one with the goatee, and Mr. Thomas, he's—" Here Mr. Webb holds out his arms to finish with unspoken 'fat.' "You address them all as 'sir' if you're called on. Otherwise, don't say anything. There's a protocol. Got it?"

"Not really. I don't understand any of this."

"So pay attention."

Reed has been paying attention. A large revolver, loaded, and pointed at his chest, did focus his mind. Still, it is a small favor that Mr. Ashton and Mr. Webb have been more forthcoming than Marie and Eddie. He decides to believe these men. They seem more concerned with uncovering truths than burying them. Assuming this is the case, then Reed's life is over and every minute from now on is borrowed time. He needs to make the most of it to learn quickly so he can get control of his life back or end it.

"How did you find me last night? One guy in the whole city?"

"We were searching for someone else, and you turned up. Mr. Ashton has got a gift for finding people like him, people like you."

"What are you saying? Like a hunch?"

Mr. Webb shakes his head. "You saw blue around folks last night, right? Those are auras. Like energy signatures. He can pick up your kind's a mile away."

Auras. Reed thinks of ghosts and ouija boards. The blue shimmers were ghost-like.

Something *is* wrong. The feeling is stronger now.

Reed's eyes return to Miss Catherine in the yellow dress. Mr. Webb's shadow dances on the picture in time with the firelight. From the wavering shadow, Reed looks behind him at the now tamer fireplace. Reed steps beside Mr. Webb. The light passes both men, but Mr. Webb's shadow dances without a partner.

Mr. Webb turns to Reed, "You're the shadow now."

What the hell? Reed waves his hand as though trying to conjure his silhouette. He points out its absence to Mr. Webb. "How can you be so fucking casual about this?"

Everything operates on set principles. Fire needs oxygen. So do people. And people cast shadows. And have heartbeats.

Lily would be better at handling this. She believed more deeply than he. Deep in her marrow. She could probably quote from the Bible a passage that would explain this. When she attended St. Joseph's, they may have taught this stuff. Latin, the catechism, what to do when the dead insist on not laying down. Like a CPR course.

"Like Mr. Ashton says, 'It isn't for everybody.'"

He gestures at the wall, the missing shadow, raising his voice. "How can it be for anybody?!" He nails each word, "It's. Fucked. Up."

Footsteps return. Mr. Ashton taps the entryway, then nods for them to follow.

Not too roughly, Mr. Webb takes Reed by the arm. He says under his breath, "If I were in your place, come morning, I'd kill myself."

***

Kyle recognizes the Lincoln and parks his own Audi beside it. As he steps from it he looks his car over. Finding a smudge, he restores the shine with a handkerchief.

Ahead of him he can see the new house. The unlit windows indicate Lady Catherine is already out for the evening, leaving Tamerlane to the men and their business.

Leaves have already begun to fall. They crunch under Kyle's shoes into the gravel. Once at the door of the manor, he bends and wipes the shoes clean with the handkerchief.

The door opens and Mr. Webb steps out in a hurry, nearly atop Kyle before noticing him.

"Excuse me, Mr. Dowd."

Shedding his leather gloves into his overcoat pockets, Kyle offers his hand, "Going somewhere fast, I see."

"To the car. Care to join me? You'll want to see this before seeing them." He thumbs back at the house.

Kyle walks beside him, "How are you?"

"All things considering, I'd rather be helping my nephew build his go-cart."

Seated inside the Lincoln, Mr. Webb says, "Let me get some notes together," then begins to dictate commands to the docked smartphone.

With what's ahead this evening, Kyle anticipates only, at best, disappointment.

"Is that new?" Kyle indicates the smartphone.

Mr. Webb beams like a child with a new toy. "The latest and greatest." He begins to describe the bells, whistles, and horns packed into it. He always has his hands on the latest gizmos as well as some prototypes from his R&D contacts.

"Sounds breakable," Kyle says after Mr. Webb completes his show-and-tell.

Kyle likes Mr. Webb. As Mr. Ashton's initiate and capable partner, he is one of the few humans to earn and keep their trust.

Kyle pulls a folded section of the *Inquirer* from his coat's inside pocket. He flicks the headline twice.

GRUESOME DISCOVERY IN SOUTH PHILADELPHIA

"Is this why I'm here?"

Nodding, Mr. Webb asks, "Want to hear the rest of the story?"

Not really. Perhaps he should have slept in tonight. This is not the start of the evening he prefers. After last night he had wanted to avoid business, relax alone or with Michael, maybe even Malcolm if the professor is free. But calls from Mr. Ashton are invariably about business. After hanging up, he skimmed the paper's headlines in case something devastating had been reported. Nothing so seismic yesterday, only this headline found in the local news section. Kyle read the scant inches concerning the murder. Little detail was given as the time of discovery had been too close to the paper going to the printers and the police's tight lid on anything that would bungle their investigation. No name was provided, but the manner of death, ritual mutilation, the suspicion that the victim was a gang member, and the very public display of the body got Kyle's attention.

No doubt Mr. Ashton, Mr. Webb, and others have been busy handling the situation to keep human investigators in the dark about the Society and its members.

"Who?"

In answer, Mr. Webb pulls up a photograph on the smartphone. Kyle sees the length of a body on a table, naked with a large hole in its torso. White skin with black tattoos on the arms. With a swipe of Mr. Webb's finger, the next picture slides into view. Close up of the face. The now-late Troy Dawson, also known as Blade.

"You're kidding me." Troy Dawson led the Rotters, a Camden gang of wannabe anarchists who have harried Lord Devlin's domain in the past. The Rotters are young and poorly organized, but numerous and reckless. That is until a truce was forged by Kyle himself. Unless a killer is found, blame would fall to Lord Devlin. The truce broken, harassment would resume. All Kyle's work would be undone.

The news is a fat stone. With its weight, he sinks further into the seat. "We have the body." That's at least something.

"We do. Took a while. We didn't learn of this till Philly PD already arrived. Had to hang back and wait till morning. Snatched it from the morgue."

"Do we have leads?"

"Mr. Ashton will have to talk to you about that. He's going to be interviewing everyone. Starting with you."

"Did you get any sleep?"

"Winks here and there. Had to run most of the day."

"Why did Mr. Ashton bring you out here?" Kyle knows of the black man's aversion to visiting Tamerlane and his not-unjustified distaste for Lord Devlin, who, in many ways, remains a Virginian planter circa eighteenth century. Kyle would run out of the house, too.

"No. No. I haven't told you about the new guy we picked up last night. Some poor fool made it all the way from Paris to Philly before collapsing in

Fishtown. So we put him in one of the safehouses for the day. All morning and afternoon I'm running down records on this guy while making sure Blade's body is secure and getting our investigation under way."

"You love it, Mr. Webb."

"I'll remember you said that."

"So who is he?"

"Reed Williams." Mr. Webb nods in the direction of the manor. "He's in there with them all. He doesn't have the first damn clue."

***

Reed is still stuck on Mr. Webb's parting words. *If I were in your place, come morning, I'd kill myself.* How? Isn't he already dead? He had been too stunned to ask.

Now in the dining room, Reed is suddenly aware of the austere silence, broken by pops from the fireplace. A pair of violin cases rest atop a nearby pedestal table. Three men gaze in his direction as Mr. Ashton takes his side.

It is easy enough for Reed to identify which of them is Lord Devlin. He's the one seated, holding court upon his throne. The man might have stepped out of one of the pictures that adorn the house, dressed in a fashion of a period closer to then than now. He wears a black tailored suit with tails, grey vest patterned like a tapestry, and silk tie looped around a stand-up collar.

Reed wants to say something, perhaps introduce himself. Then he recalls Mr. Webb's instruction not to speak unless asked a question. In fact, he all but freaks out when he notes the single chair's shadow wavering across the floor and up the wall. The men have none. He would not have noticed this had he not discovered the absence of his own shadow in the parlor. Now he cannot *not* see it.

Lord Devlin finally speaks. His voice is resonant, careening off the wood floor and paneled walls. "You may continue your summary, Brother Ashton," he says. The words have a southern drawl.

"Thank you. This is the complication I had been alluding to earlier: Mr. Reed Williams."

The men's scrutiny makes Reed feel like a medical oddity, as though he has a rare rash or growth. He won't be prodded if it comes to that.

"The suspect?" asks Mr. Thomas. He's heavyset, wearing a tight suit. The jacket would probably split down the back if he bent over to tie his shoes. Standing farther back in the room behind a podium, he holds a pen, that Reed half-expected to be a quill, but it's a fountain pen. He's taking notes. Minutes of the meeting?

"He is not, sir," Mr. Alcott answers Mr. Thomas. "He is not connected to this murder, but another. His wife was killed when he was sired."

"A waif?" Mr. Thomas frowns.

Mr. Alcott turns back to Lord Devlin, "He fled and seeks sanctuary in this House."

"An unsponsored waif? Your petition is meritless, as you should well know, Brother Alcott." Lord Devlin says coldly. "Dispatch him and waste our time no further."

That was quick, Reed thinks. From a "precarious position" to a certain one. He must not be of value after all. Just a lame horse to be put down. A mercy killing. Just as well. If there was justice, he'd have died instead of Lily. If there was justice, Reed would have a little more time to see Marie, Eddie, Ron, Clarice, and Jean-Paul dead first, then him.

But how? Reed is curious how they will do it. Mr. Ashton had said bullets won't work. And since he doesn't need to breathe, he can't drown. Maybe fire? People caught in fires can be spared pain by succumbing to carbon monoxide inhalation before being licked up by the flames. Could he?

"I have not forgotten my duties, sir. However, he is also an erif and his late wife belonged to a family of local influence."

"A pyro-sympathetic? Mildly intriguing, if true," says Mr. Milos. The firelight glints off his slick black hair and groomed van dyke beard. A scarlet handkerchief blooms from his breast pocket.

"While he was unconscious, I had him fed and a sample of his ichor couriered to New Hope. I anticipate confirmation tonight."

"Has his sire been identified?" asks Mr. Thomas, writing in his open book.

"Not Roxy's whelp, I should hope," says Mr. Milos.

"We will have a closer examination," Lord Devlin waves his fingers in a summoning gesture.

Mr. Ashton leads Reed to the throne while answering, "No, Brother Milos. This transpired in Paris. His sire is Marie de Telfour."

"That's Claude St. Croix's territory," says one.

"I thought Beloc oversaw Paris," says the other.

Up close, Lord Devlin regards Reed over his steepled hands. Reed feels uneasy and pinned by the man's gaze. Those steel eyes could bore wood. Is Lord Devlin reading his thoughts? Why does that occur to Reed? Given everything he's experienced, the idea doesn't seem crazy. He has no idea what any of them are capable of.

To Reed's relief, Lord Devlin looks down. The cord connecting them snaps instantly. Reed shudders. He understands why Mr. Webb does not like it here. Who wouldn't be freaked out?

Lord Devlin takes each of Reed's hands into his own, turning them over. "A laborer's hands," Lord Devlin comments.

"Yes, sir. He's a fireman," Mr. Ashton says.

Lord Devlin smiles for the first time. Reed sees sharp teeth. "Amusing, Brother Ashton."

Reed misses the joke. Is he the joke? These stuffy men in costumes sure are serious about everything else, but when it comes to him, it's all fucking ha-ha.

"Indeed, he does have fire in him," Lord Devlin says, releasing Reed's hands.

Yes, he does. More passion than sense sometimes. He has low tolerance for idleness and less patience for bullshit. The way they talk over his head like he's not even here. What is their problem?

Lord Devlin says, "Who was his wife?"

Reed bursts, "Lily! Her name is Lily." To hell with these stupid rules. Like Devlin's a king and Reed's some peasant. The heat in his chest rises. In the stone hearth, the fire belches as though it found a small pocket of gas. A log tumbles, throwing a spray of hissing embers.

Eyes on Devlin, he continues, "Lily Martin. As beautiful as your Lady Catherine. And I'd bet if she was murdered like my Lily, you'd want the bitch who did it, one way or another. What are you going to do about it?"

"An erif's choleric disposition," Lord Devlin observes. With his smile gone, his tone darkens, "And an erif's disrespect. The impertinence of one erif is already more than we will suffer in our domain. Is that not so, Brother Ashton?" There is an unstated jab for Mr. Ashton in Lord Devlin's glare and arched brow.

With this unexpected turn the humbled Mr. Ashton readily agrees.

"This is bullshit. I don't know what's going on, and it's clear you don't care. So do what you want. Just do it already." By now, Mr. Ashton is pulling Reed away, telling him to not say another word as if there was anything more to say.

Diplomatically, Mr. Thomas says, "Ms. Roxy Marchetti is an altogether different case. I would suggest that Mr. Williams be permitted a probationary period. During such time, he will be thoroughly educated in how he must conduct himself and how to constructively direct his gifts. For the service of all members of the House, of course."

"Are you offering to sponsor the erif?" Mr. Milos asks, fingering a growing smile.

"Certainly not. As Brother Ashton will be occupied with the more pressing matters discussed earlier, perhaps Lord Devlin would agree to have Brother Dowd sponsor Mr. Williams."

Lord Devlin cools in thought, his eyes returning to Reed, appearing to consider the idea. Looking away, Reed still steams. Angry, but with the wrong people. It should be Marie. Maybe he should have chanced charging into her last night in the Paris café. Now he questions every decision he has made since then. It's as if he died a sensible man and came back as a cowardly idiot.

"And what if this Marie de Telfour comes to collect her wayward child?" asks Mr. Milos.

Reed's attention snaps back, "Then I'll kill her."

Lord Devlin says, "We have no accord with this Frenchman, this... St. Croix. He is owed nothing. However, should the sire come, she will not be molested and she will have her case considered." He looks to his men, "Very well. Mr. Williams will be put on probation under Brother Dowd's supervision. He will be formally introduced at the upcoming masquerade." Then to Mr. Ashton, "Continue your investigation. All our resources are at your discretion. Where is Brother Dowd?"

"He's in the parlor with Mr. Webb."

"The colored one," Lord Devlin says.

"The initiate assisting me. We will need to interview everyone."

"So be it; Catherine exempted. You have leave to go. Ask Brother Dowd your questions, then have him speak with us. He shall meet our new guest."

***

"Hello, Kyle. Thank you for being prompt." Mr. Ashton sits with Kyle, speaking to him in a perfunctory manner. "I need to ask you several questions. Beginning with: where were you last night?"

"I was home. Alone."

"All evening?"

"I was working on my trains."

"So you never saw Blade or any of the Rotters last night? When was the last time you saw them?"

"Not since we negotiated the truce. They don't come here; we don't go there."

"Do you know who had motive to kill Blade?"

"Only us."

Mr. Ashton softens his tone. "What are we looking at? What will the repercussions be?"

"Could be open war again. Assuming it was a setup, we'd need to prove it soon."

"How soon?"

"Their leader is dead. Tommy would want blood. If the others follow, it would be as soon as they find out what happened. Amity, Chris, and Skoog are more reasonable—that might make for a window to talk. By now, they'll all know something is wrong, but have they got anything more concrete to go on?"

"I do not see how. He is missing and only that for now. I don't have a long list of suspects. I'm tending to agree with the set-up angle. I'm undermanned here."

"Then I'll help–"

"Father wants to see you. He has someone else in need of your help."

nine

Act Natural

" **M** ichael, my angel, you're going to break hearts. Starting with mine."

Zelda had prophesied as much on the evening Michael awoke from the evanescent dream of his human life.

And Zelda had been right. Blessed as he is with angelic Latin looks that inspire wicked thoughts, Michael breaks hearts. All over the continent.

In their nights in the California desert and the Los Angeles sprawl, Zelda taught Michael to put his innate charm to good use. Grifters, they roamed and scammed, spooling strings of jewels and swallowing beads of blood. His fingers strummed, stroked, misdirected, palmed, and pocketed. Whatever his fingers could not grasp, his words hooked, using his confidence to convince marks to reel themselves in.

Then one night it was time to go. Without so much as a wave goodbye, he put Zelda and the city in the rearview mirror of their '64 Chevy Impala he named Celestine. The road took him, as though it were a charging river, and he a caught branch. He was swept north, where he met Professor Malcolm Gold. They became fast friends. Ever rootless, Michael would journey on, but in his loops over the latitudes, he would reconnect with his friend wherever the professor next settled.

And so Michael has found himself in Philadelphia for a spell. He took to the city. In fact, this has been one of his longest stretches since California.

His Indian motorcycle thrums along Market Street. He won the cardinal red and ivory bike in a wager in Winnebago. Named Fox, it has become a symbol of the wanderlust in his heart. It's one of his few dear possessions.

Center City, Philadelphia's downtown, pulses with people out for the evening to dine or shop. Market Street runs through the chasm of sky-scrapers that looms over the city's financial district. Department stores and boutiques draw in pedestrians and turn out customers. Billboards want readers to know who to call for personal injury claims; posters ask voters to choose their favored mayoral candidate next month; and bright murals offer inspiration.

Michael dismounts his steel steed, joining the prevailing current of pedestrians, eyes open for deliciousness. Ahead he can make out the edge of Old City, to his right and across the street on his left are storefronts closed or closing for the evening.

Michael coordinates his date night with Malcolm's schedule. While the professor drones on about conjunctions, Michael puts words to prac-tice. Somewhere out here is a nibble. He feeds often so as not to need much from any one donor, leaving her satisfied, if a touch light-headed. Other times, he doesn't take anything, instead seeding a relationship to grow over time; thus, should he need someone in a pinch, he could return to collect.

Among all these beautiful faces, young and old, there are stories, lives, and dreams to be savored. Who will be the lucky one? Who would like someone to listen to her story?

People stream past Michael while he puts out good vibes. Like cologne, mood is something everyone picks up instantly. So it's important to wear happy like a balm. For him it's effortless. What's to be down about? Each evening is an opportunity to meet new companions. And each city teems with women who will find him great company. Just go with the flow; ride the tide.

His genuine smiles are returned by the women who walk by. Some even turn to look at him as he passes, pleased by his cover-model physique and his confident stride. One gawks openly, forgetting the person she's speaking to. He winks, "Likewise."

Ahead he assists an older couple fumbling with a SEPTA subway map. After their thanks, he asks with an affected twang, "Where ya'll from?"

The husband wearing a Stetson hat answers proudly, "Galveston, Texas, young man."

"I've been that way. Great beachfront. You work for the insurance company out there?"

"No, I've recently retired. Flo and I are touring this great country before we move to Colorado to live with our son and his family."

"Good man. Be sure to enjoy yourselves. Welcome to Philadelphia." Michael tips his non-existent hat.

Nearby, a woman with chestnut brown hair is locking the green door of a shop. He positions himself so that they collide when she turns. She yells in surprise and would say more, but upon seeing him, her voice dies away while her eyes grow to the size of silver dollars.

Michael retrieves the water bottle that dislodged from her hand when they bumped into each other. After snagging it, he looks up at the store's signage. A florist shop. *Perfect.*

Behind her astonished face, her mind must be racing. *I know him. Where do I know him from?* He guesses she's, say, thirty, though her owl-rimmed glasses with beaded chain lend maturity.

Michael hesitates to dispel her star-struck stupor. He could be any-one really. As often as not he lets them fill in the blank. You're that drum-mer, or you're the street illusionist I see on that cable show, or you're my sister's gardener.

Mechanically the woman takes the proffered bottle, her green eyes fixated on him as though she doesn't believe he's really here and may van-ish in a blink.

"Sorry. I'm late, I know. Did my P.A. get hold of you?" Even minor actors have personal assistants. At least they should.

"We're closed," she blurts. The bottle crackles in her hand. "I mean, don't go! I mean, welcome to Suzie's Florals. How can I help you?" She says all this in one breath before freezing up again.

"Are you Suzie? This is your shop?"

Delayed, she answers, "Yes. I'm Susannah's shop." Then she realizes her gaffe. "Oh boy! I'm Susannah. It is my shop."

"I take it you didn't get the message. S'all right. Susannah, my name is Michael. Would you consider one last customer?"

"Definitely," she answers and turns back to the green door. She takes a moment to control her quavering hand in order to slot the key into the lock.

Inside, she flips on the lights. A bell above announces them. "I really appreciate this, Susannah." He notes her ringless finger when they reach the checkout counter. "Are you all right?"

"I'm sorry. It's just... well, I feel that I know you from somewhere. Like you're famous and I should know your name."

"I get that a lot. I have that kind of face, I suppose."

She tries not to look disappointed for mistaking him for a musician or an actor. No denying his devilish Latin looks, dressed as he is in a white linen shirt, flattering blue jeans he actually paid for, and sharp-toed boots. He leans over the counter and spots a soap opera gossip magazine. He says confidentially, "Or maybe it's because people know me from *Upon Windmere Manor.*"

Her face brightens the room. "I knew it!"

Chuckling, Michael embellishes, "Catch me in my big screen debut next summer." Then to implant the idea into her imagination, he adds, "Shirtless action galore."

Her earlier awkwardness forgotten, she asks, "What happens to Draco's baby?"

"I owe you one, but don't tell a soul. Okay? Next week you learn the baby isn't his at all."

She clamps her hand over her mouth, blown away by the revelation. Must have been dynamite, because he doesn't know what they're talking about. But it's soaps—it's always someone else's baby.

"Who–"

Michael puts his finger to his lips. "Now, that'll have to do."

She nods emphatically and whispers, "Can I have your autograph?"

"Certainly. I appreciate your helping me out. Wanted to pick up some flowers for tonight."

With a professional air, Susannah circles around the counter, perhaps getting a whiff of his cologne, a clean masculine scent. At a wall, she turns on more lights and together they pass promotional cards advertising upcoming sales for Sweetest Day, Homecoming, and Halloween.

She begins humming. *How adorable.*

Once at the center of the single display room, she asks in a way less casual than she intended, "This is for your girlfriend?"

He answers equally, "Don't believe the gossip pages. I'm unattached. I'm tired of dating L.A. girls. Too... superficial." He shrugs. "Anyway, the flowers are for my aunt. Her name is Sylvia."

"That's so sweet. Is it her birthday? Or some other occasion?"

"When I'm in town I make sure to visit her."

"Were you thinking of a single flower? Or a bouquet?"

He gives a helpless shrug. "I'm in your capable hands. What are your favorites?"

"I love pansies. They have these cheerful faces smiling at you."

"I should have guessed. They suit you quite well," he says, observing a blush accentuate her smile.

Michael raises and lowers the red flag of a mailbox holding birch branches. "This is really a charming shop." With more to view, he sees a lot of love here. She has decorated the place herself, putting her personal touch on the baskets and vases, stands and displays. The hardwood floor gleams.

"Thanks."

"I'm serious. You really made this place your own. What's your inspiration?"

Surprised, perhaps, by his interest, she answers frankly. "Tight budget. I just hunt for bargains in thrift stores or trash bins."

"Now that sounds like an entrepreneur. Tell me about this one. What was this in its former life?"

"It's a breadbox. I bought it at a yard sale and took the door off." She painted it white with strands of ivy. Inside are dried babies-breath.

"Nice. What about this one?" He notes a handmade piece with blobs of Elmer's glue. "Popsicle sticks?"

"Yeah. My nephew had made it for me."

"What's his name?"

"Charlie."

"Charlie. Like the Chocolate Factory."

"He wishes."

Michael laughs, and she does likewise. They fall into the comfortable exchange of long ago friends reacquainting. He relates his humble start in Hollywood, doing local commercials till he got his Big Break and made his momma proud. While stroking her necklace near her heart, she opens up about her affection for flowers and how their arrangements bring beauty, elegance, and comfort to any occasion. Her talk more animated, she conveys the excitement of landing her first wedding that wasn't for a friend. With more success, she was able to relocate to Market Street. "Since then, most of the business is referral based."

He listens with easy attention as they drift about the shop. Under the guise of friendly banter, he considers her more closely than she might guess. Bending near her to inspect a display, he inhales the scent of her citrus shampoo. He thinks of tossing the crinkly purple band that gathers her hair into a ponytail to see the brown locks fall wild past her shoulders. By his compliments, he notes the rise of rose on her cheeks like crimson blooms and wonders where else her skin might react.

After a time, Susannah pulls together a white woven basket bursting with pansies—blues, lavenders, plums, and violets. "Well how about this arrangement? It's small so she could put it out on a windowsill, or on her nightstand, or… anywhere, really."

"She'll love it."

"I'll wrap—"

"No. No need for that. I'll take it as is." The fingers of his left hand snap. Her attention drawn away, his right hand reaches behind her ear. Pulling his hand back, he reveals a vivid blue pansy.

"Wow. Thank you." Susannah takes the flower and peers over its petals at him. An unspoken, unsurprising invitation. He returns her gaze, then leans in, "I see there is a back room. Why don't we complete the tour, and I'll sign my name wherever you wish."

Michael and Susannah share a soap-scene-worthy embrace as they stagger over the threshold of the semi-lit back room. She swats at the light switch, missing.

Navigating bins, buckets, and tubes, Michael backs her toward the counter space at the far wall. With each bang of the counter the shelving shakes above; spools of satin ribbon, twine, and tape jump.

In the weak glow of the refrigerated cases, Michael helps her out of her blouse. The pause in contact makes room for her initial awkwardness outside the shop to slip back in. Her eyes are on his. Perhaps she's in awe of his celebrity and not believing this chance encounter is real. She hadn't left the store and met him; she must have fallen asleep reading that soap magazine.

Despite his inclination to rush, he slows his pace, gently removing her glasses and setting them on a shelf. Letting her catch her breath, he wonders where on the map of her skin might he discover a discrete tattoo that is meant for her as a reminder of a love or a promise.

Kissing along her neck, he can feel through her flushed skin the thread of life. A tantalizing pulse just beneath his lips. The heartbeat. Like the steady wash of sea up upon the beach, which recedes back into itself, then resurges. Michael thinks on his time with some night surfers in Oregon. Under a full moon that threw a million tinsels onto the water, he experienced Zen-like transcendence. Immersed in the ocean, consciousness merged with its vastness, the edges of self dissolved as foam, and the infinitesimal connected with the limitless.

Blood is the flipside. Each drop an ocean of the donor's soul. You can experience the person's totality—all that the person can and will ever be. Their entire story laid open to read. An unique configuration of genes and spirit and time and chance and fate. At once an abyss of profound ache and a peak of exultation. A sublime experience.

So it is with Susannah and everyone who has come before her and will come after her.

He looks upon her, sharing in her anticipation.

After more of her clothes are discarded, Michael spots a yellow rose that plants an idea.

He knocks aside cuttings, sheets of grass green tissue paper, a pair of shears. He lifts her onto the counter. "Before my turn at soaps, I was in a made-for-tv-movie. I played an immigrant gardener seduced by the wrong woman, played by Victoria Collins. Production was ultimately canceled, but…"

He rolls up his shirt, revealing a lean muscled chest the fictional gardener might have possessed. "I got an education in love from an experienced actress." He makes a pillow of his shirt and lies her down on the counter. "Comfy?"

She nods. Her eyes track his own. He can see her breathing pick up and feel her pulse quicken. His nostrils twitch at the first scent of her personal, unmistakable perfume.

The yellow rose appears in his hand. Improv with props—so much fun.

The closed-up bulb of the rose dips downward toward her neck. It gently brushes from there to the hollow above her breastbone. He smiles over her. The buttery petals sweep over her skin, "For great personal attention, use Philadelphia's best florist: Suzie's Florals," he says with chili pepper in his voice.

The yellow velvet sways up her thighs, triggering a sharp intake of her breath followed by soft coos. She shivers. Her fingers coil his in hair and her toes curl about each other.

Upending the flower in his hand, he traces the tip of the green stick over her throat, breasts, stomach. Gentle here and there, other times he lets the thorns work like fingernails, exciting some gooseflesh without yet breaking skin. Farther along the swells, curves, and plains he continues, till at one spot, he finds that colorful mark: a jeweled hummingbird. There the thorn punctures and draws drops of blood.

Susannah flinches. He soothes her cry, looking back to her apologetically, "Occupational hazard, I suppose?"

He resumes reassuring kisses upon her lips, then journeys south once more. While tuning Susannah to perfect pitch, he anticipates his own satisfaction. Each drop's aroma of rust, wet glimmer, and infinite stories rouses his own craving. While one hand distracts with expert attention at her breast, the other softly squeezes by the nicked vein. Each red note contains her soul, flavored with her hopes and fears, and intensifies his longing. Not just yet, he thinks, wanting to indulge her a little longer.

He flips the rose once more and twirls the bloom in all the right areas of her receptive body before leaving it in her hands. Building her up to exquisite contortions, he attends her with caresses and laps of his tongue, which do not miss a bead of blood.

***

Michael leaves a message on Malcolm's voice mail. The professor does not like text messages, claiming not being able to read the combination of letters, numbers and symbols. "An illiterate alchemy," he calls it.

Susannah's sweetness still on his tongue, he says, "Hey, Mal, I'll catch you at the club after I'm finished with Sylvia. Thanks for the concert information. I'm sure she'll eat it up."

Michael had left Susannah alone in her shop, knowing she would recover in good time and have a good story to tell her friends. Not gallant of him, but he wanted to be sure to get home.

With a quick-change at his apartment, Michael repackages himself as the dashing companion of the well-to-do widow, Mrs. Sylvia Golombek. A tailor-made tuxedo helps him step once again into the role. A carnation palmed from Susanna's shop fills its buttonhole. His hair is well coiffed with pomade. Tonight he is Michael Lorenzo, M.D. and cardiologist, third son of Marco and Kate, graduate of Johns Hopkins University School of Medicine, now providing his physician skills here in Philadelphia as well as relief aid abroad.

Having traded his Indian for a taxi, he's deposited at Mrs. Golombek's home. The neighborhood is as old as Philadelphia itself. The brownstones on Spruce Street are among the eighteenth-century houses that have been restored by their owners to their historic virtue.

Up the stone steps, Michael rings the bell and smiles for the ample woman who answers the door. "*Buena noches*, Rosalina."

The live-in maid cheerfully beckons Michael inside, "Doctor Lorenzo! It is good to see you."

"Thank you. You as well. How is your brother's health?"

"He is much better. Bless you for asking."

"I could tell. There's a lightness in your eyes." He gives Rosalina a quick wink and hands her one of the plum pansies.

"Dear Michael, how marvelous to see you."

Attention drawn to the top of the stairs, Michael admires his date, "You look radiant, Sylvia."

She has taken good care of herself and many would not guess her age to be seventy-one. No one would guess his age correctly either, mistaking him to be in his late twenties, or early thirties. Like an actor, he can shade his age with the right disguise.

The older woman is wearing a sequined black dress and a silvery grey wrap. Her fingers are bejeweled, including a ten-carat diamond ring. She descends the staircase beside the track of a chair lift. The chair lift remains inoperative at the top.

Sylvia smiles, "I'm getting old, Michael. And you are as young as ever. How do you do it?"

"Women keep me young," he answers truthfully.

Chuckling, she embraces him. He leans in, kissing her cheek. "How have you been?" He puts Susannah's bouquet in her hands.

"Philanthropy will be the death of me, Michael. I cannot recall being so busy in all my life. I'm scarcely home—going to this board meeting or that fundraiser. Committees filled with loggerheads and dunderheads. Ladies my mother's age who need to be put to the rack to get them to pry open their purses. You'd think they expect to take it with them when they drop dead. Of course you must know some of what I talk about. Your work in Honduras with those unfortunate children can't go on without all this falderal."

"This falderal is how we met. Tell me truly, Sylvia, you love it, don't you?"

"I suppose," she says feigning reluctance to cede his point. "I want to give you this before we go out." She takes a red box from a secretary desk and hands it to him.

Michael slides the top off. Inside is a silver wristwatch. The second hand sweeps across the BVLGARI lettering. "Sylvia, you shouldn't have. Though I'm glad you did." Soon it's on his wrist. "Fits just right."

"I'm a good judge. I never had any trouble with my Norman. Rings, watches, shirts… I knew his size without ever needing him to be measured. Before he died, I purchased that watch, but never had the chance to give it to him. Recently I had some links taken out over at Saper's on Walnut. Now that we've been friends for over a year, I wanted to get you something special."

The Golombeks had been married for forty-nine years. It is a relationship Michael can never have, nor imagine ever wanting. Nonetheless, he does find their marriage remarkable and endearing. On their outings, Michael will probe their past. Where had she met Norman—on a blind date, shortly after he returned from his service in Korea; how did he propose—in an Italian restaurant where she uncovered the ring box in the bread basket; what did she miss about him—his snoring, she joked.

"I'll treasure it, always. Shall we go?"

Outside, the pair are seated in the back of her Cadillac. It isn't a stretch, but it is well appointed. The deep seats are soft leather with lots of leg room and space for glasses and liquor. Michael doesn't touch it, and lately Mrs. Golombek hasn't either. Her grief has turned to determination to honor her late husband's memory.

Geoffrey, the hired driver, smoothly pulls the car away from the curb.

Michael reclines in his corner, gazing at her with pleasure. Her dark dyed hair is elegantly styled, her poise perfect, the corners of her eyes and mouth creased by years of pain and laughter. She's theatrical and whip-smart and resourceful. He couldn't imagine many saying no to her velvet requests.

They met at a banquet Michael had crashed over a year ago. Under the alias Michael Lorenzo, he introduced himself as a physician affiliated with Central American Medical Relief Agency, a group that cared for the poor abroad. The ruse was a way to explain his disappearances— really a way to keep a distance. Women don't like to share, and Michael refuses to be wound around anyone's finger. It wasn't practical. They'd age. He wouldn't.

What *does* he want? she has asked him. Same as she: companionship. Women, young or old, each have their particular charms. In the older set, he is nearly chaste, preferring to string out their friendships across the continent. Should he ever revisit, he'd have a port to dock at. With the younger women, it's brief and carnal.

The driver confirms with Mrs. Golombek their destination: the Kimmel Center, home of the Philadelphia Orchestra. Ten minutes later, the Caddy arrives at the majestic brick building topped with its iconic glass barrel vault. Not only is Mrs. Golombek a season ticket holder, she's one of the Center's benefactors, currently involved with educational projects.

Inside the cello-shaped hall, the pair take their seats in an orchestra box. The warm mahogany walls make for an elegant and intimate atmosphere. Below, the orchestra tunes up and the conductor appears. He will lead the musicians through pieces of Brahms and Tchaikovsky.

She's sometimes reacts to his chilly touch, but always warms to the sweet nothings or risqué jokes Michael whispers by her ear. From what Malcolm told him, he can share details of this new conductor and compare this season to the prior one as though he really has an ear for such things.

Woven through their hushed conversation are old and new tales of her life with Norman. The engrossing stories of true love describe a place Michael has never visited. It sounds pleasant, perhaps exciting, but ultimately lonely. He cannot imagine caring for one woman for the rest of her life, to the exclusion of all others.

During intermission, the pair exits to the lobby. Once there, Mrs. Golombek clutches Michael closer. She answers his quizzical look with a nod of her head, indicating an elderly woman across the way. "That's Eleanor Hampton. An obstinate woman. She chairs the Byberry Scholarship Foundation board and the position has gone straight to her head." She tosses her head to the ceiling and makes a disapproving noise before turning to avoid the woman.

Michael gently stops her, and with a twinkle in his eye, says, "Would you like to introduce us?"

"That's a fine idea." She likes mischief too and together they walk up to her. "Why Eleanor, delighted to see you here. Alone?" The woman is about to say something, but noticing Michael she loses her thought. "This is Doctor Michael Lorenzo a close and trusted... friend. Michael this is Eleanor Hampton."

Michael takes the woman's hand and bows to kiss it. "An absolute pleasure to meet you, Mrs. Hampton. Sylvia has spoken highly of your dedication to the Byberry Scholarship Foundation. And may I add that dress looks exquisitely cut for your figure."

Breath escapes the woman. Michael catches Mrs. Golombek enjoying the reaction.

Finally, Mrs. Hampton asks, "Have we met before?"

"Maybe you saw him at the Wyatt affair this past summer? I'm sorry—were you not invited? Well, we must be going. It was good to see you again, Eleanor."

Out of earshot, Sylvia says, "She nearly collapsed, the poor thing."

Her arm in his as they circle the lobby, she says, "Michael, your visits are too brief." Her voice tells of many decades of smoking Virginia Slims. "I know your relief work takes you to Central America quite often, but won't you consider a longer stay? I'm sure there are colleagues who can take your place."

"I am very dedicated to the Relief Agency, as you know. The faces of the children are so beautiful that it is difficult to leave them behind."

"You do such important work. But please tell me you will you be attending the Martin Foundation benefit?"

"When is that?"

"The Saturday before Christmas. I would treasure your company."

"It would be my honor to accompany you. Tell me: do you know if they need a florist?" He doesn't hear her answer as his attention is taken away. "Would you pardon me for a moment?"

Michael strides over to Malcolm, throwing up his hands in a gesture of exasperation. "What are you doing here? I'm working."

"Am I intruding on Operation Gigolo?"

"Casanova. Operation Casanova." Michael knows his friend has deliberately misstated it. Riling up one another is half the fun they share. But there is something in Malcolm's demeanor that suggests something is weighing on him.

"I am here on Brother Kyle's behalf as it seems he has urgent need of us," says Malcolm. "I have Celestine double-parked. We're to meet him at the club. Presently."

"You're killing me." He sighs. Then he whispers, "Your mother is quite ill. It's dire. You're in need of my assistance. So act like you're begging me." He nods toward Mrs. Golombek behind him. "Understand?"

Malcolm frowns but puts his hands together and gets on his knees in a pleading gesture.

Michael nods and pats his shoulder in reassurance, then returns to Mrs. Golombek.

"My deepest apologies, Sylvia. It appears I am needed more elsewhere tonight." He kisses her after some explanation and further apologies, then assures her that he looks forward to making it up to her very soon.

Grabbing Malcolm by his arm, Michael hurries with him out the door where Celestine awaits. Its body is pearlescent aubergine with a cream leather interior. Malcolm takes the wheel.

"Stink Pink: a friend who's down." Michael initiates a word game they play where the solution is a pair of rhyming words with same number of syllables as Stink Pink, Stinky Pinky, or Stinkity Pinkity.

"A glum chum," Malcolm answers easily, absently.

"So? Shall I guess? Let's see: you discovered a pair of students in the lab mixing metaphors without protection? Or one of your lectures finally set a record of mass boredom-induced comas? Ah! I know: you were offered tenure and you're not sure how to explain to them how long of a commitment that is."

"Two of those were not humorous the first time you told them. One did have the merit of novelty. Ha."

"Something *is* bothering you."

"Leave it alone."

"Something serious." Michael thinks about what could upset the professor. Very little fazes the man. A graph of his emotional state over time would nearly be a flat line. What kinked the line in the past? Then it occurs to him.

"A woman!"

"How could you possibly have deduced that?"

"I remember when you were this way with Hannah. So long ago I nearly forgot about her."

"Nonetheless, there is nothing to discuss."

"Nonsense. You're going to fill me in while we're waiting for Kyle. You're in luck—tonight I'm Michael Lorenzo: physician of the heart."

chapter

ten

The Unseen

K yle enters the converted council room with a deep bow of his head.
Those before him nod in return.

Seated on his throne beneath the gaze of a King George III portrait,
House Master Elias Devlin is flanked by his courtiers, House Secretary
Gideon Thomas and House Master of Rites Sebastian Milos.

Another man stands near the fireplace, his expression unreadable in
the snapping firelight. Head tilted down, arms out before him, the man
examines his hands as though they belonged to someone else.

In the bright fire, Kyle notices the flames slant as though a breeze
blew. They slant toward the man who doesn't appear to notice, absorbed
as he is. He must be the one Mr. Webb had been speaking about. Reed
Williams. All at once Kyle understands why he is here and what will be
asked of him, but he maintains a neutral expression nonetheless.

Lord Devlin stands, looks up at Kyle and claps him on the shoulder.
"We trust that Brother Ashton has informed you of our delicate situation."

"Yes, sir. Troubling, but I'm certain Brother Ashton can keep it in
hand. I will help all I can."

"Let us hope so. However, we have a different task for you. We will
need to impose upon your time."

"Yes, sir." Kyle had been on the mark, once again. Here it comes.

Lord Devlin motions to the man, "This is Mr. Reed Williams, and he is in need of your tutelage."

"Sir... with respect, I believe I will be of more use assisting Brother Ashton. My experience with the Rotters—"

"Without doubt, Brother Ashton will avail himself of your counsel. Should he need your diplomatic or lethal talents, you will provide them. For now, however, we require you to attend to Mr. Williams."

Kyle wonders if his wincing at the mention of his lethal talents has been obvious. None of the men show it. He certainly hopes those talents will not be necessary. He has done his time. Enough with killing.

Lord Devlin's hand grips the shoulder of Kyle's suit jacket and draws him close. Though Lord Devlin is four inches shorter than him, Kyle sees a man of a stature that outsizes most; one accustomed to having his words heeded, his instructions followed.

Speaking confidentially, Lord Devlin says, "Do this for us, Brother Dowd, and we will consider hastening your ascendancy. Free to be your own man. Brother Milos and Brother Thomas warrant it."

The two men give solemn nods.

Kyle's surprise is obvious to Lord Devlin who gives a knowing smile. Yes, it is a magnanimous gesture. Lord Devlin need not offer Kyle anything, just utter the command and Kyle would do his best to fulfill it. Such is the bond between sire and child. The Rite of Ascendancy would sever that bond and establish Kyle as master of his own destiny. And here Lord Devlin is offering ascendancy at least years, if not decades, sooner.

Though he has no reason to regard Devlin's pledge as insincere, Brother Thomas will record it and Brother Milos will perform the rite when the time comes. It seems too generous.

Kyle regards the man, Mr. Williams, who looks back, expectant, ready to leave. About six foot, he wears off-the-rack clothes with sleeves a tad too short.

Kyle would be responsible for this man.

He doesn't have the first damn clue, Mr. Webb had said. Since this Reed Williams has fled his sponsor, Kyle would have to teach him everything. If the arrangement stretched to a long-term one, it would be formalized in ceremony, then Kyle would have to look after Reed as if he is his own for decades. So in essence, Lord Devlin is offering Kyle a trade—one shackle for another. Not such a sweet deal after all.

***

By the time Kyle and Reed reach the Audi, Mr. Webb and Mr. Ashton are on the road. Kyle wonders if Mr. Webb will get more than cat naps during all the interviewing and legwork ahead. Running down the who and the why—a tantalizing mystery that Kyle will not now get to solve.

Instead, he has become a babysitter.

Brushing leaves from the crevice at the bottom of the windshield of his car, Kyle eyes his new charge. The taciturn man speaks with his hands; they rub together, working on some tension that isn't abating.

Inside the manor, Kyle could only smile and acquiesce to Lord Devlin's request. *Oh yes, it will be my honor to sponsor this fledgling.* Albatross more likely. This onus brings childhood to Kyle's mind. When they were kids, Kyle had been often burdened with the company of his brother Kenneth. Five years Kyle's junior, Kenneth spoiled Kyle's plans with his friends: sneaking into the movie theater, smoking behind the pharmacy, exploring the junkyard at night, running errands for Mr. Alvio.

Now Kyle has to be more careful in his plans. A tag-along will crimp his outings just as Kenneth had.

Kyle draws in a breath and releases it to center himself. This isn't the correct attitude and Kyle tries to reframe the situation. Make the best of this. Here is an opportunity to help. The man needs to touch solid ground and plant his feet.

Wordlessly, the men get into the car. Kyle pushes the ignition button. Here he can appreciate Mr. Webb's delight with technology. Just push a button and start a car.

Reed asks, "Do you have a cigarette?"

"We can stop at a convenience store on the way." Kyle tucks a slip of paper into his inner pocket. "Mr. Webb gave me your address. We'll get you home, but first we need to talk, to get acquainted."

Why should he do this alone?

Kyle says, "Hold on a moment," then undocks his cell phone from the console.

The list of those who are available and willing to help is short. Kyle can only think of two. The first person doesn't answer the phone, but the second does. "Hello, Malcolm. Is Michael with you? Get him. I need to see you both. At the club. Yes, now. See you there."

As Tamerlane disappears into the darkness, Reed says, "Mr. Webb said I should kill myself. But he didn't get to the how part."

Direct. Kyle likes that.

For his part, Kyle's expression doesn't change. He peers out at the dark road, with its ghostly trees along the periphery. Part of him, the old Kyle, would be happy to be rid of Reed. Mr. Webb's advice would do them both a favor. But Kyle won't heed. And he understands Reed's state. Kyle, the new Kyle, had also wanted to take one more life—his own.

Kyle says, "Wait for morning. Open your blinds and smile at the sun."

"That's it? Sunlight?"

"That's it." After a pause, he adds, "You won't do it though."

Reed turns in his seat, disbelieving, "What are you saying? I'm a coward?"

"You should not have awakened to this side given the trauma. But you did. Takes a great deal of willpower. You were holding onto something. Still are. You grasped it and pulled it close."

"Yes." Reed says in a sigh of understanding.

"Your wife?"

"Yes." Reed says.

"Lily, correct? She must have been a special woman." Reed nodding, Kyle continues, "Aside from the stock husband answer—beautiful, smart, funny—tell me what was different about her. What about her brought you back?"

"She asked me out."

"That's all? She asked you out?"

"She's like that. She's gutsy. She goes for what she wants. I'm a fire-fighter, and I'll go into burning buildings, but she's more courageous than anyone I know. She won't let her family tell her who to be. She's Catholic. A real believer. That takes courage too. To have that faith and live it. She told me that's where her strength comes from. That there's a God and that He has a plan for us."

God came up a lot in Kyle's old life. Often by those who pleaded for their own lives.

God don't kill me!

Jesus save me!

Please, God have mercy!

The Man never did intervene in Kyle's work. Looking back, Kyle wishes He had. One jammed gun, a blind-spot, or slow reflexes may have been all the miracle his targets needed. Some nights his old life seems just a dream or a bad movie that stays with him after the curtains close. But too often, it presses close, so he's nose to nose with every man he murdered.

"You believe that? That God exists and He has a plan?"

"I never thought seriously about it till I met her. She was so certain. And she didn't speak of her faith in a preachy way. It would just turn up in conversation as casually as comments on the weather or how her day went. Well... most of the time. It could get on your nerves sometimes, but I guess it was like me and my buddies going on about sports, you know, getting worked up about favorite players, amazing plays, or bad calls.

"Anyway, I wanted to live in that world of hers. Things made sense with her. I think I converted. I must have, but I can't remember." He groans. His hands rake his hair, "I need to end this before I forget to."

"Isn't suicide against God?"

"I'm dead already."

"I know what you're going through—I do—"

"Don't tell me it will get better!" Reed says, smacking the dash in front of him, cracking its surface. The glove box door swings down, aghast.

Kyle had been prepared for yelling, but not damage to his car. He brings the Audi to a stop on the desolate road. Harsh red hazard lights flash on and off in the dark. After looking pointedly at the fissure in the wood trim, Kyle fixes Reed with a glare. "You want to hit something, you hit me. Not my car." He takes a breath. "I have it coming, believe me."

"I'll get it repaired."

He waves the offer off, annoyed. "You don't know your own strength." Then in a softer tone, "You came back, Reed. You came back."

"Great. I came back. Does Lily a lot of good now." Reed shakes his head, turning quiet. He resumes, "You know, I got through my entire adult life being single—self-reliant, independent, having fun. No complaints. Then I met Lily and its as though I really hadn't lived a single day. I fell for her so hard that it scared me. It didn't make sense to be turned around so fast. With her it was like she had always been in my life. Like my shadow that I finally realized was there beside me. She told me that's what a soul mate is, and that I was hers as much as she was mine."

Reed's voice quavers at the end. His eyes shine, "Now she's gone. All those years alone..."

Reed doesn't finish his thought, leaving Kyle to realize that he has been with two grieving spouses in as many nights. Not superstitious, he nonetheless marks the coincidence and let's this moment pass without a word. This is the aftermath. These are the days and years that he never saw. Kyle shattered worlds and never gave it a thought. Some of those men deserved worse than he had delivered. But not everyone. Not Stanley. Not Mrs. Whittaker.

Reaching to snap shut the glove box, Kyle says, "You can choose to make the best of it, Reed. Salvage some good. There can be life after death."

"What kind of life? I'm losing my memories. I can't live without them."

"It could be a blessing. You'd have a clean slate. You know what some people would give to be free of their past?" Kyle envies his carefree friend, Michael. "In any case, how do you know for certain? As I said earlier, this has been traumatic for you. Surely some memories will get lost in all the violence and grief. Maybe you're simply panicked or you're overthinking. Try to remember… how about your first pet's name, or recite the Pledge of Allegiance, or the teams that won the past five Super Bowls."

As Reed does so, Kyle resumes driving. "Look, we'll get to a store soon. You'll get your fix. We'll make this right. We'll make a plan."

***

The Wawa convenience store is brightly lit except for one darkened cooler, its beverage contents overlooked. Slick hot dogs roll endlessly at the end of the counter; to their left are two spools of instant lottery tickets, a canister of red licorice, and a yellow placard warning minors not to purchase alcohol or cigarettes. A woman with tangled hair and a grey fleece jacket unzips a pouch to count out cash.

Behind her, Reed clenches his hands tight together, feeling their bones. Seven months, thousands of miles, and death to be so close to a fresh pack of cigarettes. Yet he must wait on this woman scrounging for change to avoid breaking a dollar. The cheated take-a-penny-leave-a-penny tray is empty.

Left to huff in place, he turns Kyle's theory over and over, not finding the explanation for the gaps in Reed's memory comforting or sound. Though he recalls the Super Bowl and World Series winners, he has difficulty with the names of dear friends, or even who his wrestling coach was. He had needed Mr. Webb's help with where the Atlantic City photo strip was taken.

Electric beeps from the cash register prompt Reed forward. With the woman's exit, Reed steps up to the counter. The clerk with the mustache turns away without acknowledging him. Astonished, Reed waits. Perhaps he needs to check on something before waiting on him. No. He takes a sip from his paper cup while checking his cell phone.

Except for the chirps of the phone and the drone of the appliances, the store is quiet. Reed plants his hands on the counter, his expression quickly decomposing from mild annoyance to heightened agitation. An array of cigarette packs, cellophane-wrapped satisfaction, taunts him from beyond his reach.

Out of patience, he yells like a thunderclap. The clerk has such a start, he may have lost bladder control. The phone has fallen to the floor. His jaw tight, Reed speaks and points. With trembling hands the clerk gives Reed a pack of Camels and refuses Reed's money. Ultimately Reed leaves the euros on the counter and exits the store.

Halfway to the car, Reed hears Kyle call from the corner of the pavement at one end of the storefront. Reed changes direction, realizing Kyle doesn't want smoke in the tidy Audi.

"Problem?" Kyle asks when Reed reaches him.

Reed already has the cellophane off the hard pack, taps the pack against his palm and lifts the lid to slide out a white stick. Testy, Reed answers, "I'm standing there right in front of him. He ignores me and plays with his damn ringtones."

"He didn't see you."

"Obviously." The cigarette is in his mouth, and he opens the Wawa matchbook, tearing off a paper match.

"I mean he *couldn't* see you."

"What are you saying? I was invisible?"

"No. More like unseen. We don't register consciously with most humans, as long as we don't do anything overt—like shout at them. We fade into the background. Not foolproof—kids and some exceptionally intuitive people recognize us as you'd expect. But most just pass us by without a thought."

Just as what had happened when he and Lily walked to their hotel, passing by Marie as though she wasn't there. They didn't see her. Like the couple in the French café didn't see Reed. And the woman outside the apartment didn't see Mr. Ashton. Like a ghost. Or like Mr. Webb said, a shadow. No one notices shadows.

"That's creepy."

"Like anything else, in time, you'll learn to control it."

In practiced succession, Reed has the match head pressed between the striker and cover, then pulls out the lit match. The sizzle of the flame coming to life stokes Reed's anticipation as he brings it to the cigarette caught in his lips.

Kyle stays his hand.

"Come on!" Reed says, nearly spitting the cigarette out.

"Look," Kyle nods toward the match head. The bright flame doesn't rise. Rather, like a tongue, it flicks in Reed's direction.

Kyle blows it out. "Try again."

The second flame behaves the same way. As Reed slowly lifts his arm, the flame bows downward as though trying to reach him.

"What does it mean?"

"Strike a third and be done with it. We'll figure all this out together."

Reed puffs on the cigarette. The sharp taste and the ashy smoke reunite with Reed as fond friends, but the nicotine has yet to join them. Reed walks back and forth past Kyle, taking in deeper lung-fulls.

When Reed gets halfway through the second Camel, Kyle says, "While I was waiting for you out here, I've been thinking. If Marie was here, right now—"

Alarmed, Reed breaks stride, "Is she?"

"No. But if she were... If she came to realize the terrible wrong she had done—if she had a personal revelation—and she asked you for your forgiveness, would you?"

"You're asking me this now? Hell, no." His hands shake drawing out the third cigarette. Edgy, he snaps off two match heads instead of lighting them. Finally, one flares up, as does his heart. The heat returns.

Reed says, "Lily would. Wouldn't even wait to be asked." Now lit, he takes a drag on the stick, trying to coax out a fix that will settle his nerves, soothe his heart, quiet his conscience. "We disagreed on that. She believed it was a gift you gave freely. You gave it, not for your own sake, but for the sinner's."

"Very Catholic of her," Kyle says. Then, perhaps disappointed, he says, "But not you."

Wincing, Reed rubs at his chest as though he pulled a muscle. "Kyle, while I've been pinballing around this city with you and your buddies, in my mind I'm going back and forth on who to kill first. There's Marie and Eddie—they'd go quick. Then there's the three fucks who tortured Lily. I don't have the words for what I'd do to them. Then there's me, sooner than later. And somewhere in there, I'd have to find some way to tell her family and beg their forgiveness."

Unmoved, Kyle says, "They're not helping," meaning the discarded butts.

Reed crushes the last one into the cement. "No. They are not." He tucks the pack into his breast pocket.

Kyle catches sight of something and stomps away, making big gestures with his arms. A large rat with a dark coat, hurries out of sight.

Returning to Reed his says, "Rats—you never know with them."

Reed rolls with it, "Ok…"

Returning to the previous topic, Kyle says, "There was nothing you could have done, Reed. Lily would have known that."

Head down, Reed smolders inside and out.

"Revenge then," Kyle says. "You know you'll have to prepare. At minimum, that means not killing yourself. But for effectiveness, you'll need to do as we say and learn from us." He takes out his car fob, "Let's go."

In the car, as they leave the parking lot, Reed asks, "Mr. Ashton said I could take a bullet. Is that true?"

Kyle says, "I'd rather you take his word for it than for me to have to show you. In most ways, we are difficult to kill. We don't age or die of disease either. All told, I'm still young, perhaps about your parents' ages."

The man appears to Reed to be in his forties. Mom and dad are way past that.

"Lord Devlin, my sire, is about as old as 'We hold these truths…' Though, he never held those truths. Still doesn't."

This explains Lord Devlin's outmoded attire and the old manor frozen in the eighteenth century. "Now I understand why Mr. Webb doesn't like him."

"Exactly. For all I know, Devlin may have once owned Mr. Webb's enslaved ancestors."

"Unbelievable."

Kyle continues, "But in limited ways, we're quite vulnerable. Sunlight for example. Fire for another. Both destroy the ichor."

"Our blood," Reed says unsettled by how he's beginning to grasp this reality. "And because I drank Marie's ichor, I have some of her memories?"

"Yes." Kyle spares looking from the road to lean toward Reed, saying, "And this is important—from now on, be careful who you drink from. Only from those whom you trust. You're sharing something deeply personal. Intimate. When done freely between partners, it's beyond anything a mortal experiences. Ichor is not just a fluid, it's our essence. Like human blood, but more potent."

A drug after all. "Is the bond permanent?"

"Between sire and child it can be severed. Between others, it weakens on its own over time."

"Good, then let's get that done. I don't want her in my head any more."

"That won't happen tonight."

Of course. At every turn, Reed smacks into a glass door. What appears as a clear path ahead turns out to be another stunning obstacle.

Kyle says, "There's a ceremony. And you have to wait about fifty years. Plus you have to be a member of the Society."

"A society of monsters. How civilized."

"Yes. We have rules, rites, customs. Like a fraternal lodge, where full members are equals. Lodges are called Houses. Each House has a Master; ours is currently Devlin. The Society of Brandywine, based on a compact of the same name, goes back further than Devlin's human days."

Reed notes how Kyle didn't flinch at the word monsters. "You're kidding me with this shit."

"Suffice to say there are codes of conduct as well as benefits. Mutual support and aid. Consider yourself a pledge on probation. One of our clubs is on Vine Street. That's where we're heading."

"And Lord Devlin's your king?"

"No, but he seems to like the trappings of one. He's master of the house—the First House. Each house has elected officers with responsibilities and privileges."

En route, Reed listens to Kyle read out the manual, not following along really well. "What are you saying about sponsors and novices?"

"Let's not get in the weeds of terminology. There's much to learn. That's why there's this preliminary process, to make sure—"

Reed cuts in, "To make sure they share the same interests and dreams. Right, I get it. A lovely courtship. You should make an online dating service out of it."

They wind around City Hall, the largest building of its kind, topped by the city's founder, William Penn gazing toward Fishtown.

"I will put that in the suggestion box. For now I need you to watch yourself. I know you're overwhelmed right now, but do you feel clear up here?" He points to his own temple. "A sign of hunger is when you start to fixate on things. Like your mind won't let go of an idea and keeps chewing on it. Or you find yourself counting things, like tiles in the ceiling."

"I'm good."

"Excellent. Mr. Ashton said he fed you."

"When was this?"

"Some time last night when you were unconscious."

Reed scowls. Left at the mercy of others. First Marie, now Ashton.

Reed says, "Blood," realizing that the hunger Ashton had warned about was blood.

"That's the high cost of living. Fresh and human, but you don't need a lot at once if you do it often enough. Thus you don't have to kill anyone."

"What a comfort."

Reed touches his teeth, feeling along the crowns.

Noticing, Kyle says, "They come out when you need to feed."

So, so wrong. He doesn't want fangs or to chug from people like they are cans of Yeungling beer. He puts killing himself at the top of his list again.

Gingerly, Kyle pulls the car into the club's parking lot. A clump of young people mill about.

Like an accusation, Reed says, "You chose this."

"Excuse me?"

Kyle parks in a space marked with a RESERVED—VIP ONLY sign.

"Mr. Ashton said this was a gift for those who choose it. I'm curious how the pitch goes, Kyle. Is it like a job interview when you get down to haggling over health care plans, vacation weeks," he then sweeps an arm to encompass the Audi, "a nice company car."

"It isn't—"

"At what point do you discuss blood, 'fresh and human'? Is there a instructional video for biting people on the neck?"

"Not the neck; you may nick a vital vessel and cause them to bleed to death."

"I'm serious." Reed raises his hand, "Who says, yes, sign me up?"

"We each have our reasons, and I was a different person than I am now." He turns off the engine.

Whoops and hollers accompany college kids leaving the club. Headlights of arriving vehicles sweep over them.

"So then why did you?"

"It seemed a good idea at the time."

"Now, it isn't."

"Now, it's different. I see things more clearly. I have a chance to do the right thing."

"Do you hear yourself? Do you realize how crazy all this shit is?"

"Like I said, you can take the good out of it."

"And Devlin—he's your sire, right? So that means he gave you the gift. Why did he choose you?"

"I was a good… salesman."

"He needed a salesman?"

"I'm a very good salesman. A closer."

"Yeah," Reed says. Opening the car door, he adds, "I believe that."

chapter

eleven

Bedlam

T he motley throng of patrons stands in some semblance of a line,
impatient to be let in Club Bedlam along the Vine Street Expressway.
Some are men in makeup, some women in rubber, others with tattoos for
sleeves admiring those with metal biting their skin. They all snail their way
up to a bouncer named Scissors. Large silvery shears dangle from the bull
neck of this silent man with the well-deserved reputation of discerning
genuine IDs from fakes. The latter are snipped in two and their owners
forbidden to return. Those who are accepted pass through the featureless
steel doors that lead into the club.

Both pass after Kyle signs to Scissors that Reed is with him.

Noting the Halloween costumes and make-up, Reed says, "What are
we doing here?" The place doesn't appear to be his or Kyle's style.

Kyle informs him that Mr. Milos and his wife own the club, providing privileges to their kind here. A place to be themselves without undue
attention as well as a place to pick up a drink.

Once inside, bass-heavy music beats their ears as their eyes take in the
tableau. Directly ahead is the main dance floor that is packed with people
channeling the music with their bodies. Beyond that is a long metallic bar
bathed in ambient blue light. Bartenders dash about mixing drinks for the

customers. Booths are fastened to the walls and multi-level scaffoldings and catwalks flank the dance floor. Patrons line the rails or sit in cozy niches ten-to-twenty feet above the grind.

In a lettered brown t-shirt, the DJ holds the shell of his headphones to his ear while mastering the cacophony from his glass enclosure. Below him, Reed follows Kyle, his hands sealing his ears to abate the thunder of music. He squeezes through the glut of the bizarre. Strange hands and warm bodies brush and feel along him. There's haze and shifting colored lights; sweat, latex, beer, smoke mingle in Reed's nose.

They reach the back where the decibel level drops over booths patrolled by waitresses. Reed observes two men engaged in animated talk. The one seated, dressed in shirt, tie, slacks, and gym socks, looks up at the other. The friend, dressed in formal-wear, stands with one foot planted on the bench. This one notices them first, breaking off mid-sentence to smile wide for Kyle, "Hey, man!"

Kyle stiffly accepts the one-arm hug. "This is Reed Williams. Reed, this is Michael and Malcolm."

Michael instantly has a hand out for Reed, "Pleased to meet you."

The moment Reed sees him, Michael feels familiar. Like a friend he lost touch with and is happy for their reunion. "I'm sorry, but we know each other, right?"

"You know me now." Turning to Kyle, Michael indicates the suit he is wearing by brushing his fingers across the fabric of the black jacket. "Why did you have Malcolm interrupt my evening with a woman whose favorite subject is me?" He draws his sleeve back to reveal the silver wristwatch.

Kyle leans in to examine the watch. "Very nice, Michael. She has good judgment in watches."

"Not in men, however," Malcolm quips.

"We're coming from Tamerlane. We're going to help Reed get adjusted to the way things work here." Kyle hopes tonight goes smoothly. Michael and Malcolm can take Reed off his hands night-to-night. Likely, Michael will appreciate another buddy when Malcolm is unavailable, leaving Kyle free to continue his agenda.

Michael spreads out his hands, "This couldn't wait till tomorrow night?"

"We'd appreciate your help." Kyle swallows, noticing that he is sounding like Lord Devlin. "In any case, tomorrow night you'd be busy getting cuff links."

"Well, Reed, come sit and settle a dispute I'm having with Professor Oblivious here." He scoots inward so Kyle has room and Malcolm does likewise for Reed. "Now Reed, let's say you're a professor and you've got this gorgeous foreign exchange student coming to you for help with her studies." Here Michael's voice changes to a plaintive falsetto, "Oh professor, you have to help me! Words are hard. I need your personal attention."

Kyle gives a faint chuckle and Reed smiles, while Malcolm is less amused.

Returning to his normal voice, Michael continues, "But she's your ace student! Then, last night, she takes your hand." Michael reaches to take Reed's hand, "Like so, she gazes into your eyes, and asks if you'd like to show her your apartment. Now tell me she's not interested in extra credit."

"May I remind you that she's betrothed?"

"Not yet, Mal. He's in South Dakota."

"South Africa."

"Just as far. So, Reed?"

"Sounds like she's interested. Why not ask her out? Then you can be sure." Reed says surprised with himself. For a moment it all passes for normalcy. Just buddies hanging out. Good company.

"Of course she is. I knew I liked you, Reed. See Mal, you need to grab this woman. Hell, you should be grateful she's giving you the time of day. Have fun for once."

Malcolm says, "I agree. She is a *rara avis*."

"Wouldn't dating your student violate some university policy?" Kyle asks.

"It is a consideration that Michael fails to appreciate," Malcolm says.

Michael rolls his eyes at this.

"I assiduously endeavor to honor the teacher-student code. Such professionalism is my armor, shielding my reputation. Any potential display of dereliction must be deflected. And yet..." Malcolm finishes with a long sigh.

"Yet you are torn," Kyle says.

"With her, I would risk a fatal crack to that armor."

"Sounds like love—for a robot. You're all head, man. No heart," Michael says.

"I am in love. It is a decidedly damnable dilemma. The boyfriend's proposal could not have come at a more inopportune time. Grace will return home at the semester's end. To attempt to convince her to stay out of love would be selfish, wouldn't it?" He isn't a robot, but he isn't human either. He'd fail her, somehow. Best not to try, to not risk hurting both of them. "In any regard, it is moot. End of discussion." He says this with a finality that Michael decides not to press on now.

"So Reed, what's with the warm handshake?" Michael asks.

Kyle answers, "Reed, it appears, is an erif."

Michael makes a face of great alarm, as though he had opened a closet door and found the bogeyman on the other side.

"What? What does it mean?" Reed asks.

In a faraway voice, Michael says, "You're the chosen one. The prophecy foretells of a man named Reed who will bring balance to the Force, unite all Middle Earth, and free Zion!"

Reed can't believe what he is hearing.

A beat passes before Michael snickers, then thumps the table and gives a whoop of laughter.

Kyle reassures Reed, "That's Michael trying to be funny. There is no prophecy."

"Should have seen your face, man."

"Funny," Reed says sourly. "Mind if I smoke?" He taps out a cigarette and sticks an end in the corner of his mouth. As had happened at the Wawa, the new flame bends toward Reed. He has a notion that the flame could reach for the cigarette tip. The flame quavers, lengthening toward the tip, but not quite reaching. Reed pulls closer so he can get the light before it burns out.

The others watch mildly.

Reed wonders why it even occurred to him that the flame could be guided. Does he have some new instinct?

"A little more finesse, add some card tricks and you can take it on the road," Michael says. "Bar mitzvahs, kids' parties, nursing homes."

Kyle picks up the thread, explaining to Reed that all of them can recover from the most grievous wounds in minutes if not hours, see auras around people, and not age; and each have gifts of their own, such as an affinity with fire.

Reed is skeptical. Part of him still finds all of this outlandish, like some comic book world with its own rules, societies, and logic-defying powers. But there is an undeniability to this shadow world he's dying in.

Michael realizes, "Wait. Reed's new? Like just off the dock?"

"Airport actually. He's a waif."

"So, he's not Roxy's?" Michael asks.

"No. But we will need to find her." To Reed, Kyle explains, "She is an erif too and your best bet to learn how to control that fire."

"Without Lord Devlin knowing?" Michael says, "She's not welcome in Philly, or has that changed?"

"It hasn't changed." Kyle believes the woman remains in Philly solely because she isn't welcome. "Reed is in an unfortunate situation. His sire, Marie, killed his wife, Lily, on their honeymoon."

Michael winces, giving Reed a sympathetic look, "Sorry man."

Reed nods his thanks.

"Lily Martin of the Martin family," Malcolm states. "They are bene-factors of the Wharton School."

"How did you know that?" Reed turns to Malcolm.

"You were wed this past Saturday at St. Joseph's. The reception was at a country club in Blue Bell and attended by an estimated 1,100 guests. There was a write-up in the *Inquirer*, probably because the mayor, promi-nent businessmen, and one state senator were in attendance."

"Malcolm remembers everything he reads," Michael says. "The Martins have that foundation I've heard about. Wow, small—" Michael grabs Kyle by his shoulder, pulling him close while slouching down till he's nearly under the table.

"What's wrong?" Reed asks the question on the others' faces.

"Saw this girl I know look my way," he whispers.

"So?"

"So, I forgot her name. A woman doesn't like it when you forget her name. I didn't call her either. A woman likes that even less."

Malcolm says from the corner of his mouth, "She's moved on."

Straightening up, Michael does a double-take. The unnamed woman at the end of their table frowns at him, her arms folded across her chest. "Hi, Michael."

"Hey! Hello. Hiya."

"You never called me," she says, empty drink tray on her hip.

"I lost your number. Had it in my phone, but I lost the phone."

"Bullshit," she says drawing out the word.

"It is certainly not. I admit I don't deserve a second chance. I was just telling the guys here how I hoped tonight you'd be on shift. I wanted to see you again. If I were avoiding you, why would I come here?"

She looks around the table as though seeing the three others for the first time. "Really?" She now holds the tray across her front, "What are you all dressed up for?"

Indeed, Reed was the only one without a jacket and tie. Michael says, "Good question. Earlier we were at a concert at the Kimmel Center." He puffs himself up, "I look handsome, right?" She nods a bit. "We had a great time the other night, yes?" She nods some more. "Who else shares my kink, but you?" She smiles.

As Michael climbs out of the booth, Malcolm gives him a satisfied smile.

After the pair leave, Reed asks, "How did she notice us? I thought we were unseen."

"She saw Michael. Everyone notices Michael. Especially women."

"He's very familiar. I swear I know him from somewhere."

"He has that effect on people."

To Malcolm, Reed asks, "Can you tell me more about my wedding?"

"I was not present."

"I mean from the article. Do you have it?"

"I do not possess the printed matter, but it is indelibly printed on my grey matter. I can recite it for you." With a nod from Reed, he "reads" the article to him.

"Fuck!" Reed stands and paces for a moment, running his fingers through his hair. "I don't remember any of it." The pair watch as he trails away, talking to himself. "I remember the night before. My dad, brothers, and Chuck were at the hotel bar..."

Malcolm says to Kyle, "Apropos of alcohol, I saw one of my students here earlier. Academically, he is not in a position to squander hours that would be better spent studying."

With an eye on Reed now and again, Kyle counters, "Time away from the books can be good too. Recharges the brain."

Malcolm gives a dismissive snort. "That young man was emptying shot glasses of whiskey. 80 proof has likely poisoned the brain cells that held answers to Friday's exam. Clearly, he has already pickled the synapses governing judgment."

With a fresh cigarette in his mouth, Reed returns to the table. "Can ichor take away memories?"

Beside him, Michael appears triumphant. "Got their numbers. Hers and her friend's."

"Did you get their names?" Malcolm asks.

"Mary Jane and... Gwen. Ha! So what are you all talking about?"

Kyle says, "Reed is concerned that he's losing memories of his human life. Reed, I'm certain you're fine. There is a lot to take in."

"There are crows in my head. I swear they're stealing my memories." He fears it's getting worse. When will there be relief?

"I lost all mine. What's the Latin, Malcolm?"

"*Tabula rasa.*"

"*Tabula rasa.* Right."

"All of them? How long did it take?"

"Not long. First night I woke up, they were all gone."

"Everyone's different Reed." Kyle again tries to assure Reed. He doesn't need the man unraveling and losing control of himself.

"Great story," says Michael. "It's the Summer of Love and I wake up in the back of Celestine—that's the '64 Impala convertible I would come to inherit and pass on to Malcolm. I don't have any idea of where I am. Come to think of it, I don't know who I am. All I know is there is the most gorgeous woman looming over me with beautiful stars spread out behind her in a cloudless sky. It's quiet. Not a breeze or a coyote howl. Just her and me and the desert." Michael smiles as serenely as he had that night, looking up to the exposed duct work above them. "She tells me her name is Zelda. I can just about smell her now." He sniffs, raising up his nose. "Cloves and jasmine. She has brown hair with flowers in it, reaching her waist. She's wearing a loose white blouse and a peasant skirt. And she was straddling me like I was a Harley Davidson."

Kyle leans into Michael, eyes sharp, "Reed doesn't need to hear this."

"So you have no idea of your human life?" Reed asks. The man's breezy attitude causes Reed alarm. "You don't know if you were married? You look about my age, aren't your parents still alive?"

"Well, no. Does it matter?"

"Matter? Of course it matters. Did this Zelda ever tell you? Aren't you curious? How do you even know you had a choice?"

"Choice? What's he talking about?"

Kyle answers, "Reed wasn't sponsored. Marie did it the old-fashioned way."

"What would any of that change, man? Life is good. If shit happens, step out of the way, and just move on," Michael says. He smiles but not with a whole heart.

Reed straightens, growing more agitated, thinking of Michael's whole life erased in one night. And he's fine by the sound of it. Like he lost a penny or something else trivial. In one night—gone! *How long do I have?* He can feel feathers brush his neck. "Stop pecking at me!"

The lit tip of the cigarette blazes as it drops, leaving a line of ash on the table.

Before the others can react, Reed shoves his way toward the club's exit.

twelve

Home

When Reed escapes from Bedlam, Kyle, Michael, and Malcolm pursue him like orderlies trying to catch a patient. Those in line might mistake Reed for a rowdy drunk, but may not know what to make of the steam wafting from his body. It takes the three of them to corral Reed to a corner of the club's parking lot.

Michael is scalded where he grips Reed's arm. "What the hell are we going to do?"

Kyle gets in Reed's face. "Talk to me."

Despondent, Reed says, "You don't believe me. I'm telling you I'm this scarecrow and crows are pecking me apart. They're stealing my memories. I'm going to lose her!"

"Reed, listen to me. Calm down. You're going to hurt somebody and panicking isn't going to help you. Calm. Down."

Reed makes an effort to relax. The others do the same.

Michael suggests, "Maybe writing your thoughts down would help. Like a diary. I saw a movie where the guy tattooed his body with clues about who he was."

"There is another solution." Malcolm points to Celestine parked nearby.

Inside the car, Reed lies on the back bench. The professor has lent him his phone with its voice recorder app ready to go. Reed taps the REC icon. His tight grip on the phone strains the aluminum chassis while he sputters every thought in his head, trying to transcribe his life into a digital file. The crows are real. They're going to eat him till there is nothing left.

"I like Tasteykake Chocolate Juniors!" Reed lists favorite treats as well as foods he hates such as turnips au gratin.

He jumps from recipes to high school. The jostle of bodies against one another in the hallways, the metal slam of locker doors, the gleam of the polished gym floor and the squeak of sneakers on it. He had dated a girl named Cynthia Langford. He pledged adolescent love so she would wave him to third base. Now, he doesn't feel anything for her. Not a single moment of their time together carries emotional weight. Like it's someone else's story he half-listens to.

"I remember summers at Wildwood. I was afraid of the jellyfish, and I can still feel the stinger on my leg from the time my cousins came with boogie boards. But I loved the salt in the spray and the power of the ocean; how it could pull you anywhere it wanted."

Reed's recollection proves to be deteriorating asphalt, some stretches are smooth, such as sophomore year when he and his dad spent weekends fixing up a Dodge Charger, while other moments are suddenly swallowed up in sinkholes just as he utters them.

Then before he realizes it, he's on Marie's road, her thoughts sputtering from his mouth. Vivid as his own life, he's on a catwalk where he can hear the clack of heels on the platform, the strain of a fake smile, wide eyes in the bright lights.

"Fuck," he says, mentally retracing his route back to his own life. "Once, I stole a pack of baseball cards and candy. Dad found out. He was the angriest I ever remember. He made me take them back and apologize to the clerk."

Another memory of Marie's seizes Reed. Cold hands grab his arms and lift him as easily as a pillow. Just torn away from his companion. Down an alley, he screams in fright and struggles in vain. Then he's released, set back on his feet. Before him are the deepest eyes he's ever seen. He falls into them, like plunging headlong into a warm pool. Weightless, he feels safe and far removed from the world. He floats in a void. Then distantly he feels someone draw him. There's a prick on his arm, his wrist. Lips press there. The wrist turns warm and wet. He's still miles away. He has forgotten who he is. His panic is gone. There is only this moment. He wants his captor to kiss him, to touch him, to hold him. Steadily he grows tired. Already closed, his eyes are heavy with lethargy. He'll fall to the ground, but instead sighs into the man's strong arms. Don't let go. He thinks it, but did he say it aloud? His tongue feels thick. Don't let go. Don't ever let go. I'm just going to sleep now.

***

Malcolm and the others stand a respectful distance from Celestine, as though the yards between serve as a privacy curtain. He can't hear Reed, but his body language practically narrates stories of apparent amusement the way his torso rocks and his face contorts with laughter.

Michael observes, "He's having it rough."

Ah. Malcolm reassesses Reed's convulsions as fits of joviality. Mourning makes much more sense.

Michael says, "Do you think he's crazy?"

"Possibly it is madness," Malcolm says. "Perhaps a disorder such as dissociative amnesia."

Kyle says, "Or he is simply overcome with grief. He isn't thinking right. Let him do what he needs to do in there."

They all turn aside. A trio of young women, each clinging to one another, staggers past them, reeking of vomit.

Michael says to Malcolm, "We haven't finished discussing you dating this Gracie girl before it's too late."

"It is, in fact, too late. No doubt she will complete the coursework of my class, and her studies generally, and soon enough, earn her degree. Then she will return to her home and to her suitor, who undoubtedly lacks the capacity to truly appreciate her as I do."

Michael steps closer to him, raising a finger to emphasize his point. "The fact is that you don't have the *cojones* to tell her about how you feel."

"She had already made her choice," Malcolm says in a sharper tone.

Michael matches, "You didn't give her a choice. The boyfriend was the fallback option. What are you afraid of? The worst is that she'll say 'no.' You can live with 'no', Malcolm, but can you live with, 'if only'? The fact is, that if you don't do this, you have a very long time to regret it."

Kyle steps away from the pair, not in the mood to referee. Retreating to the Audi, he checks the tires, then looks over for any scratches or dings in the body.

He has gotten a lemon of a deal with Lord Devlin. His own fault for not having looked under the hood to learn that Reed may be on the verge of a mental breakdown. Not that it would have made a difference to Lord Devlin.

Some memory loss is not uncommon. Kyle had been truthful about that. Everything has a price. One does not come back to life in cherry condition. But Kyle had never heard of this kind of piecemeal amnesia. Then again, he never heard of Michael's all-at-once either.

It's probably best to get Reed home. Being in a familiar environment may help his mental state. Reed might find comfort in seeing his own stuff, reminiscing over family pictures, and finally sleeping in his own bed. The four of them could work out a plan together so that Reed has something to focus on, tasks to accomplish.

They're all still at it, when Kyle turns back his attention. Reed yelling into the phone. Malcolm and Michael having words.

Michael says, "…you put her on a pedestal. Now you're afraid to climb up with her."

Kyle gets between them, "Let's go."

"Reed's still confessing in there," Michael says.

"Let him. You two drive him home. I'll see you there."

***

Reed has stopped talking. Sprawled out in the back of the car, he takes no notice, instead reliving another moment of personal horror. Unwilling, but knowing he has to face it to understand his final human moments.

Gouts of blood coat his skin slick and sticky. His limbs turned heavy with numbness while his struggle slackened. Peripheral vision shrunk while his heart rioted in its cage.

Marie lapped at the end, getting the last of the heart's blood. At that moment, she concentrated, willing her ichor into her mouth, the black overwhelming the red coating her tongue, gathering itself behind her fangs. She sealed her mouth over his discolored cold lips till the ichor— Reed rubs his throat at the memory—the ichor entered his mouth and slunk down his throat, diffusing along the way into blood vessels, riding the innumerable tributaries, zeroing in on the heart where the substance pooled in the now lifeless organ's four cavities.

Reed dies all over again. The horror of it clings to him, permeates him like smoke in his clothes.

"Fuck!" Reed cries, pulling himself up, finding Malcolm and Michael in the front seats of the moving Impala. "Where the hell are we going?"

"Your place," Michael says, his hands on the wheel.

"Good. No offense, but I don't want to see any of you again."

Michael asks, "Are you all right?" when glancing at Reed in the rear-view mirror.

"I'm sick all over. I don't know how you're all okay with this. It's as though part of me is at war with another part of me. I'm losing more than memories—I'm losing connections to people. Human people." He thinks of the plane ride, the Wawa, the club—how part of him felt detached, indifferent, even superior. How part of him looks upon his withering humanity with approval.

His vision has slid back to the movie black-and-white, everything in sharper focus or purged of extraneous detail, like he's seeing a truer picture somehow. The sluggish blue encircles Michael and Malcolm.

Each man glances back at him and he waves a hand by his eyes, black as midnight in Hell. "How do I get rid of it?" When he kills himself, he doesn't want his mother to see these freaky eyes.

Michael says, "Relax Reed. You probably shifted unconsciously. It happens. Just center yourself."

Reed sits stiff on the seat bench. "How is this normal?" Closing his eyes, he breathes in rhythm. In, one, two, three. Out, one, two, three. More calm, he opens his eyes and finds color again. Sitting up more, he says, "How is all this a secret? What we are? What we can do? How could I not have known about it?"

Michael says, "Don't be hard on yourself. How could you have known?"

"Although there are innumerable novels written about us," Malcolm says.

"TV of course," Michael adds.

"Plays, poems, and prose..."

"Movies. Did you watch that *Only Lovers Left Alive* movie?" Michael asks.

"Graphic novels. Video games. Those pen-and-paper diversions I understand are common on campus. Yes—you'd like the film."

Michael shrugs apologetically to Reed, "See? I guess there was no reason to suspect at all. Say, who's up for a driving game? Stink-Pink, Reed. You know it?"

***

The others arrive at Reed's apartment building a minute after Kyle. He approaches the purple Impala and peeks through the lowered driver window. "I'm going to go inside. Wait here till I call and say it's okay to come up." To Reed he says, "Give me your key."

"Why can't I come up? Is Marie here?"

"Just stay put, Reed. I can handle myself."

Kyle returns to the Audi, popping the trunk and then popping the lid of a steel case with foam interior. Snug tight is a Colt pistol. He opts to attach the suppressor and after slapping in a magazine, shuts everything and walks into the apartment building.

That Marie may be here in the city has already occurred to Kyle, but he chose to keep it to himself. No need to get Reed even more worked up. If she has come, she may have either gone to a hotel to secure a place for the coming day or headed directly here. And if she came here, has she already left after finding the place empty? Or maybe she remains to surprise and capture him once more.

At door number 721, Kyle stops to examine the jamb. No sign of forced entry. He gently tries the knob. Locked. Pressing his ear to the door, he listens for a moment. He hears something faint and indistinguishable. A minute passes. No voices. No footsteps. If it is Marie inside, the Colt would not kill her, but it would hurt a great deal.

He turns to look down the hall and glowers. Reed, Michael, and Malcolm have stepped out of the elevator. He goes to meet them before they come any closer. "Was I not clear that you were all to stay in the car?"

"I'm not waiting in the car like a coward, Kyle," Reed says.

"You don't know anything, Reed."

"I'm not going to run anymore. I know that."

"I don't care. My job is to keep you alive. If she's in there, I'm going in alone. She doesn't know me and what I'm capable of."

Michael asks, "Why do you have a gun? You look like a professional killer."

"What did you say?" Kyle says. "Never mind. Reed, is there a fire escape?"

Reed nods.

"Stay put. I'm checking the back."

"What if she's here," Reed says.

"I don't know that. And I will need to. You three stay till I open the door." Here Kyle's eyes turn black and his teeth sharpen in a warning sneer. "I mean it."

Kyle quits the building and circles via the alley to the back of the apartment building.

Climbing up the steel frame, Kyle reaches the seventh floor and locates the windows of Reed's apartment. A light is on in the larger of the two windows. A seated shadow projects on the drawn drapes. A human? Kyle moves to the second window. He used to be better at this, getting into places without raising alarm. Brute force, then. With the butt of his gun, he breaks the window. He slides gingerly through its lower half, and plants his feet.

***

Reed can't stand this waiting. He's had to shut up Michael several times so that he can hear nothing. What's taking so long? Will Kyle be able to talk sense to her? He doesn't feel Marie tugging on his thoughts as he had last night.

A man's shout can be heard down the hall from Reed's apartment. Then two men shouting, then quiet. Reed forces his way past Michael and Malcolm. They run after him.

"Damn it!" Reed realizes Kyle still has the apartment key. Instead, he backs up, readying to slam himself into the door when the door flings open to reveal Kyle there, calm but wary. "Get in here. Malcolm, up front."

By a chair stands a fifty-something man with silver and black hair. His hands are up, throwing a long shadow cast by a lamp. There is no sign of anyone else.

The four form a semi-circle before the man, blocking exits from this living room to the hall, kitchen, and bedroom.

With the gun put away, the stranger talks to Reed, apparently recognizing him.

Reed doesn't and cannot understand the fast-clip French. "What are you doing in my apartment?" Is he some errand boy for Marie? He will chuck this man across the Atlantic like a skipping stone.

The man makes gestures as he speaks which do not help at all.

"Do you know what he's saying Malcolm?"

"Perfectly."

Four pairs of eyes look at Malcolm expectantly.

Then Michael prompts him, "Will you tell us?"

Malcolm says something to gain the man's attention. They have an exchange.

"*Merci.*" Malcolm explains to the others, "This man says his name is Aleron. He means you no harm. He says Lily is alive, and he apologizes for the corpse in the closet."

part
III

thirteen

Bliss

The first morning in Paris, Lily wraps a white terrycloth robe about her and crosses the suite to answer the rapping upon the door. While Reed brews coffee, she had requested a newspaper to be sent up as a keepsake, perhaps for a scrapbook. She thanks the young hotel employee with several euros.

After setting *Le Monde* on a glass-top table, she takes her phone and moves to the windows that are framed with floral patterned drapes. Haloed in morning sunlight, she thumbs through a sports app. A smile brightens her face, and soon she's bouncing on her toes.

When Reed emerges from the kitchen, a Hotel Le Hervey emblazoned cup in hand, she holds the phone to her chest.

"What are you smiling about?" he says as he saunters her way. Wearing only a towel, he looks like Mr. August from a calendar of firefighters. Broad across the chest, brawny muscles, arms that are tireless and capable of anything. She loves watching Reed at bat in the softball league. The way his shoulders and arms flex when he swings and the power the muscles deliver. The satisfying smack that means a double, maybe a triple. The sweat on his brow and the dirt in his day's stubble. And she loves that smell on him after a great game.

She teases in a sing-song voice, "I know something you don't know."

Understanding lights his face. He holds out his hand, "Give it here."

She backs away, shaking her head, and dangling the phone.

He barks in laughter, "You're killing me."

He puts the cup down and swipes for the phone. She jumps away. When he lunges a second time, he gets her instead. Scooping her, he carries her over his shoulder. The phone falls to the carpeted floor, but he ignores it; he takes her to the other room and tosses her in the bed. Before she can sit up, he's already on top of her.

He says, "Tell me the score."

When she refuses, he slips his hand inside her robe and pinches her hip. She gives a squeal, which only prompts him to do it again. Soon she's nearly voiceless and relents. "Eight to two."

"Phillies?"

"Of course." Like Reed, she's a Phillies fan. Baseball had been a way she bonded with her father. He would take her and her brother to Vet's stadium, making a day of it. She cherishes her almost tangible memories: the thunder-crack of the bat, the roar of cheers, the hot dogs goopy with ketchup, the sun-melted blueberry water ice.

The day they tore the stadium down, she cried.

Now she and Reed spend the season using her father's club seats at the new stadium. Their first game together was when the Cardinals played and lost. They lost last night as well.

Reed gives a delighted whoop, then kisses her. "One more win and we're in the Series."

She kisses some more, then gently nudges him off. "We still have to finish getting ready to go."

"We don't have to. We can stay here."

"I thought you didn't like the room."

When they had checked in, Reed had a fit, saying, "It's bigger than my apartment." She could nearly see his mind estimating the cost per square foot of the suite, the pink Portuguese marble, Persian carpets, dazzling crystal, chintz silk, and fine furniture. It didn't matter to him that they were not paying for it. He simply didn't like the extravagance. Wasteful. "We're not here for the hotel," he said. She reassured him that it was only while they were in Paris. The rest of the trip they would stay at hostels and with her relatives.

Reed concedes a little, tracing a finger over her shoulder. "I like the bed. With you in it."

She meets his gaze, thinking on last night between the sheets. The delicious passion they had shared. She feared that she would be inhibited, but he tore that away with her shirt, then her skirt, then her unmentionables.

Though spare with words and maddeningly stoic in expression, in physical love Reed was effusive. He fired her up with his hands. They are always warm, like hearthstones. Thinking on those hands kindle her even now. They were strong where they needed to be, and at other times exquisitely delicate.

Drawing him close, wanting him, kissing him, she says, "We've not explored the whole bed, yet."

***

Their first days in Paris are heavenly, greeting Lily and Reed like a gift, full of promise, found on the doorstep. The bright-blue sky vaults above and Lily feels so giddy and light she may well float into it and brush up against the azure.

Not a cloud. Not a shadow.

She is ebullient as though exploring Paris for the first time. All that was once familiar is fresh once more. The pace, the smells, the alarms, the cadence of speech, all strike her as though Paris has changed her hairstyle, gotten a tan, and bright new wardrobe.

In a way, she *is* here for the first time. She is a new person after all, having the Sacrament of Marriage on Saturday. She and Reed became one flesh at St. Joseph's, attended by friends and families, ordained by Father Lillrose, and witnessed by the Lord.

And now she is Mrs. Lily Martin Williams, a new name for her new life. At the hotel she had not responded when the clerk called for Madame Williams until Reed gently nudged her. So she repeats the name, saying each pair of syllables to everyone she meets.

"*Je m'appelle* Madame Lily Martin Williams."

Inseparable, she holds Reed's rough hand to keep grounded. Through him she gets to experience the city all over again. Her eyes watch his reactions. Will he love it? France was her idea. Had she suggested or insisted? Reed never gave the wedding planning, much less their honeymoon, a lot of thought. For him, they were dates on the calendar, but for her, it was a long-held dream finding its twin in reality.

Reading her thoughts, he reassures her. "It's great."

At one of the open-air markets, Reed follows her under the series of white canopies flapping in a breeze that stirs up.

Lily says, "People come to the markets because they are less expensive and tastier compared to the supermarkets. Most of the food is brought in fresh from nearby farms and ports."

Reed says, "Makes Reading Market look like a lemonade stand," while they survey the offerings. Some he recognizes—like cherries and olives, apples and string beans, a spill of nectarines, whole flounder and filleted sardines, heaps of shrimp, chickens roasting on spits—others not, like black radishes, purple carrots, and *potiron* or French pumpkins, their nut-brown rinds sliced open to reveal thick orange smiles. Amongst them, on little blackboards, are the prices with commas instead of periods marking the decimals.

Grocers weigh, wrap, bag, and chat with customers who touch, shake, thump and taste the goods.

Reed sniffs a gnarled quince.

In the restaurants he observes how she shares the same eating habit as the locals. "I consider it as more thoughtful. Almost meditative." She keeps the knife in one hand throughout their courses, using it to push food onto the tines of the fork, then placing the fork overhand into her mouth. "It's part of the overall culture here. Mealtime is an experience. It's leisurely, giving you time to savor the foods and enjoy your conversation. The wait-staff do not rush you. They're salaried."

She teaches Reed how to request ice when his soda arrives without.

He says, "*Je voudrais un peu de glacons, s'il vous plaît.*"

"*Parfait.*"

"The food is really good," he says. "The chocolate is amazing. Back home it's chalk in comparison."

Taking advantage of the temperate weather, Lily and Reed agree to shuffle their itinerary in favor of outdoor spots.

In the Chaillot Quarter, gregarious starlings welcome them. The couple strolls the avenues, passing elegant mansions turned embassies, peeking into fashion boutiques, and filling paper bags with market stall offerings.

At Rue Benjamin Franklin, Reed hands Lily his phone and poses beneath the blue street plaque. He is tickled by the idea of walking in the inventor's footsteps when he had resided in the area centuries ago.

Sprawled on the ground by the Trocadero, Lily and Reed watch the tourist groups not at all different than what they might see in Philly. Even in autumn, tourists spring out of the buses and subways in all directions.

Wearing rumpled clothing, parents chase boisterous children, shouting in fast-clip gibberish. Many ask strangers to take pictures, many more form lines at attraction entrances. Tour groups wear matching shirts or hats. They squint to orient themselves on maps, swarmed by beggars with pleading hands out front, and by thieves with filching fingers from behind.

On a tablecloth borrowed from the hotel, they lounge, letting their feet rest. From the bags, they put out hunks of cheese, brown bread, fig jam, sandwich meat, crisp veggies, wine and mineral water, and an apple tart.

Reed taps her foot with his. "Look, Lil."

"Aww," Lily melts at the sight of a baby girl asleep in a stroller some yards away. Lifting her sunglasses, Lily can see the girl's long lashes, adorable bow lips, and the most serene expression of innocence.

"Bet she's a screamer," Reed says.

"No. She's an angel."

They have discussed children before, happily agreeing on wanting a large family. Reed, because he is from one himself, and Lily, because she isn't. He is one of five siblings, while Lily has only a brother.

In a past conversation, Reed said, "It should be boy, girl, boy, girl. That way each of the girls would have an older brother to look after her."

"Our girls will do well themselves," Lily said.

"If they are anything like their mother, that's true. But if they have to deal with the types of boys I grew up with, then they'll need brothers."

"That's why they'll be attending private school, like I did."

After lunch, they cross the river to Champs de Mars.

"Over ten thousand tons. Took over two years and three hundred men to build it." Reed has memorized the Eiffel Tower brochures Lily gave him. What she could use as a sleep aid—dimensions, tonnage, kilowatt hours—Reed pored over like it was a spy thriller novel. "It's 1,051 feet tall; add another half foot on hot days."

He recites more engineering statistics as they cross the Tower's shadow.

She joins the queue for the elevator, but notices Reed taking a different way. "Where are you going?"

"You don't want to take the stairs?" he says teasing.

On the observation deck, Lily feels overwhelmed. There aren't a lot of moments when her dreams match up with experiences, but this is one such time: sharing this beautiful day and this stunning view of Pairs with her husband. She feels blessed to be alive at this moment with Reed on a picturesque day.

Nonchalantly, she wipes a tear away while Reed envelops her in his strong arms—the safest place in the world.

The wind defeats her attempts to placate her hair.

"Isn't it beautiful?"

Reed nods by her shoulder.

Lily isn't sure how much time has passed when Reed breaks their embrace to request a picture of them. The accommodating gentleman and his companion chat with them. Turns out they are not only Americans but live in Chester, Pennsylvania. After pleasantries, they move on.

At night, they walk off their dessert. Reed drapes his leather jacket on her shoulders to keep off the chill.

Reed hears it first, glancing behind. Soon, accordion music reaches her too. They turn around. Coming their way is a gaggle of musicians. Among the half dozen accordions, there is a concertina, a guitar, bongos. The players bounce, kick, and strut toward them.

Lily laughs and claps to add her own percussion, delighted by the energy as much as the music. Reed gets out his phone to record the whooping procession.

The troupe is lively, their fast finger-work whistling an infectious upbeat tempo. Like an ambulant party. Lily thinks of New Year's or Mardi Gras where strangers cheer together, embrace, wish the other better times. They flow around the couple. Pantomime smiles circling once, twice, then continue cavorting down the avenue.

Reed hugs Lily with one arm from behind, letting her lean back into him as she watches the retreating cacophony while he captures them digitally.

Strangers hands' bind Lily's arms. A chill breath by her ear, then a slimy tongue worming down her neck, sends her body into revolt and her heart into thudding panic. A short man and a tall woman already haul Reed apart from her. His phone hits the pavement her feet no longer touch.

fourteen

Abducted Twice

Their abduction spins Lily's mind like a top. She can't comprehend the impossibility of what's happening. In an instant she's gone from delight to dread. Clutched by someone's strong hands and walled in by two other someones, she feels claustrophobic, pressed in by leering men and a woman.

Reality reasserts itself. The man who holds her stinks of tobacco. A second man wearing a checked scarf and a woman with fuzzy cat ears on a headband leer at her. They move to flank her. In the new gap, Lily can see she is in a small green area with empty benches and trees that are taller in the dark.

Yards away, Reed is held by a woman who looks like a model—statuesque, imperious, and wearing fashionable clothing. A shorter man with oily hair bends Reed's arm behind his back, subduing Reed with ease. Her man grimaces in pain, and she screams.

Tobacco Man seals her mouth with his hand.

She feels smothered and gags.

Reed tries to reason with them, offering to reach for his wallet and give them all that is inside it. "Take what you want and let us go."

She is doubtful they understand his English.

The model strokes Reed's face, shushing him gently, like a mom trying to calm a distressed child. While gazing at Reed, she speaks in French to Lily's captors, "Do what you want with her. Dump the body in the river when you're done."

What kind of mugging is this? Her heart gallops, but at its center is a calm denial. This isn't happening. They are on their honeymoon, enjoying the City of Lights before beginning a go-go-go tour of the country, historic churches, and her family's ancestral lands. Who gets mugged in Paris on their honeymoon?

Her mind rockets up to heaven prayers for protection.

Tobacco Man snuffles at her long black hair and hisses French rudely into her ear. "We'll tell you when to screech, little mouse," he says, removing his hand.

Lily wrinkles her nose and strains to stretch her neck away from him.

Reed yells to her to be brave, that she will be okay.

"That's right, love," the stocky man says with a British accent. Taking backward steps, he adds, "We're all mates here."

They are being separated. Realizing this, Reed's expression turns to anger. His face reddens enough to boil over. When his temper runs short, he is a brick from the oven, impossible to handle and has to be left alone to cool. Maybe it will help him overpower the pair. He makes efforts to break free. But he cannot plant his feet to gain leverage. The model and the Brit just lift him in the air like a sack of straw.

"Reed! Don't hurt him!" All three erupt in the laughter of bullies. She loosens an arm and reaches for him only to have it snatched back and pinned to her side as though soldered there. Her mind searches for some magic phrase that will free them. Despite their jocular demeanor, Lily knows the situation is grave. A cold notion plinks through her—she fears she is seeing her husband for the final time.

Checked Scarf steps in front of her, blocking her view once more. Warm tears spring up. They are going to beat her or rape her. She tries to be brave and not show how truly terrified she is. It is happening so fast—pitched from dream to nightmare, an amusement ride gone fatally off course.

Won't anyone help them?

She tries to reassure herself. Reed will make it. He is strong, the strongest man she knows. He can handle a skinny model and the Brit who's half Reed's size.

When Checked Scarf grabs her ankles lifting her, she blurts in French, "I'm wealthy! Let me and my husband go, and we'll pay you anything. We won't tell anyone. I can wire any amount and you'll let us go. Please!"

They all pause as though giving the proposal due consideration. They even set her feet down on the ground. Lily's eyes plead, trying to coax a change of heart by willpower alone. She can't hear Reed anymore. Have they left with him? Please be safe.

The woman with the cat ears steps over, "It's not your money we want." In an eye-blink her features change. The whites of her eyes are now fathomless black and cruel lips part to reveal long sharp teeth.

Lily falls back and screams. Now they toy with her as they move along, shoving her from one to the next like a game of keep-away. "If we take our time with her, we can suck on her all night," says one.

At the edge of hearing, Lily detects a distant noise growing louder. Checked Scarf licks his fangs suggestively, while Tobacco Man takes hold of her once more. His cold hand slides down her soft neck.

"Hail Mary, full of Grace..." she begins to recite.

He pulls at her blouse, popping buttons off. Against her white skin, rising with the panicked hitches of her chest is her crucifix. All three flinch. It glimmers in the dark.

"... now and at the hour of our death."

Lights come on in the darkness. All of them squint at the bright spotlight. An engine noise roars. Checked Scarf and Cat Ears are knocked away like bowling pins. The bowling ball, a Peugeot, strikes the pair with enough force as to dent the bumper and crease the hood. Lily and Tobacco Man are nearly hit but for scant inches.

In seconds, the driver springs from the car, rounds the hood and charges into the man left standing. His fist impacts the lower back, around the kidneys. Then he strikes the throat and trips him. From the ground, Tobacco Man looks up and gets a solid foot in the jaw. Then the driver whirls, grabs Lily up in his arms.

"Let me go!" she says.

Having deposited her in the passenger seat, the man hurtles back around the car. Lily reaches to get out of the car, but stops herself. Incredibly, all three are recovering. Checked Scarf unsteadily gets to one foot. His other leg is perhaps broken, the pain evident in his anguished face. Cat Ears hisses while holding one arm with the other. Tobacco Man sits up and spits out a long canine.

Breath caught in her throat, Lily's eyes widen. The windshield is a movie screen playing a horror film. Headlamps throw the driver's shadow toward the shambling pair. They don't throw their own. Their flat black eyes eat the light, reflecting nothing. They're teens, or just a bit older—perhaps a third the man's age. His black and silver hair reaches the collar of his gumshoe trench coat.

Tobacco Man manages to tag the driver on his way by, but misses his grip. Nonetheless the driver stumbles and falls onto the hood of the Peugeot. All three close in, moving now with more ease as though Lily has overestimated the trauma they suffer.

With the element of surprise and a one-ton vehicle spent, he hasn't a chance. Sneering taunts resume as they too realize this. Tobacco Man nearly has his hands on the driver. The driver pulls something from his trench coat. Lily thinks he has un-holstered a gun, for they stop in their tracks. The object glows in his hand. Her attackers' expressions turn to agitation. Lily pairs this reaction with its twin minutes ago when her blouse was torn open, revealing the crucifix. That's what's in his hand.

Their attention is fixed on its palpable ethereal light. He pushes off the car, brandishing the crucifix as they take a matching step back. Their eyes become slits, hands become visors. Another step and they fall back again. The man waves it as a torch before the mob, then bolts for the open car door, slamming it shut behind him.

Thrown into reverse, the car pulls away. Tobacco Man ineffectually bangs the body of the car. All three pursue and aren't losing much ground. Their faces are normal. Did she imagine their inhuman features out of fear?

Lily's hands brace the dashboard. This is senseless. Why is she being abducted from criminals? She slides into the driver as he puts the car in a sharp turn. Now the car faces forward, shifted into drive. Clumps of earth are flung into the air. Lily struggles to buckle the seat belt. Cat Ears leaps onto the trunk. Lily screams, but the woman slips off when the car thumps off the curb and turns up the street.

The car lurches through traffic. Gasping, Lily takes in the stale air of the car. A mistake. Already dizzy from the wild careening of the car and high emotions, the smell of offal, grease, corn syrup, smoke, and soiled socks, causes nausea to swell inside her. She's going to vomit.

"*Arrêtez*," she says quietly, while holding her forehead.

Honking cars and screeches of tires pass them. Lily looks down. The odor is down there, where her feet are lost in a swirl of trash. Wrappers of fast food and candy, twine, newspapers, coffee-stained paper cups, cigarette packs make the mélange of litter.

"*Arrêtez!*" she says urgently. Lily finds a used paper sack in time to vomit into the unrolled top. It's almost a full minute before the heaving stops.

As though handling a dead rat, the man pinches with two fingers the top of the sack and tosses it through Lily's window. In the same manner, she discards a napkin she has used to wipe her chin.

Then she feels him on her left arm.

"*Êtes-vous blessée?*" Out of breath himself, his hand searches along to her shoulder, then her neck. He's thorough there. In clinical fashion, he examines from under the jaw down to the base and all around. Before he continues farther, she pushes the hand away.

"*Je vais bien*," her tone sharper than she had intended.

Relenting, he glances repeatedly at the side-views of the Peugeot and the rearview mirror, panning it left, right, up and farther down.

Adrenaline dissipates from her system. With a clearer head, Lily recognizes that she is not likely being kidnapped. Usually, victims are bound in the trunk or knocked out with a gag of chloroform, if movies are any guide. She's been rescued.

Centered on the dash stands Mother Mary. Her porcelain arms are open, palms up. Her painted face has a serene expression. Lily mouths, "Thank you."

Lily dares to look back. There is no sign of the gang. But she is being taken in the wrong direction. Away from Reed.

"We need to go back," she says in French.

The man makes no sign of hearing her. His attention is on the road as though pointedly not looking at her.

She looks at him. His trench coat cannot hide the middle age bulk creeping up his otherwise solid form. Unshaven, with a mane of silver hair, he appears as a noble king dethroned.

She shivers at the sudden cold and realizes Reed's jacket is not on her.

At an intersection, he asks where she lives so he can return her there.

"My husband's still back there. We can't just leave him."

"Out of the question," he says in dismissive French. "I will not return you to danger."

Lily doesn't want to argue. Every second, every mile she's away from him, the more her desperation grows. She's suffocating as surely as that evening when she had been caught in the fire.

Where is Reed? What's happened? Has he gotten away from them? Who were those people? How did they get so close to her and Reed without them noticing? Are they a gang?

Please, God, let him be safe.

"We just got married. We're on our honeymoon."

"I'm sorry. He's dead as surely as you would have been."

"Don't say that!" Her hand flies at his face of its own accord. As the man touches his reddened cheek, Lily appears as though she had been the one slapped. She holds the offending hand close to herself and says subdued, "I'm sorry. I'm sorry."

He nods once, accepting her apology without looking at her.

"What is your name?"

He doesn't answer for long moment. His eyes cast down at the steering wheel. "Aleron."

She has a vague recollection, perhaps from a movie-of-the-week, that humanizing people, such as using their name and other details, creates empathy. "My name is Lily Martin Williams. My husband's name is Reed. Reed Williams. He's a good, beautiful man. He has brothers, and a sister. And nieces, and parents. They all love him and want to see him again." She sniffs. Her hand touches the statue's feet. "You're a Catholic like me. In the name of Mother Mary, please take me to him."

fifteen

Misery Gets Company

A leron turns the car around as Lily's heart slips into the seat underneath her. She realizes he may be right that Reed may be dead. He could prevail over two, but if the others regroup... She shakes her head, refusing to consider what may happen.

As they approach the area they had fled only minutes ago, the Peugeot slows. Lily tries not to blink and miss spotting Reed or the others. Only a troupe of teens, a pair of inebriated men, a woman and her St. Bernard.

Aleron parks the car and escorts Lily across the street. Reaching the curb she breaks into a run. She hurries in one direction, then back the other way.

This is the spot.

"Reed!"

At least she thinks it is. Now she isn't certain. She orients herself so that she faces the direction they had been a short while ago. The musicians came up the pavement over there. Lily guesses where she and Reed stood to watch them shuffle off. Their backs must have been to their attackers, who bundled them off. She moves to follow herself into the park. Over there must be where the three corralled her. Then her knight galloped in. Yes,

149

there is a furrow of churned grass and dirt where the Peugeot had come or gone.

Shuddering, she's back in her captors' unyielding grips, feeling helpless once more. Did she imagine their dreadful faces? Those demon eyes and teeth. She saw it all clearly, but it is too fantastic to believe. They got up from being struck by a speeding car.

"Reed!"

She looks around herself, feeling utterly alone and vulnerable. She wishes she had pepper spray, a taser, *something*, to defend herself should the wrong people answer her desperate cries. Sobs return. Where did they go? Her legs no longer support her. On the ground, she spreads out her arms. How did this happen? How will she find him?

Her fingertips brush something leathery. In the dark she had missed it. Her hand clutches the jacket and draws it to herself. Her tears wet the collar as she pulls it on. The sleeves are much too long. She can smell him in it. She's not going to give up. He has to be somewhere. She's going after him and not ever letting go.

Lily finds Aleron dozing on a bench like a vagrant. She touches his shoulder. Her wet cheeks already speak for her. "He's not here," she says in French.

Rising, he reaches toward her, seems to think better of it and turns away, resuming his habit of not looking at her. As they reach the Peugeot, she says, "We need to go to the police."

"Impossible. I should not have intervened. Much is already in jeopardy."

Cracking open the door, she says, "You did, and I won't leave. Not without Reed."

"The police cannot help you."

Lily sinks into the Peugeot, her feet submerging once more in the morass. How can this man stand being so untidy? With closer inspection, she discovers it is not all garbage. Amid the wadded refuse swirl newspaper clippings pasted to card stock, fashion magazines, photos, twine, a mallet, notebooks with pens in their spirals. Like pulling a fish from the water, she draws up a pair of binoculars by its leather strap, then lets it go.

The car is a bachelor pad on four wheels.

Curious now, she further inspects the car's interior. On the rear seats are pillows and a blanket, a SLR camera in its form-fitting case, a plastic folio with a missing top crammed with hanging folders packed with papers.

"Why can't they?"

Preoccupied with driving once more, Aleron fumbles to answer. "Euh. They are incompetent. Inspector Clouseau could teach them better police work."

"Then take me to the American embassy."

"You are an American? Your French is more elegant than most Parisians."

"Is the embassy near here?"

"No difference there. Just more Clouseaus."

"Don't be absurd." Her hands brush her hair back while she thinks of what she'll say at the embassy. Would it still be open? Of course it would. It must for emergencies such as this.

"I will take you to your hotel. I presume you are lodging at one."

He makes a series of turns. Lily wonders if he knows where they are now; she doesn't. "We're wasting time. My husband is out there. Still in danger."

Aleron stares ahead. Thinking? Reconsidering?

He slows the Peugeot, looking for a spot along the curb to stop. "I will leave you here. You can take a cab wherever you wish to go."

"Pardon?" She says, at first thinking this to be a poor joke. Then alarmed, she says, "No. You have to tell the police what you saw."

"What did I see?" he says, part challenge, part feigned ignorance. "Delinquents? Two French teens, an older Romani, an Englishman who looks like he's lived in a bar all his life, and a... a retired fashion model. They just decided to get together and assault you and your husband? For what? For money? Did they take any? Did they have weapons? Why couldn't your husband get away from an unarmed woman not even half his weight?

"Perhaps the police will suspect you. That you made it all up. Maybe you hated your husband. Maybe he cheated—"

Lily slaps him. No regret this time. She wants to say, "How dare you," or "He would never." But she can't reconcile why this man would save her life then dismiss her plight. Why had Aleron saved her? With a car? A car that looks more slept in than driven.

How had he seen her predicament? Just by coincidence, he drove by at the right time, saw a woman being harassed by a gang? At a distance, in the dark? And seeing this, he decided to intervene with a car? It was amazing. He plowed right into two of them and got her into the car safely.

And Aleron had known exactly what to do. He knew to take out his crucifix. The three feared it, just as they feared her own, like the metal was radioactive. She hadn't imagined that.

Lily gasps, "You know them."

Recovering from being smacked, he says, "I do not understand."

Recovering the binoculars, Lily waves them as damning evidence, "You were on reconnaissance. Who were they?"

"I use that for bird-watching," he says unconvincingly.

"What are you—a private investigator?"

In a quavering voice, he says, "You are excited, and your imagination leaps too far."

"You didn't happen by. You knew them. French teens, a Romani, an Englishman, and a fashion model." Indignant, Lily shoves Aleron's shoulder, again and again till he faces her. "You know them."

She digs up a magazine from the mess on the floor. She had glanced at it earlier. The woman who had held Reed poses on its creased cover. It's dated more than two years ago. Lily hadn't recognized her at first, partly because she didn't think to make a connection, and because the woman on the cover looks vivacious. Carefree. Whole somehow. Unlike the woman in the park who was missing something vital.

Aleron turns green at the discovery.

Lily jabs her manicured finger at the woman's glossy face. "I am not leaving this car without the truth. My husband is out there and you're the only one who knows what really happened."

"You don't know what you're asking. If your husband isn't dead, then he may as well be."

"What is wrong with you? You rescued me and now you want to throw me away. Tell me the truth!"

"The truth," Aleron scoffs. Then to himself, "I should tell her. I should." He reaches into the mess, finds a small photo album and hands it to her. Inside aren't pictures, but newspaper clippings. He taps on a one-column story only a few inches long describing a sex abuse ring busted in a coastal town in Ille-et-Vilaine of the Brittany region.

"I am not understanding the connection." The headlines of the other articles share the same theme in other locations at other times. She recalls similar sensational ones in America from time to time, like a disturbed man who kept a pair of women locked in his basement, parents who caged their children, or men of the cloth who distributed child pornography.

"Abuse so depraved, to just *read* about..." Aleron stills himself for a moment. "In many instances, the police did nothing because of political pressure from above. Cases were closed, evidence went missing, or witnesses' credibility were undermined. Even reporters were threatened and their files confiscated.

"Sometimes the abuse went on for years. Sometimes for decades. And I kept thinking on how these pits were often in neighborhoods where I may live or you may live. What about the men delivering the post or packages, or landscapers, or maintenance workers. Or the neighbors walking their dogs or knocking on the door to borrow a wrench or a rake. They never heard a cry? A scream? They saw nothing unusual—strangers coming and going at all hours of the day and night?

"Then I think maybe they did know, but didn't want to know. They did hear, but didn't want to hear. It's too unbelievable and mundane at the same time." Aleron says to himself, "Damn shadows. Right at their feet and they don't see them."

Lily would like to think she'd be the neighbor who spoke out. As a teacher, she has taken training to recognize signs of abuse in children. She gathers that Aleron has taken it upon himself to do the work of the police and reporters, to obtain his own evidence and expose... what?

He says, "And just as those investigations were shut down there, the same can be done here."

She considers his point but won't accept it. She says, "You saw. You saved me, right? And now you're not alone. So whatever the truth is, you can tell me. Aleron, tell me."

"I won't tell you." He hurries to add, "I'll show you."

He crawls halfway between their seats and rummages behind them. She hears snapping plastic and scattering paper. After pulling himself back, he hands her several thick packets. Their open ends reveal photographs inside. Large ones, used for examining detail or showcasing in portfolios, slide out onto her lap. While Aleron drives once more, she turns the stack in her hands and flips through it.

Taken in the evening, often at some distance, the pictures had captured the subjects' backs, profiles, and faces. Candids. Like those taken by a private eye.

Or maybe those taken by a member of the paparazzi. In the glamorous scenes depicted, the fashion model turns up in evening gowns, expensive heels, and makeup. Lily scowls at the sight of her smiling and carefree, and looking like a slut in those clothes. How could this be the woman involved with violence? Who'd believe it? But she does look grand, damn her.

All the more so when arm in arm with a man who strikes Lily as a Gaulish noble—long locks, thin mustache, peacock suits. Royalty out among the commoners, they remind Lily of her own parents attending private galas, her mother resplendent with jewels, her father exuding charm.

Some pictures pull back, showing an entourage of men in dark suits swarming them from the exits of museums, music halls, hotels to the doors of luxury cars, of which, Aleron got closeups of the license plates.

Halfway through the stack, Lily wonders why she should bother to continue, when she notes a shift. Soon all this glamour disappears. In the subsequent pictures, the solitary model wears casual clothing, sunglasses in the dark, hooded sweatshirts or coats with upturned collars. No makeup, no king, no courtiers.

She disappears into nightclubs below ground, then emerges with her hands shading her face, her shirts untucked or torn or stained. The final closeup shows her chin blotted with blood.

Does she get into fights? Who's smacking her around? Why does she go back?

While putting the pictures back in their sleeve, Lily glances out the window to get her bearings and failing. The road follows the Seine lined with docked houseboats. The gangways, less steep now than in the summer when the river flows at its lowest, bridge the land and boat decks.

What is Aleron's interest in her? His work here might cover a period of months, at least. Cover, perhaps the woman's fall from grace, from her chin up and smile open, to head down and eyes wary. Did she age out of her career? Did her prince break up with her? Or was it drugs?

Maybe it's personal for Aleron.

Questions with no answers. She says, "You said you'd show me, but these don't mean anything."

"We're nearly there," Aleron says subdued.

"Where? Who is this woman, Aleron? Clearly, you've known her for a while."

The Peugeot slows and does a three-point-turn. Parking in spaces punctuated by London plane trees along the river, Aleron turns off the engine. With the headlamps off and engine silent, the night seems more alive.

He turns to Lily. She flinches upon seeing his storm-grey eyes. They contain such desolation. He says, "Madame, please do not persist in this or you will end up living in a car with only memories for company. I do not want that for one so young and beautiful as yourself."

"She really hurt you, didn't she? She took someone from you, like she took Reed? Who is she, Aleron?"

"Her name is Marie de Telfour. She is my fiancée."

sixteen

One Heart Beats Between Us

B ased on the paraphernalia of a private investigator, the scopes, camera, notebooks, and refuse of hand food, Lily had expected Aleron to confirm he was a disinterested observer. Instead, *she's my fiancée*. That is all. No biggie. Private eye, fiancée, what is the difference? Lily feels foolish for having believed any part of this evening could be straightforward and sensible.

She clutches her necklace, feeling the metal crucifix while taking the moment to process this. She blows out a breath. But her words aren't calm, "That woman *is* your fiancée? Still? What kind of game is this?"

Aleron shakes his head, "I assure you this is no game."

The woman must be deranged. And does being engaged to her, *still*, make Aleron unbalanced as well? Lily considers that they are some perverse couple, feeding off each other's kinks, like sado-masochists. This Marie de Telfour indulges in terrorizing tourists while he watches with vicarious pleasure. Or rides in as a hero, some Munchausen syndrome by proxy, where Marie inflicts pain on people so that Aleron can save them from it.

"Unbelievable!" She hurries to unlatch her seatbelt and get out of the car. She slams the door shut and huffs ahead, unsure of where she is going or what she will do when she gets there.

She hears Aleron getting out of the car, but she won't look at him. She quickens her pace, "Stay away."

She doesn't hear him follow. With the chill of the October evening, she pulls Reed's leather jacket tight around her. In the distance ahead of her, the headlights of an approaching car appear. Maybe she'll wave the driver down when he nears. Hopefully he will be willing to take her to the police.

But then she thinks of what she'll say to the police. With what Aleron had just told her, she needs him more than ever. Fiancée. Fiancée! Just as she turns to go back, he's already running toward her, grabs her, then rushes her back and into the Peugeot.

"I'm sorry—" she says to apologize, not out of a sense of having wronged him, but because she needs to persuade him to confess whatever he knows about Marie and what Marie's done to her and Reed.

But Aleron makes a noise for her to keep quiet while he grabs the binoculars from the floor by her feet. He peers through them. Lily looks out. The car she had considered hitchhiking in pulls over and parks across the street from them, some hundred yards ahead.

He whispers, "It's them." He hands her the binoculars and slumps lower in his seat, "This is what you wished to see," then adds, "You must keep quiet and out of sight."

The car zooms wildly into her view. She steadies the binoculars in time to see a man in a pea coat closing the driver door, then stroll to the rear of the car. By the trunk is another similar figure raising the trunk lid. What comes out of the trunk aren't groceries or six-packs of beer, but a full-grown man whose arms are tied behind him and his mouth gagged.

Lily gives a shout.

Aleron whispers a firm, "Quiet. No matter what happens."

The hostage appears South Asian, face florid, eyes bugged out, cords of his throat taut in a scream. Lily hears nothing, and if the men do, they don't pay it any mind. Close up, before the two men turn in profile to escort their hostage, she can see their eyes. Pitiless black.

Lily whimpers.

In quick-step, the three cross toward their side of the street. If they continue straight they will reach a houseboat with an emerald deck that gleams in the glow of tiny lights strung aboard.

Dump the body in the river when you're done.

Do something. Do something. Do something. Reed would do something.

Lily lays on the car horn.

Suddenly alert, Aleron swipes Lily's hand away, "They'll see us!"

They certainly heard them, stopping in their tracks and turning to look in their direction.

She returns her hand, making urgent wails with the horn, enticing one of the men to come investigate.

"Stop!" A frantic Aleron starts the car.

Lily can see the hostage take off in the opposite direction. "I couldn't just watch!"

Launching the car down the street toward the men, Aleron asks, "What are you doing?"

Lily climbs into the back seat, "He won't be able to open the door tied up like that."

"What?!"

Lily clears off the boxes and cases, then braces herself while Aleron swerves around the nearer bad guy, leaving him behind, then gaining on and passing the second. He whips the car sidelong to the hostage. Lily pops the driver-side door open, waving at the man, signaling him as though he were a plane taxing to the gate. "Hurry!"

The hostage dashes around the car instead, scooting past the trunk. "No-no-no!" Lily pulls the door shut and locks it before the pursuing bad guy reaches it. He punches at the window. The breakaway glass crumbles onto her legs. Lily scrambles backward as the he reaches for her. In a second his head and arm are in the car grasping while she presses against the passenger-side door. She thinks on what Aleron had done in the park. She holds out her crucifix as far as its chain will allow. Though not nearly as large as Aleron's own, hers does glow and has the same effect. The man squints, blinded.

Aleron floors the gas and the car lurches into a turn, whirling the man away from the car into his buddy. The car zooms past the fleeing hostage and Lily thinks that Aleron will leave him behind. But he brakes about thirty feet ahead, giving Lily time to open the passenger-side door.

Sticking close to the car, she waves again at the man, "Safety! Safety!"

This time he heeds her, diving into the car. Aleron is already on the move once more before Lily gets her door closed. Now he's going in reverse, back toward those devils. He goes erratically up the street, and it's clear the men don't know which way to go to avoid being hit. Ultimately they dive aside.

Aleron makes an arc, rams the rear of the Peugeot into the driver door of the bad guys' car, then changes gear, speeding away.

***

While Aleron takes a circuitous route, Lily undoes the knots of the hostage's gag and bindings. Perhaps in shock, the man rambles in a language Lily doesn't understand, nor does he acknowledge her while she checks him for injuries, finding none. When they believe they lost the would-be murderers, they drop the man off at a hospital.

When the Peugeot approaches Hotel Le Hervey, sighing to a stop, vested valets leave their stand and part to either side of the car, unable to hide their disapproval of the busted front end. The hood looks like the cracked face of a boxer at the end of a fight, the bumper his split lip.

Aleron follows Lily through the entryway of the hotel. But for two clerks, the floor is empty. Unsurprising, given the late hour of a weeknight. She should have been asleep hours ago and her body knows it. Fatigue settles over her mind, dousing lights there. Undeterred, reason carries a candle, trying to make connections in the dark.

At the door of the suite, Lily rests her forehead, closing her eyes. She and Reed had left through this door this morning, laughing. She cannot remember what got it all started; Reed was just in a silly mood. Their ghosts run through her, causing her to tremble. Drawing in her breath, she unlocks the door and steps into the sumptuous room.

The turn-down service has left the room fresh. A pleasant contrast to the Peugeot. Walking past a vase of gardenias set on a small table, her spirit lifts just a bit. Everything is crisp and renewed. Like their first night here.

In the closet, she hangs Reed's leather jacket. She smooths the black collar and pats the cuffs. She wants his arms in the sleeves again and feel them around her. *I will*, she promises herself.

Aleron haunts the entrance.

While she paces the room, her thoughts run around like her wound up students, never settling in one place for long. What she had just witnessed; what she and Reed had themselves endured; what Aleron had said about Marie being his fiancée.

Her hands shake, "They would have killed that poor man, yes?"

About to answer, Aleron checks around himself, then steps inside the room just enough to close the door. "Yes. It's a scheme I learned about.

They abduct people, often immigrants, and bring them aboard the boat." He hesitates to say, "And discard the bodies into the river."

Lily holds herself, "That's what they would have done to me." Unable to get calm, she makes her way to the couch, "And what they will do to Reed?"

Aleron hurries to help Lily before she collapses. Once she's seated, he steps back and says, "I don't believe so."

"No?" She tries to be hopeful. "I don't understand. What do they want with him then? They didn't want my money. They laughed."

"I can make tea if you'd like." In the kitchenette he pokes around.

Shaking her head, she says, "Why were you spying on your fiancée? What's wrong with her? Drugs? Or did she have some mental breakdown? Is she crazy?"

Aleron presses his palms together, "It is not that she is crazy."

"Then what?" When he doesn't answer, she prompts him, "Just tell me."

He lets out a sigh. "She is not human."

Lily groans. A giant's thumb and forefinger pinch her head. She massages by the temples, "I'm very tired, Aleron. I'm trying to understand, and I'm not interested in your nonsense."

"You saw them. Their eyes, yes? Their fear of Christ the Lord?"

"I don't know."

Aleron's arms drop to his sides and he turns about nodding, expecting and accepting her skepticism. "It doesn't matter."

"Then what? Aleron? You knew she was violent, right? She's done this before." She realizes this as she says the words, rousing herself to press more. "Abductions and murders. You knew what to do. How to handle them. Why didn't you stop this sooner?"

Aleron responds with indignation that bites Lily back. "Now that you are in my position, we'll see what lengths you will go to save his soul and what transgressions you will allow at the cost of yours." Seeing the effect of his rebuke, he softens his tone and draws closer to her. "Marie and I are both damned by her condition. So it is with you. My inclination was not to intervene at all. Perhaps I should not have. It might have been less cruel."

"How can you say that?"

"I can't save everyone. I just want to save her." His shoulders fall as his shoes point to the hallway door. "It is better that I go."

"No. Please. I'm sorry. I'm tired, and I'm scared for my husband. Just tell me he's okay."

"Marie doesn't intend to kill him but to recruit him. Why and what for, I do not know." He falls silent and takes his cue to leave when she yawns with sleepiness.

"Please… I don't want to be alone." Thinking on the state of his car, and her part in it, she suggests, "We can make the couch comfortable. There are extra blankets and pillows in the closet," she pleads with her whole tired, pained body.

Appraising the room, he says, "It is not a Peugeot, but I suppose it will do."

***

Slipping between the drapes, the morning sunlight crosses a fallen pillow and moves up the bedside, to caress Lily's cheek. The bed sheet is drawn tight around her body. One hand grips a knot of it.

In the twilight between sleep and consciousness, dreams bleed into reality and contradictions are overlooked. Reed is here. He is not here. They are in his apartment, and they are in the suite.

She mutters for him to wake and make a fresh pot of coffee. But she already hears the distant noise of motion and banging, telling her that Reed is in the kitchen. When the dark roast lifts his mood, his morning glower will civilize into a smile, and he will return to her with her cup, saying, "Morning, sunshine," as both an endearment and a way to mock her caffeine-deprived disposition.

Her hand releases the sheet and seeks out his form on the bed. Fingers sniff pockets under the coverlet, finding only absence. Not even his scent in the laundered linen. Then all at once she understands he is not getting coffee. He is not here at all. The empty space prompts her to open her eyes, which begin to spill tears. Feeling halved, it is as though she awoke an amputee. For minutes, the lump of blanket with her head poking out shakes with sobs.

There is a knock on the bedroom door. The intrusion startles Lily who only dimly remembers having asked Aleron to stay. She sits up and wipes her reddened eyes and cheeks, and swipes her hair from her face.

Clutching the blanket, she shambles toward the door, unlocks it, and plunks back into the bed.

"I remember this morning two years ago," Aleron says from the door. "You are handling it better than I did. The pain that morning was worse than the night before. I threw and kicked everything in sight. I was heart-sick, and I was furious with myself for not having done more. I didn't know what had happened to her. She could have been violated or dead or worse. As I would discover later, it was all three."

Through a hiccup of dying sobs, she says, "That is not helping."

He steps toward the bed, extending a cup of coffee.

From her blanket cocoon she reaches out, taking the cup. After a vitalizing sip, she thanks him.

Aleron sits on a stool near the bed. "I did not have anyone to help me, not for a long while. But I can help you. I could assist making it easier for you, if you are determined to see your husband." He scratches his beard along the jaw, "That morning, I felt terrified, lost, broken, like my breath was stolen from me. That is why I intervened last night. I saw it happening again."

"You are saying that what happened to Reed, happened to Marie?"

"And what happened to me, I pray, will not befall you. The day I began looking for Marie was the best one I had in two years. I am without employment, without a home, without friends. This is the most I've spoken with someone for quite some time."

Lily unwinds the bedding and straightens her legs. "But you did find her. Before last night." Her expression conveys the unspoken gap in his story. Two years to find her? Two years following her? Two years of doing nothing to stop her? "Then if you know where to find her, you will know where to find Reed. We should go. Now," she moves to stand.

"They will be asleep. We will look tonight."

"I can't wait till then. Reed can't either."

"We will have to. They are only active at night and she has many homes. The one on Ile de la Cité is well guarded. If you wish my help, you will listen. I do not expect to convince you. You will have to find the faith to believe. You will need to. Without it, you will not see, you will not comprehend, and you will not be able to help your husband. Finding him will not be the problem. The problem will be saving him."

***

Lily makes a plan. "This is what we'll do. I am going to shower. You will then do the same. A long, thorough one. And while you're in there, I will order breakfast. Then you are going to explain everything you know and how *exactly* you're going to help my husband. Understood?"

The showerhead has the perfect pulse and pressure to make the morning more bearable. With a clearer head, Lily realizes she must consider what to tell Reed's family.

Affectionately, both families had admonished them to forget their phones, forget them, forget the world. Just have fun. Her last communication was a text to her mother's phone when they arrived at their hotel. Now their loved ones have gone to bed certain Lily and Reed are having the time of their lives. She absolutely doesn't want to wake them from that dear illusion.

But Reed's mother and father deserve to know what happened. The thought twists in her belly. She holds herself under the splashing water, unable to rehearse her side of the conversation further than, "Hello, Bobbi."

She backs off the idea of calling the Williamses first. It's too impossible. Howell and Bobbi had long ago made Lily feel welcome and part of their family, as though Lily grew up next door. Her imagination too great, Lily could hear their hearts shatter over the line.

She could call her own parents. Slightly less daunting for Lily, and for an altogether different reason. They had difficulty accepting Reed, especially, her mother, Anne. Of course, she and her mother disagreed on many, many things over the years. Lily wonders if her mother would be capable of withholding judgment in her tone for once.

Charlie, then? She and her brother get along as well as siblings do. Declared enemies one moment, best friends the next. And whenever she needed him, he had been there for her.

While the question remains unresolved, Lily finishes in the bathroom and emerges wrapped in her plush robe. When Aleron takes his turn, Lily calls room service. She orders to her taste and trusts that Reed's usual fare will be sufficient for Aleron's appetite.

On the sofa where he had slept, Lily notes Aleron's deflated trench coat. The coat had been shining armor last night. What really gleamed was the crucifix he produced from its inner pocket. Is it still there? With a quick look back to the bedroom door, Lily inspects the coat, wrinkling her nose at the stale odor. The item is easy enough to find. She is surprised by its weight. A reassuring weight, cast in silver with high detail of Jesus outstretched and transfixed. It does not glow now, but throws the sunlight. Somehow it had power over her attackers. They were repulsed, blinded, maybe even afraid as if Aleron had been waving a torch and they were soaked in kerosene.

She should pray now. She had made sure that she and Reed said their daily prayers. With the white noise of the shower helping her focus, she kneels before the sofa. So often she has prayed for her family, her students, strangers undergoing hardships, the pope, the president. Now at this moment she prays for herself. She wants strength, resolve, and her husband to return safe. She knows that she should also pray for those who have wronged them, that they should seek redemption, feel remorse, ask forgiveness. But she does not have it in her heart now. They cut that part out.

Drawn by curiosity, she looks through the remaining jacket pockets. Amongst the lint are several matchboxes, a silver lighter, and a small bottle like miniature liquor bottles sold on airplanes. Its label has faded and its content is limpid. A nip of vodka, perhaps?

A final item is a photograph folded in half. Opening it, she almost doesn't recognize Marie. It is a studio portrait of her before a neutral backdrop, showing Marie posing with confidence and openness. Her complexion is warmer than Lily remembers and less gaunt. She doesn't resemble a killer.

She replaces all the items and makes a call to housekeeping before dressing for the day.

Aleron emerges from the bathroom wearing Reed's robe. Reed had filled it out more nicely. He looks at the cart of food with surprise and hunger. Lily beckons him to join her at the table where plates, utensils, and condiments are set. He piles starches and breakfast meats and syrups into one mass. Starved, he nonetheless dines rather than devours. He thanks her for the hospitality.

The coffee hasn't fortified her to face the day, but for his sake, with effort, she manages a small smile.

"Where are my clothes?" he asks, suddenly sheepish about his state of undress.

"I had them burned."

"Pardon?"

"They're being laundered. Someone will be by to measure you for new clothes."

"That is not necessary."

"It is a favor to us both. You had mentioned needing faith to find Reed. I'm not ready to believe you, but I am willing to trust you to do what you promised. Now. Please, tell me about Marie."

seventeen

Missing

L ily contemplates her light buttered toast. Without an appetite, she
is nonetheless famished for the information she expects Aleron
will provide.

Except he remains silent, but for the chewing.

She clears her throat, as her mother would, to prompt him to speak.
But unlike her mother, who would feign interest in her fingernails, Lily's
eyes cut to his, sword-sharp.

Aleron kisses jelly off his thumb, saying in French, "I know the wrongs
Marie has committed. And I can imagine what your feelings are for her.
But I ask you to consider that she is a victim too. We all are. And the man
responsible is still out there."

He swallows yolk-sopped bread and a slice of cantaloupe. "I am much
older than Marie. We are an unlikely pair. You must know the feeling
of being with the person who brings you to life like no one else. She had
energy of youth and I saw things as new again. Until I had met her, I
thought I was past needing companionship. But when you're with someone like that, you don't want a moment away from her. Yes?"

"Yes," Lily says, recalling the feeling when she had been treated for
burns and smoke inhalation. In her hospital room, surrounded by her

students' cheery hand-made get-well cards, she formulated a plan to properly meet her man, who, for the time being, she named Logan. Once free
of the I.V.s, monitors, and prodding nurses, she would visit the firehouses
that responded, speak with each of the houses' captains, and discover the
identity of her hero.

The Fishtown station lieutenant helped arrange for Lily to meet
Reed—even better than Logan—when he was on shift. All went as she
planned—until he turned her down.

Reed came around the fresh-washed fire truck. In a snug blue tee
shirt, he was an engine himself. Strong and expertly built, with pistons
for arms.

The words she prepared forgotten, her fingers drummed a tin of cookies she brought while she stumbled to explain that she was one of those
caught in the recent three-alarm fire.

"I remember." He took a step closer and noted her bandaged arm,
"You're all right?"

"Yes. That's why I'm here. To thank you in person for saving me."

Reed nodded, "You're fine. Good. That's thanks enough."

Lily approached, offering the tin and her hand, "I'm Lily Martin."

He gave one firm pump of her hand, "Reed." Then he took the tin
and popped open the lid. He examined one of the sugar cookies shaped
like a dog.

"They're meant to be Dalmatians. I couldn't find firefighter molds. I
hope there's enough for everyone. I wasn't sure how many to make. I know
there are rules about donations like these."

"We appreciate it. These will be gone in no time."

Lily smiled, wondering what to do with her hands now.

He replaced the lid, "The guys told me about you and your family."

Was it a bad thing? Should who her family was matter?

He said, looking concerned, "That wasn't your place, was it? I heard
they're still investigating the cause."

"I was visiting friends."

He looked her up and down, but his thoughts were a mystery. When
it appeared he would turn to leave, she said, "How about dinner? Have you
been to Xavier's?"

Now she could read him. Awkward for her putting him on the spot,
his posture tensed. Delicately, he said, "Um, I can't accept."

Unable to hide her disappointment, she rolled up on her toes and then
settled with a sigh. "Oh."

"Look. I get it, but understand I was just doing my job. Everyone here is trained for it. It happened to be me who found you. Any of the guys would have done the same."

He backed away, "It was good meeting you." He shook the tin, "And not to be picky, but I prefer the peanut butter kind."

She waved a silent goodbye. After he disappeared behind the truck, she surprised herself, saying aloud, "But it *was* you."

She heard him turn around in his steel-toed boots and come back. "Excuse me?"

"It was you. I understand it could have been anyone, but it was you. You saved my life. Perhaps people say that a lot to first responders, but I want you to hear it. You saved my life," she said with a hitch in her voice that she tried to flatten out. "And I'm so thankful. It may be a job to you, but it's someone's life. Please don't make light of what you do."

She turned around, feeling her eyes sting, and headed out through the open bay.

Behind her he shouted, "I'm often at Angelo's on Girard. Maybe I'll see you there."

All that seems a lifetime ago. Yesterday morning, Reed had sat where Aleron sits now. She rubs her arms trying to conjure Reed. *This is surreal.* How abrupt life has changed for them both. One second enjoying the impromptu performance of street musicians and the next second yanked out of normality.

Aleron saws into his ham, "She liked that I was older. I had experience. She trusted me like a guide in an unknown land. Like me, she attended church. It grounded her in her professional life. She had seen other models get chewed up by the profession and didn't want to follow the same fate."

He rises to his feet, cinching the robe's belt under his paunch. He walks to her right, then back, running a paw through his silver mane that glints with the light of the late morning sun.

"I have to tell you all of it. Even if you never believe me."

While he paces, Lily grows concerned he will shake apart. Years of quietude, having no one to speak to, confide in, have come to an end. A steam valve has broken, and the energy released animates his body in the telling of his tale. He punctuates his French with sharp gestures and at times Lily wonders if he realizes she's even here.

He isn't recollecting, he's reliving.

"We met at a museum. My trade was photography. The camera and light are easier in my hands than a brush and paint. But I would visit the masters for hours at a time. It was at the Musee de l'Orangerie that I saw her. Do you know of Monet? His *Nymphaes*? She was absorbed by it, as I was of her. I recognized her of course. A fashion model. In front of me she was more beautiful than in the magazines. But of course the magazines smudge out all the character from a person's photograph. They conceal real beauty.

"I had a better physique then, though I was no Adonis. No silver or belly or beard. As with any man with a beating heart who sees such a woman, I wished nothing but to cause her delight—to smile, to laugh. I don't recall how I got the nerve to speak to her, but I introduced myself."

He extends his hand to Lily. "I'm Aleron." This coaxes a small smile from her, but not her hand.

He makes nothing of it, continuing. "We discussed Monet. Mostly, I listened. One of her favorite pieces was his *Blue Row Boat*. She liked to picture herself on that boat, drifting about lazily, reaching over the side to dip her hand in the languid water. It relaxed her.

"We talked more of Monet and other artists, then our professions. A photographer and a model. Kismet. We agreed to look for each other here again. And we did. One time I convinced her to come to my apartment where I had a studio. I must have been persuasive. She agreed, and we had a photography session. I chose the best one and kept it for myself. Here..."

He fishes out the photograph from the pocket of the trench coat still draped over the sofa and holds it out for Lily to admire.

Lily feigns not having seen the photo before. With a polite glance, she says, "Very nice."

"She is. That is the Marie I love—beautiful, confident, full of life. What I said in the car last night, about the abuse scandals... When we dated, Marie opened my eyes to the issue. She was very protective of her modeling friends. The profession has predators who take advantage of naive young women. It's a very challenging business, even in the best of circumstances. Marie often invited the girls to join her at church, or art exhibits, or just to her apartment. She'd chaperone or keep in contact with her mobile. Anything to help keep them confident and away from trouble. She was very determined, very driven.

"Now... Now, she's different. Something is missing."

"So what happened?"

"She lost her shadow. I'll come back to that.

"I proposed at the same spot as we met. Nothing elaborate, just one knee and a question. The patrons surrounding us applauded when she agreed. Truly the happiest I had ever been. She often called me her lion, her protector. I felt my life had started when I met her and then I felt like a child, full of energy, wanting to explore the world with her. We would marry and travel. No itinerary. Just go.

"That night we dined at her favorite restaurant. The attack came as a surprise. But it should not have. I can remember this feeling I had. A sensation that we weren't alone. As though someone unseen was watching us. I would find out they can do that. The shadows, they may stand beside you and you'd never know it. But I'll come back to that also.

"So, I was not mistaken: we were watched. After dinner, Marie and I walked holding each other as you and your husband had last night. One moment it was little nothings of conversation and the next I'm on the ground. It happened so fast, I initially assumed that I had tripped. I was about to laugh at my own clumsiness, expecting when I looked up to see Marie offering her hand to help me if she wasn't laughing herself. Instead I heard her scream. I looked up and reached my arm out to her, which was absurd as she was no longer near me. She was in a stranger's arms. A stranger who moved with ease despite holding a protesting woman. He didn't appear to be running. Rather he took great strides as though on stilts—I don't know how else to describe it. By the time I found my feet, he was turning a corner.

"I ran after him, turning the same corner. I didn't see either of them. No sign. I heard a car start off in a hurry, but I was too slow to get a good look. She was gone. Like the earth swallowed her up."

At the end, Aleron's voice thins and he blinks his eyes.

Lily pours him a glass of water, and he gulps it.

"Who took her?"

"A shadow named Claude St. Croix. I didn't know him. I didn't even have his name. In fact, for months the man I pursued wasn't him at all. I did not have anyone to help me. This is why I intervened last night. I saw it happening again."

Lily feels her own shame for having ever questioned Aleron's motives. He had saved her life and only wanted what she wanted: their lovers back.

"I didn't know what to do. I felt nauseous and brainless. All night I had searched for her. I called her mobile, leaving urgent messages. None were returned. Eventually I made my way to the police and reported her missing. I described the man as best I could. One detail of his dark face was that he had a severe under-bite and his lower front teeth protruded out—kind of like a deep-sea fish. L'Anguille is what I called him. He worked for St. Croix, I would learn. He had abducted Marie and took her to his master.

"I told the police we didn't have enemies and I could not think of anyone who'd want to harm her. They speculated that it could have been any number of reasons. Ransom, an obsessed admirer, or, perhaps, I made it all up.

"I resolved to find Marie myself. But like the police, I had little to start with. I could not entertain the thought that she was halfway around the world. In order to work, I needed to assume she was still in Paris and that some slip-up by the man who had her would provide me a clue to his whereabouts.

"I grabbed my camera and a notebook. I went straight away to the scene of the night before. I spoke to the staff and any regulars about what they might have seen. I wrote every name down, every detail they could recall. No one had anything useful to provide, but I felt purposeful. I took pictures of our every step. I tried to recall the man who took her. Dark complexion, average height with a nose down-turned and under-bite. He moved fast. Faster than I had seen anyone move.

"I canvassed nearby stores and homes asking if they had seen my Marie. No one had.

"I just fell apart, not realizing it was going to get much worse. There were some brighter moments, but too few. False hopes, setbacks, realizing my fiancée resembled less of herself each time I saw her. While I have done shameful things and lost everything trying save her."

A knock at the door quiets him.

"The tailor," Lily says to Aleron as she goes to the door.

His arms straight out and legs apart, Aleron stands like a robed paper doll. Behind him, the short, balding tailor unspools green tape to measure Aleron's neck, neck to shoulder, shoulder to elbow and elbow to wrist.

Lily had requested shirts in three shades of blue and one green, each in several sizes; she hoped that one of them would be suitable. Lily had sized Aleron based on her brother, before middle age might one day thicken his middle. The two were otherwise almost the same height and frame.

The tailor pronounces the measurements while digging in the open sacks for packages of shirts.

"That one," she approves.

Declining further measures, Aleron finds slacks for himself; Lily had ordered practical khakis. With fresh socks in hand as well, he secludes himself in the bathroom. After a short moment, he returns to the room wearing a bright blue shirt that fits, though the cuffs of the slacks are are rolled up. The tailor bows his head and takes his leave with the remainders.

Aleron says, "I have not worn anything new for years. It is a good feeling—to have a woman care for me. Thank you, Madame."

Just then, dressed in crisp clothes, freshly showered, a handsome smile, Lily glimpses the happier, slimmer Aleron. Not bad.

He reaches for his trench coat. "We should bring my car up. You will find my notes helpful and maybe credible."

Thinking on the busted state of the car, she says sincerely, "I must apologize for what happened. I promise to fully pay for the repairs."

She double-checks that she has her room key in her purse before meeting Aleron in the hallway. He continues where he had left off, heedless of who may hear him here, or in the elevator, or in the lobby.

He described his concern about when to inform Marie's family that she had been abducted. She had a mother who would fret, but he was indecisive and put it off.

Lily nods, "Yes, I've thought of that and feel the same. I've decided to call my brother and go from there."

"I had called her agency the following morning, informing them that their talent was kidnapped. I assumed that would get the word out.

"Then, I think it was two nights after she was taken, Marie phoned me. She was on for about a minute. Long enough to tell me that she was fine and that I must leave her be.

"The phone number was restricted and my attempts to call back were for naught. Thank God she was alive, but she didn't sound like herself and why wouldn't she want to see me or tell me where she was?

"A story was taking shape without my realizing it. Before the week was out I went on assignment at a gala held at the Pompidou Center. With my camera in hand, it became easy to get lost in the work. All that existed was inside the frame. I was wrapping up when I spotted her. I was certain it was her. I only saw her back, but I knew the silhouette of her body and the skin her backless dress revealed. She glimmered with opulence I'd never seen before.

"She was at the curb, and I immediately ran in her direction, shouting her name. She sunk into a limousine and just as she did, she turned her head and I saw her face. It was Marie and I smiled as big as I had when she said, 'Yes,' less than a week ago. But it quickly disappeared. Marie didn't smile back. Her expression was cold, and it brought me up short. She shook her head once. Then several men surrounded her. One already followed her inside the dark interior of the car. Another was a youth with long hair, and the third was L'Anguille.

"I shouted for her again. But the door closed and the limousine pulled away. Stunned, but still this time I was alert enough to photograph the car including the license plate."

In the lobby, Lily arranges for the Peugeot to be brought around and for a bellhop to appear with a garbage can and a dolly.

Lily asks Aleron, "She didn't recognize you?"

"I couldn't tell. But it appeared that was so. I didn't know what to think."

The Peugeot is brought up and the valet hops out. Lily and Aleron step outside and pop the car doors and trunk open. She assists him in pitching trash into the wheeled grey barrel, setting research and the rest of his belongings secured inside the trunk, which despite the damage from yesterday, still worked.

"I want this cleaned inside and out and filled with gas before it's returned it to the garage," she says to the valet.

"Why don't we go to the garden?" Aleron suggests.

She looks at the beautiful sky. "No. I can't sit any longer. I have to feel I'm doing something."

Earlier in the suite, Aleron had mentioned retracing their steps after Marie was taken, giving Lily ideas of her own.

A short walk later, the pair are in a print shop. Lily zaps over photos she has of Reed on her phone to the shop's wifi network. From this, she, Aleron, and the clerk construct a decent flyer.

After the ream of color prints are lain in the recycled cardboard box, Lily's hand trembles over the top sheet. Reed's face takes up the middle third of the page. Proclaimed in 80-point letters above him is the word MISSING.

chapter

eighteen

Last Kiss

W hile the valets bring the Peugeot around once more, Lily and Aleron put the fliers into the hands of those exiting the lobby. She tries to explain to the guests what had happened, but few break their strides to the revolving door, half-listening, glancing at the paper with half a heart.

"Please call, even if you only think you've seen him!" she says to their retreating backs.

"Where do we go from here?" Aleron asks.

"Back to the beginning."

In the car, Aleron navigates the day's traffic. Beside him, Lily plucks a folder from one of the folios between her feet. A clipping from a gossip magazine states that Marie had felt threatened by an unknown stalker and took precautions by employing bodyguards till he was apprehended.

"I was the stalker," Aleron explains. "Stupidly, in those early days, my actions set myself up for this conspiracy. Very clever on her keeper's part, framing my following her, leaving demanding messages on her mobile and at her agency, taking unwanted photographs. Instead of being a concerned fiancé, they flipped it so that I was an obsessed ex-lover. The inspector, who I appealed to for help, now not only had closed the case, but said that if I persisted in harassing Marie, she would press charges."

Lily says, "How horrible."

Aleron waves a dismissive hand. He says, "In retrospect, not surprising with what Marie had told me before. About unsuspecting youth getting in over their heads, sometimes due to their own moral compromises, other times... Well now Marie found herself in the position that she had tried to avoid: a captive of powerful men."

Aleron says in a lighter tone, "Things became interesting when I found her at a charity event with plates costing more than I earned in a year. She was accompanied by L'Anguille among others. She looked incomparably beautiful, but distracted. Her smile was false and her laugh hollow. I knew how she looked and sounded when she was truly delighted.

"But I kept my distance, armed only with my camera. Not once did the escorts leave her for a moment long enough for me to get close. Before the party was over, they were departing. A sedan awaited Marie and L'Anguille while the others took a different car in a different direction. I hurried to get in my car to follow the sedan.

"We were driving in a part of town I would have preferred to avoid. They were quite overdressed and likely to get mugged so late in the evening. But perhaps, that was their intention.

"By the time I had found a spot for my car, they were out of theirs and walking into a club. I was not permitted to enter—members only. While I tried to think of a way through, I heard an alarm go off from within. The doors burst open and I got swept away by evacuating people. Now back on the street, I noticed out of the corner of my eye a side door. It was a steel door that had been thrown open with such force that it banged on the brick wall. Out tumbled Marie, L'Anguille, and two men. They were fighting. It was like those cartoon melees where it's just a ball of arms, legs, dust, and stars. I couldn't be sure what was going on, only that Marie was hurt.

A patch of rough road jostles Lily in her seat. She can hear its springs groan. The smell of upholstery shampoo refreshes the air that had previously been sullied by refuse.

"I ran over to her where she was knocked to the ground. Around us the three men were still fighting. I heard broken glass, swear words, invocations of God and His Son, screams. I cried her name and she looked up, her dress torn, but I didn't see any gashes in her skin. No blood. For a moment I was relived, but then I saw her face. Her eyes were entirely black and her teeth were sharp like an animal's. In an eyeblink her features were human, and I thought I imagined it."

He pauses to look at Lily, "But we both know I didn't imagine it."

"'Aleron,' she whispered like a question. I took her hand in mine. It was cold, but I didn't mind. I was holding her, and I sobbed with joy.

"But like every bright moment in my life recently, it quickly dimmed. The fight was over and L'Anguille hoisted Marie up to her feet and ran off with her, just like that night at the restaurant. I went to run after them, but someone hooked my ankle and I fell. When I rolled over one of the two men, bloody and hot with anger, grabbed my shirt. He yelled something and I thought he would strike me, but I was angry too. I might have caught up to Marie if he hadn't stopped me. Then we both heard a groan and turned to see the other man slumped against the brick. He listed to his side, blinking to stay conscious and clutching a wooden crucifix that glowed."

Aleron has fallen quiet, perhaps as much to rest his voice as let Lily digest it all. The crucifix turns up again. Lily had believed the combination of fear and adrenaline caused her to imagine her crucifix warding off her attackers. Just as Aleron's had a few minutes later. Just as this man had saved himself from L'Anguille. *Miracles.*

All Aleron has been through—for what? And how does Reed fit into it?

As they approach the park, Lily is struck by how different it all looks in the daylight. The gold cast on the greenery seems to have cleansed the horror of last night, promising only serenity from now on.

Lily scowls at it.

Under the birdsong, people feed pigeons, a dog plays, a couple on rented bicycles wheel past. Just another day. The area should be cordoned off with police tape and detectives ducking under it to comb the park for evidence. Behind barricades, people should gawk with curiosity and sympathy.

After Aleron finds a spot to leave the car, Lily divides up the fliers, handing him his share. On the sidewalk, he hands them out to those seated at bus shelters, benches, and outdoor tables, while she engages those in and around the park.

"Were you here last night?", "Did you hear screams?", "Did you see cars racing away?", "Have you seen this man?"

Each "no" chips at her resolve and stings her heart. The next phase of canvassing nearby businesses doesn't improve her mood. Many stores had closed by that fateful hour, but the shopkeepers promise to keep an eye out and have no problem with her posting a flier in their windows.

Aleron tears off bread for Lily when they return to a bench near the Peugeot.

"You should eat more," he says.

"I'm not hungry."

He makes a harrumph sound and nothing more.

Lily brings Charlie's contact information up on her phone and drafts a message:

I NEED YOU TO CALL ME. ONLY YOU.

Her thumb hovers over the SEND button.

"Who is Charles," Aleron asks.

"He's my younger brother. He's probably already in a morning meeting." She looks at him, "I need to talk to someone. Someone else."

He nods, "You two are close."

"He was the first in my family to welcome Reed. He knew how much I love him." She leaves out that Charlie had shared the same skepticism of Reed as their parents. In point of fact, Charlie had been an insufferable ass in how he treated Reed. But he *was* the first to come around, and when he did, he followed Lily's directive to apologize, which Reed graciously accepted.

Her best friend, Margot, in whom Lily can and has confided everything, would be a better person to vent to. Like Charlie, Margot is beginning her work day in an office; her field is environmental law. Lily can picture her, dressed in business attire, sipping herbal tea while reading her horoscope.

Early in their friendship, Margot had a casual curiosity about astrology and other forms of divination. Once at a fair, she pulled Lily into a tent to have their Tarot cards read. There was nothing in those cards about last night.

But Lily wonders if she tells Margot all that she has seen, that her friend would be too credulous. That she'd read more into Lily's plight than actually is there. Perhaps Lily needs someone who will be more skeptical.

She'll think about. She reassigns the message from Charlie to Margot, saves it, then pockets the phone. With a long sigh, she says to Aleron, "What else do you have?"

Lily finds a batch of pictures in the middle pocket of the folio, among other items, Aleron brought for her from the car. Cleaning her fingers from the veggie wrap she partially ate, she places the large glossies in her lap and flips through them. Several are of Marie from different distances and different occasions.

The next few don't need Aleron to identify. There's no mistaking the face with the pronounced lower jaw and smashed downward nose as belonging to anyone but L'Anguille. He did have a cold-blooded, eel-like quality about him, ready to snatch pretty fish in his maw. A bite of sympathy swims through Lily. Last night, she had felt what Aleron felt then.

Aleron watches her with a mild expression.

Lily replaces the photos. She creases the folio flap so it won't spring back while her fingers walk along the cardboard pockets, manila folders, and loose papers found within. Unable to see any organization, she decides on a spiral notebook missing its cover.

In many places within, Aleron's script is barely decipherable. Dates, appearing in the upper right corner of each page, are about the only consistent element. Notes about the police inspector, the museums, the stakeouts, L'Anguille. Sometimes the writing is kept within the blue lines, but often notes are written slantwise or upside down resembling her students' inexperienced lettering.

Lily sips her green tea through the plastic lid. After the notebook, she finds a legal-sized re-closable envelope. Aleron stays her hand before she can unwind the red thread from its button. "No one is to see those. I only keep them because to throw them out would be a desecration." As he takes it, she notes handwritten on the envelope two words: Lex Talionis. Punishment befitting the crime.

"Here..." He digs into the folio for more pictures. "You should recognize them."

After the briefest glance at the first picture, she shuts her eyes, feeling surrounded, closed in, suffocated, just as she was last night. Aleron taps the photograph as though striking a piano key. "That's Eddie—Marie's first."

That's right, love. We're all mates here.

"The Englishman," she says.

"Yes. He's a puppy dog at Marie's feet; follows her everywhere. But he's dangerous, and he likes what she has made him. I saw it that night when she had met him. I was watching her watching him. He was in a fight that started in a bar and poured into the street. He got thrashed by three sodden louts. He got the worst of it, but he kept getting up, grinning. That is, I presume, what Marie liked about Eddie. A brawler, he kept getting up."

Aleron points to another, "This one is Ron." Tobacco Man—Lily can still smell that unfiltered cigarette while the man pawed her body. Lily's skin breaks into a sweat, feeling the man's fingers again play at her throat while his taut arms hold her close.

She shakes away the disgust for a moment. The two remaining gang members who held her legs at one point are lovers Jean-Paul and Clarice.

Perhaps prompted by her physical reaction to the pictures, Aleron leans in. "You saw their true selves." She looks at him, asking with her eyes if she truly did. "Don't think about it. Just accept it for now, and it'll be easier on you later."

Aleron sits back and finishes his coffee. He wipes a glob of apple filling of a *chausson aux pommes* off his new shirt and looks across the park. His eyes settle on children running by their mother, or maybe nothing at all. His tone turns reflective. "Before Marie, I had dated a woman who had a young son. One day at a park, we sat on a bench and watched him play. I soon noticed another boy—maybe two years old if that—walking in an odd fashion." Aleron springs to his feet and presumably imitates the boy. He turns in a circle with his head down, then lifts each foot as though he had stepped in gum. Then pointedly, Aleron looks up at the sky. "It was a cloudless day like this." He regards her once more, "I realized what fascinated the boy."

He expects her to guess what that was, but she is not up for playing. She only shrugs, "What?"

Aleron points up at the sun, then to the ground. "His shadow. He discovered his shadow."

Lily had such experiences when she had assisted at a day care center. The children didn't know what to make of this thing stuck to their feet, following their movements, swinging its arms and turning its head in childish mimicry. She thought it was adorable, but the children often didn't.

"The boy cried," Aleron says when he takes his seat. "Many of us have gone through that. Then we forget it. We outgrow it. And as adults we don't even think about our shadows. My point is that Marie, L'Anguille, the others *are* shadows. They look like us, act like us, but they're darker, exaggerated versions of us. They're overlooked. Unseen. Till something happens, till we see their true selves and we remember the fear we had as children."

Lily finds the idea disturbing for its implications. She asks tentatively, "And Reed…?"

"He's another. Or will be soon." Aleron picks up the story from where he had left off. "The two men who fought L'Anguille and Marie were Benoit and Roland. They sought to cleanse the city of such…" He says delicately, "Inhuman creatures—their term. I thought them mad, but after seeing Marie that night, I wasn't so sure. Benoit had a concussion and I was expected to assist Roland until he recovered."

Aleron had no intention of joining them or killing anyone. Not L'Anguille, nor even St. Croix. But if he hadn't joined them, who would protect Marie the next time they struck? Besides, he could learn from them. And three were better than one. More eyes, hands, resources. He lent his apartment as a place to meet and plan.

"They bickered like a married couple with cutting remarks that would be forgotten. Often they threw up their arms over tactics and theology. Benoit, a Catholic, was practical and plotting, while Roland, a non-believer, was impatient and impulsive. During their days, Roland worked as a machinist, while Benoit worked on a doctorate of divinity. And several evenings per week, we would go out hunting. Shadowing the shadows. I felt my joining them brought bad luck for many of our outings resulted in nothing.

"I was much older than both and didn't have their energy. They seemed to thrive. In the car, we took shifts watching through scopes, sipping coffee and chatting. Benoit wrote down their activities and places they would frequent. I took photographs. If someone was in danger, they left me to keep the car running while they intervened. Returning alive was victory enough, but often only that. Especially if they pursued L'Anguille, who escaped every time."

Aleron tosses cups and napkins into the trash bin with Reed's poster stuck to it.

"Apparently, just a few years before Marie was abducted, there was something akin to an underworld war, like your *Godfather* movies, mafia families skirmishing over territory. St. Croix seized power from another. Benoit and Roland may have inadvertently helped him by having killed some of his enemies. They didn't care. Sides didn't matter to them since they all needed to be destroyed.

"St. Croix had to replenish his ranks. Many like Marie were just plucked from their lives. Roland didn't know the reasons people were chosen. Maybe St. Croix saw something in Marie that kindled his interest. Perhaps her remarkable beauty, or her resilience. She outlasted many of the others who either were killed or killed themselves, horrified by what they became."

Lily sits floored, her jaw hanging open. History is repeating. Marie and Reed have been shanghaied, pressed into service without warning or say. A gang war where no one can be neutral.

"Reed's a new recruit?"

He shrugs. "The war is over. He joins the others as Marie's shadows. But I don't know what she's after."

"Reed will be just like them?" Her chest hitches just thinking of her husband's sweet brown eyes taking on a demonic glint.

Aleron takes her hand in his. "I'm sorry, Madame Williams. I'm not trying to cause you pain. But perhaps you are beginning to believe. Tonight we'll know for certain."

He continues to describe how he finally caught up with Marie. For weeks she was still chaperoned by L'Anguille and others. Often they would disappear into a nightclub for hours at a time. Sometimes paramedics would arrive and take a man or woman out on a stretcher.

The trio agreed to just observe, not intervene until the right moment. But the first night Marie was unescorted, Aleron leapt at the chance. He was out of the car before Roland or Benoit could stop him.

"She looked hauntingly beautiful. She was flirting with a man, perhaps a little younger than I. He sipped his drink while she just held her glass. She coaxed him off his stool and led him to another part of the club. I followed. She allowed him to touch her, and she responded. She pushed him through a door to the storage room. I put my foot in the frame so the door didn't close. Through the crack I saw them. She unbuttoned his shirt and kissed his chest. Then he gave a cry of pain.

"I burst in and the man stood up, more embarrassed than hurt. Marie turned and glared at me. I had never seen her face so ugly with anger.

"The man ran out and I went in. She licked blood from her lip. I called her name, trying to keep my voice calm, though I was both frightened and excited. For a long moment, it was as though I was facing a leopard—would she pounce on me or leap into the trees? Something was being worked out in her mind. When her expression softened to sheer confusion, I ushered her out.

"I wrapped my arm around her, holding her close as we left the club, wondering how she came to be alone. Maybe by then her keepers trusted her to be out on her own. Or maybe she escaped them.

"I don't know why she trusted to leave with me either. I repeated to her that she was safe now, that she didn't need to worry any longer. She said nothing for a long while.

"We went to my apartment. Roland and Benoit followed us in, apprehensive. She wandered the rooms, feeling things with her hands and eyes for some texture of memory."

Lily interjects, "She didn't remember you at all?"

"Not initially. When she came upon the picture, framed on a dresser then, it unlocked her memories. She picked it up and remembered what room it was taken in. Finally she spoke my name." He holds himself, crossing his arms over his chest. "We embraced in relief and happiness."

"She was cold, but I didn't care. I just wanted to continue holding her. Nothing else mattered.

"In time she told us all she could about what had happened to her. She said that St. Croix was mad, and others have told her so. She feared she was mad as well, that a part of him was now in her."

Aleron shakes his head, shutting his eyes. After a moment he continues.

"'I have nightmares,' she said. 'I'm on a blue boat that has broken to pieces. I cling to the beams so I don't sink into the black water, but little by little, those pieces splinter. I have less to hold onto.'"

Aleron grows sorrowful, his eyes turning to grey storm water. "She said the terrors plagued her even when she was awake. That there were times she could feel the cold water around her legs. The memories of her life prior to the abduction were scattered and out of reach on that dark sea."

"'I don't think there's much of me left,' she had said."

As the night went on, Aleron had tried to be optimistic. They were together again. And could always be. Whatever was wrong, they could make right.

Benoit told them that in the popular lore he had been reading, transfusions can cure afflictions such as what Marie suffered from. But she surprised them all, saying that wouldn't work as she had no blood to transfuse. "I don't bleed," she said.

"She put my hand to her chest. It was cold like her hands. Cold and still. She didn't have a heartbeat. She said a black substance collects there instead."

Now it was Lily's turn to lend comfort to Aleron. She gently rubbed his upper back as he spoke.

"She also told me that she could see people's hearts as though they shone through their chests. The hearts told her their secrets: the light would say this person was venal or cowardly, that one noble or heroic. Roland took copious notes as Marie spoke to us. He and Benoit asked lots of questions, but there were gaps that she could not fill, learning what she did know from St. Croix and L'Anguille.

"Marie realized the late hour and said she had to go back to St. Croix. I protested, not understanding. Why couldn't she stay with me in the apartment? 'Because they'll come for me and they'll hurt you. He tugs at me.'"

Aleron points to his left temple, "She said it was as though she could feel him pull on a cord that she was at the end of. An insistence that she go to him, but its power had weakened and she could resist for a while.

"She said I had a good heart, but that I should give up on trying to save her. That St. Croix was too powerful. Numerous times she thought to destroy herself. She was afraid for me and was afraid she'd forget me again, and if she did, it would be forever."

Aleron's voice grows hoarse and his cheeks are wet. "We kissed like it was our last. Because it was, because after that night, we never spoke again."

nineteen

The River

A leron knows of a restaurant that will seat them early before six o'clock. They will spend the time between now and sundown having a meal. Aleron informs Lily that they might not have the opportunity to eat again for the rest of the night, so it is important to have energy and resolve for what will come.

Inside the eatery, Lily parts the red curtain that separates the vestibule from the dining room. The semi-dark place is the kind of hole-in-the-wall Reed would appreciate—a local fixture rather than a tourist draw. The chummy atmosphere is intimate and the décor is a yard sale. Scarcely one second-hand item belongs with another. Different styles of chairs and tables are crammed together so conversations and elbows mingle with their neighbors.

Evidently, Aleron is a regular. She notices several of the customers and staff look his way in recognition. A pair of patrons snickers as he nears them, but their smiles falter upon seeing her. They find a solitary table by a staircase where cheeseboards dangle by their handles like Christmas tree ornaments. Each has a coat-of-arms painted on the wood.

"Who are they?" Lily indicates the men.

Aleron looks in their direction, then all around the room, before answering. "Regulars." He folds his hands together and says quietly, "Last time I was here, I told everyone about Marie and what had happened to her, to us. They found it… entertaining. In my defense, I was drunk at the time."

A waitress excuses herself from chatting with a customer draining his wine.

"Welcome back. This is your supermodel girlfriend?" the woman asks none too quietly. The men chuckle.

"She is not a model." He turns to Lily, "You aren't, are you?" He rises and shouts, "Nor is she my Marie. Go back to your drinks."

"Pardon me," the waitress soothes while handing out menus. "Drinks while you are deciding?"

Aleron says, "Allow me to suggest the onion soup. Quite excellent."

Lily adds the soup to her order of roast Bresse chicken and vegetables, making a show of a hearty meal for Aleron's sake.

After the waitress leaves, Lily can see the kitchen through a large cutout in the wall. Above it on a mantelpiece is a clock made of a cross-section of a tree, its numbers painted in black Roman numerals and its hands are stopped.

When the bowl and plate arrive, the food has the sudden appeal of suet. Despite Aleron's urging, she is not in the right frame of mind to eat. She pokes at the cheese-skinned burbling soup.

"How did you come to speak French so exquisitely?"

"Heritage is a point of family pride. I am a Daughter of the American Revolution on my mother's side, while my father's side is French. The Martins fled to America during your Revolution. Along with our family lore, lineages, and traditions, I was brought up immersed in French, and I spent summers here visiting the family branch that remained."

"Here in Paris?"

"No. They live near Orleans. We were going to visit them later in our trip."

"Where would the two of you have gone today if you had never encountered Marie and me?"

It takes a moment for Lily to recall their itinerary. With all that has happened it feels like the honeymoon was just a dream. "It was to be Reed's day. We'd go wherever he wanted. I know he wanted to see the Roman ruins and examples of great architecture. So we would visit Notre-Dame and the Cinémathèque Française, for example."

"Is he an academic? Perhaps, an historian?"

"He's a firefighter and carpenter on the side." She takes a sip of her Burgundy pinot noir and warms to the topic. She finds comfort in discussing Reed. Her preoccupation with his kidnapping gripped her like a vise. Now, chatting as though with a dear friend, the tension unreels and she opens up.

"We had been dating for some time when Reed took me to a workshop he rents. It is a neighborhood cooperative that provides space and tools for hobbyists. I did not expect to find it as fun as it turned out to be."

She describes to Aleron how Reed had showed her around the shop. She was astounded by the array of tools hanging from the walls or stowed in drawers and toolboxes. Chisels, planes, files, clamps, awls, drills, presses, saws, hammers, and on and on. Some had such a specific function, she wondered how often they were used.

"Measure twice, cut once, safety always," he told her as he snagged goggles and gloves.

"What are you going to do?" she asked.

"*We* are going to work on a project."

"Oh really? What kind of project?"

"You'll have to see for yourself. Put these on."

She donned the goggles and he adjusted their strap for a snug fit. She hadn't worn gear like this since high school chemistry class.

He guided her to a low table with a toothy metal disc rising from its center like a shark ready to chomp. While she inserted ear plugs, he adjusted the table's handwheels a touch, then flipped on the machine. He stood behind her, "Now we're going to cut some pieces. Take it slow." His hands, firm and assuring, moved hers to the guide handles. She could feel his steady breath by her ear. Smell his aftershave along with the wood shavings that kicked up in front of them. Smoothly they pushed the planks toward the silver blur, one after another. She was mildly disappointed there weren't more pieces to feed.

Over her glass, Lily says, "If Reed taught shop at my school, I would have taken his class."

Aleron smiles a touch at her reminiscence. "What did you two craft?"

"I like to collect greeting cards. There's a stationery store that I frequent, in an area of the city called Manyunk, that sells cards made by local artists. Anyway, I helped him with the sanding and staining the wood and later he put the pieces together. He gave it to me gift-wrapped. It was a chest, maybe the size of a large toaster oven, where I can store those cards.

And it had a drawer for stamps, stickers, and pens. He carved my name on the lid."

Aleron's says, "That is a very thoughtful gift… How did you meet?"

Lily briefly recounts the fire, the rescue, and her pursuit of her hero. By the third date, she knew she wanted to marry this man who was markedly different from any other she had dated.

Aleron transfers the neglected chicken from Lily's plate to his own. "An angel, indeed." He carves up the poultry into small bites. "And yourself? What is your occupation?"

"I'm a schoolteacher."

"Truly?"

"Yes. I teach children with learning disabilities."

Lily can see that he wants to ask something more.

With her prompting, he says, "Pardon. Your suite at Le Hervey…" He considers his words, then drops it.

"Is extravagant," Lily completes for him.

"Pardon, it is nothing for me to know."

"It's all right. My family is wealthy. Old money as they say." She looks to the wedding band on her finger a moment. "We were going to check out tomorrow, actually. I wanted Reed to have a wonderful time, but I don't think he cared for the hotel. It was too much. He just wanted a bed to sleep on."

"A practical man."

"He is. He is," she says in a reflective tone. "My mother said that I intentionally chose him to hurt her. My mother and I have a complicated relationship. I think I'm too much like her."

Recalling her mother's interventions, Lily says, "A few times, she'd bring up a past boyfriend of mine, to remind me how well he was doing, and that he was still single or single once more. As though I'd realize my mistake in breaking up with him, leave Reed, and run back.

"Mother never questioned that Reed was a decent, caring man. But she was certain money would come between us."

Aleron titters—then laughs to the heavens. He waves his arms, as though to cancel a bad play. "Pardon. Pardon."

Lily nearly laughs as well. In light of all that has happened, the issue of money has come to seem petty.

"My father came around sooner than my mom. Reed made his daughter happy—that's what mattered to him."

When it comes time to pay the bill, she reaches for the tab. Aleron snatches it away. His laughter gone, he says in a tone that is reproachful, "I am not completely destitute."

***

In the Latin Quarter, Aleron drives around the same several blocks. Lily is nearly dizzy and certainly impatient. Though night has fallen, the pace is lively—a mix of cafés, markets, electronics shops, and fashion boutiques, all below apartments. The evening is crisp, well lit by lampposts, strings of LEDs, and vehicle headlamps.

Finally, an empty spot appears where there hadn't been one on the last lap. Aleron parallel parks while Lily peers about herself, trying to see evidence of Reed, or at least, Marie.

Aleron leaves the engine running and turns in his seat to reach for something. "Of course," he says to himself, pulls back the trunk release and exits the car. She watches him hug along its body, so as not to be swiped by a passing motorcyclist, and disappear behind the trunk hatch. In another moment, he appears beside the rear door, transferring items from the trunk to the rear bench seat. The first is a steel case that he may use for his photography equipment. A second trip deposits a black drawstring sack and one of the accordion folios of notes.

Aleron returns to the driver seat, his binoculars strung around his neck. He says nothing and gazes casually across the street to the café. One hand holds the binoculars over his chest, ready to bring them to eye-level when needed, the other hand idly tapping the leather wrap of the steering wheel.

For a long moment he seems to have forgotten she is sitting next to him. What are they waiting for? How long are they to sit here?

"Is this your plan?" Doesn't he know where Marie and Reed are? "You said you can take me to see Reed." Had she been wrong to trust this man? She had been patient all day, minute by minute, hour by hour not knowing where her husband was and whether he was safe. She managed only because tonight there would be a payoff.

Aleron raises the binoculars and lowers them. "You will see him. Marie frequents this place, often meeting her little shadows here." He rolls down his window and leans out to look rearward. "No one yet."

He sits back once more, taking the binoculars up. "See the case behind me? Open it."

Lily unstraps her seat belt. To reach the case she has to lie across the console between the front seats, her body nearly halfway in the back. When the latches are undone, she hesitates a moment, suddenly cautious about lifting the lid, no longer sure there is a camera lens inside. No, not a lens. But what? Packed in the grey foam are black straps attached to something. She hauls up the headgear.

"Thermal imaging scope," Aleron explains through the rearview mirror. "Careful, it is expensive." He checks the street once more before taking the headgear. "Allow me to put this on you."

"Me?"

"Yes. It will help you see."

She bows her head while he adjusts the many straps to make a snug fitting. The equipment is heavier than it appears and adds an odd weight to her head. Each turn and dip of her head feels exaggerated.

"A gift from Roland. Hold on." He presses something and her vision blinks into a world of black-and-white. Aleron explains that the more heat an object gives off, the whiter it will appear while cooler objects are darker. Aleron is an unearthly sight: a phosphorous, almost featureless, white silhouette before her. Beyond him, smaller white silhouettes walk left and right across her field, looking flat. Depth is hard to judge in this monochrome world. Eerie but somehow beautiful.

"Can I take this off?"

Aleron shows her how to lift the scope up on its hinge, so that she can see unaided as needed. "Shadows are not warm as you and me. We use this to spot them in a crowd. Takes getting used to."

Lily isn't sure what he means. Then she asks, "Where are they?"

Aleron resumes looking through the binoculars. "They will be here in time. Patience."

"No. I mean, where are Roland and Benoit? Can they help us? Maybe they can look for Marie elsewhere. In case she isn't following her routine."

"Shh! It's Ron."

Lily sees him. A scowl etches Ron's face. He marches, shoulders hunched like he is balancing a chip on each shoulder. Aleron trains his binoculars on him and likewise she switches to the scope. Among the flat white bodies, Ron nearly disappears, so dark compared to the others around him, blending with the background. Flipping the scope up,

Lily can readily see Ron reach the café door and knock aside a couple as they exit.

Aleron instructs her to look through the café windows without the scope. Lily leans across Aleron, nearly in his lap as she peers out the window. A number of people crisscross, but yes, there are several who stand apart. "That's Marie!"

"Your husband is inside, farther back with Eddie."

"Where?! Where?!" Her heart beats faster, elated and frustrated at the same time. She can't see anything! Where is he? "I'm going in." She struggles with the straps. "Get this off of me!"

He ignores her, keeping his focus on what is unfolding inside the café. Finally she is able to pop the buckle and toss the scope in the back where it lands on the foam and tumbles off onto the seat.

"Reed escaped to the back. Wait!"

But she is already out of the Peugeot and bolts across the street. Cars honk and screech, drowning out what Aleron is shouting. Before reaching the café, Aleron gives three blasts of his horn and points down the street. Lily looks.

Reed.

Reed is alive!

She can scarcely believe it. Seeing him now, it feels as though they have been apart for half a year.

He has come running out of the parking garage. He doesn't see her wave and doesn't hear her shout for him. He runs down a perpendicular street and she pursues. He's already at the end of the next block by the time she spots him again. She can't gain on him. The distance is growing.

At the block's mid-point, she hears the Peugeot honk beside her. "Get in!" Aleron leans over and pushes the door open. She jumps inside, huffing from the exertion of shouting and running for dear life. "He runs so fast. I have never seen him run like that."

The Peugeot hauls fast too, just as it did last night, weaving through and turning sharply. They're heading toward the river, the same direction Reed has gone.

"There!" She spots him bounding across the last street before the Seine. Thank God he got out of that café and away from Marie.

The Peugeot blares, brakes, and blasts through lanes of traffic. At the next red light, Lily sees Reed disappear down the great stairs to the river's bank. Aleron maneuvers the car as close as possible, parking over the curb.

Lily bolts, shouting. In the distance, she sees his profile kneeling by the river. He's kneeling at the edge and staring at the river as though waiting for something to pop up out of the chill darkness. He's shaking and for a moment he looks so vulnerable. It causes Lily to lose her voice. She runs down the stairs, but before the final step, Reed stands and runs away. By the time Aleron reaches her side, Reed is out of sight. At his touch, Lily erupts with tears and turns to cry on his shoulder. Aleron simply holds her as the river churns past them.

twenty

Faith

" C ome," Aleron urges Lily to follow him. The pair hurry back the
way they came, their footfalls echoing off the stone. Aleron grunts
up the steps, his pace slowing. Lily reaches street level first and scans the
pedestrians on the pavement, the crosswalk, the bridge. No Reed. He
moves so fast.

Aleron gets in the car and she reluctantly joins him. Strapping herself
in, she asks, "How will we find him now?"

"They are looking for him as well. We need to be cautious."

He drives up Quai Saint-Bernard. At the next traffic light, he says,
"Speak of the devil…"

"What?"

"They are there. In the black Fiat."

Lily spots a Fiat making a left turn onto Saint-Bernard, heading away
from them. "You're sure? I didn't get a good look."

Once the light turns green, Aleron follows. Compared to last night's
reckless derby, this drive is a country stroll. Still, Lily fears that Aleron
might lose them to a traffic light change.

Where has Reed gone? He might have crossed over the river at the first
opportunity. Which means none of them have a chance of finding him. Is

that a good thing? As long as he's not found, then Marie can't harm him, but that also means that Lily can't reunite with him. She tries to catch sight of him, perhaps his head is down, trying to appear inconspicuous, or standing in a shadowed door frame.

While Aleron shadows the car, he varies his distance, usually not drawing any closer than three car lengths, allowing other cars to get in between, and even pulling over as though to park.

Soon, the Fiat makes a series of left turns.

"Are they onto us?"

Aleron shakes his head. "Perhaps, she's listening for Reed. I presume as a cord connects Marie to St. Croix, so does one connect her to Reed."

As they pass closed stores and pharmacies, a police station, Metro entrances, Lily phones the hotel. The person at the desk hadn't seen Reed come in, fails to reach anyone in their room, and takes Lily's message to deliver to Reed when he does come through the lobby.

The wild goose chase continues. "Are they going to do this all night?"

Aleron says, "Wouldn't you?"

The circling seems to come to a stop as the Fiat now travels north returning to the river. This time the car turns right onto Saint-Bernard and crosses the Seine at the next light. Proceeding north by north-east, the car picks up speed. Why would they think Reed is out this way? The hotel is well to the west of their location.

The answer becomes clear when the Fiat takes the on-ramp to a highway that Lily knows will link up with Autoroute du Nord. The car bolts like a rabbit weaving lanes as it heads for—"The airport," Lily realizes. "Reed's going to fly out?"

Aleron says, "If they're following your husband, then that would be the only place that makes sense." He hangs back, "We have some time."

"I know." A trip to Charles de Gualle airport normally has taken Lily more than thirty minutes. But she's never asked her driver to floor it.

On her phone, she discovers a final flight to Philly that's nearing the boarding window.

The distance increases between the cars. "Don't lose them," she says. Impossible to say how far ahead Reed is, or if he's at the airport, or if he's completely elsewhere, but as for them, Lily estimates it would be a miracle that they get there in time. Traffic signs count down the kilometers. Aleron regains a bit. The flight status updates to BOARDING.

The lights and signage of the airport appear and once on the airport grounds, the Fiat shoots up to the departures terminal. Marie gets out, but remains by the car, looking at the porters and travelers entering and exiting the airport. Piqued, she digs a heel into the pavement. The hand clutching a phone drops to her side.

The screen likely reads what is also displayed on Lily's own phone: DEPARTED.

***

Like players to the locker room after losing the Big Game, Lily and Aleron return to the suite silent, demoralized, and defeated.

During the ride, Lily had gazed vacantly at Aleron's Holy Mother. Her mind turned over the last moments by the river. If only she had run faster or shouted louder, Reed might have noticed her instead of running off like a spooked deer. Why had he gone to the river in the first place? Why was he kneeling there?

Inside the suite, Lily wraps her arms about herself. It is lifeless here. She sighs onto the corner of the bed.

Aleron remains by the entrance, opening the door just wide enough to peer down the hallway before closing it again. "We shouldn't stay here."

"Wait," she holds up a hand while looking down at her feet, trying to reel in a thought.

The Seine scene surges through her mind. Something is missing. Why did Reed stop there? His silhouette had recalled a mourner knelt by a gravestone. He trembled, perhaps crying.

Dump the body in the river when you're done.

"Dump the body in the river when you're done," Lily whispers in French. She bolts from the bed to repeat it to Aleron, explaining that those words had been Marie's last night. "Reed thinks I'm dead. He went to the river, because he believes I'm in it." But she turns away, uncertain. "But Reed wouldn't have understood Marie."

Aleron speculates, "But Eddie might have told him."

"Then that seals it. If he thinks I'm in the river, then there is nothing for him here. He'd go home. He must be on that flight."

Lily begins to gather her things, wending through the rooms, "We are flying out tomorrow morning."

Aleron returns to the entrance of the suite. "Hurry."

Despite his urgency, Lily folds or rolls every article of clothing with care before putting them in their cases. Hers and Reed's both.

Aleron leads the way back to the elevators while Lily peers over the elliptical stairway to the lobby floor. With no sign of Marie, they have the Peugeot brought up and the luggage put in. Not an easy task, but finally each piece fits.

Then Lily and Aleron wait in the car a block up from the hotel. Aleron has a wait-a-minute moment, "Did you say, '*We* are flying out tomorrow morning'?"

***

Before the wheels of the jet lift from the tarmac, Lily is asleep. Exhaustion smothers her consciousness. Any dreams she experiences are not remembered.

Somewhere over the Atlantic she awakens. After a long stretch of arms and deep yawn, she pulls up her thin airline blanket. Airplanes are always chilly.

Beside her Aleron sips red wine. There's a glass for her too.

She is grateful that he came. There had been much back-and-forth about that—all on Aleron's part. Initially he refused on principle of not wanting to prolong his company for her sake. He was sympathetic to her point that when she finds Reed, she will need Aleron to help Reed understand what has happened. But questions arose: shouldn't Aleron remain in Paris to watch Marie? And what if Reed hadn't left for home after all?

The essential fact is Lily doesn't want to go alone. She realizes the immense imposition it is for Aleron, and she checks against her inclination to press her point. In the end, Lily gets her way. Aleron had agreed, wanting to see Lily reunited with her love. He never visited America, so there is that too.

There is something else Lily had realized, and she presently recalls when Aleron offers her his coat for warmth. In this short period of time, she has grown to rely on Aleron's guidance. Despite her misgivings and mistrust of him in the beginning, she trusts him now.

"Have you slept?"

"A little," he shrugs.

"How do you manage, Aleron? All these months alone? It's not even two days and I can barely hold on." If she could just talk to Reed, just let him know that she's all right. No matter how many miles they've covered, Reed seems always stuck at the horizon. Out of reach, with his back to her.

"Faith. And the fact that there was nothing else for me. I didn't have a life to get back to. Before Marie, I had nothing and so it is again."

"What about Roland and Benoit? Where are they now?"

"Well, we do have time and wine." He sips again.

She raises her seat to the upright position and reaches for her glass. Merlot. Warm merlot.

"Some time after the night we had brought Marie to my apartment, Roland's usual informant had directed us to an address in the 11th *arrondissement*. It was much as you would expect—a dilapidated block. While I waited in the car, they tracked back and forth on the street, checking their equipment and their surroundings. The abandoned building before us was a gloomy slab with small windows on each floor. We were told that a shadow feasted on his victims here. Through the lowered window of my car, I used my scopes to find signs of him.

"There was a man's scream. We all heard it. A sharp male voice suddenly choked off.

"They ran inside. I considered going, but also thought it better to keep the car ready to go. In any case, there was a pale hand resting on the door where the window would be.

"'You do not belong here, sir,' L'Anguille said in a tone that was not threatening, but nonetheless gave me a start. I thought I would die right then from a stopped heart. 'With them,' he nodded toward the apartment building. 'Their cause is not your own. You should leave.'

"He took his hand away and made to follow Roland and Benoit.

"I found my voice and my anger, 'You took Marie! Why?'

"He stopped to answer. 'Only St. Croix, my master, can answer why. I simply fetched her.'

"'Tell me where she is.'

"'I do not know where she is. Recently she has chosen to sleep her days in places other than St. Croix's home.' He turned in profile to me, the street light on his protruding jaw making his scowl all the more severe. 'I expressed my displeasure to St. Croix on his allowance of her liberty. He has made it plain that my opinion was not valued.'

"I believed him. From what I could guess, this St. Croix was like a father overindulgent with a favorite daughter. Perhaps L'Anguille was jealous of Marie? Still, I was unnerved by both L'Anguille's candidness and his lack of interest in harming me that night.

"'Please, how do I—how can she be human again?'

"He looked at me with a bloodless smile, 'Why would she wish that? If there are souls, your bodies make such poor vessels for them: mortal, debased, weak. St. Croix, and we his children, are a new breed for a new era. So unlike the old order that was burdened by conscience, his blood cleansed the stain of our former humanity. And like the waters of Lethe, his blood washes away our memories, our past lives but dreams forgotten. She does not remember you, sir.'

"There was another scream. Then he said, 'I suggest you consider Marie dead. Mourn her and return to your life. They cannot help you for their time is up.'

"Before I could say more, he moved in that eerie way that seemed to fold distance. In no time, he was inside the building where Roland and Benoit ran to.

"His words chilled me, yet I would not believe what he had said about Marie. Could not. Marie remembered me that night. And why would she leave St. Croix's protection?

"I killed the engine and ran after him. Once inside the hollow building, I could hear the faint echo of voices. Roland, Benoit, and a third person who wasn't L'Anguille. I would learn later that it belonged to their informant, Luc. He was the one who screamed. As an act. As a trap.

"Upstairs, I sought them out, navigating the debris on the floor so as to avoid announcing myself. I prayed that I might find them before L'Anguille. Stepping into the hall I caught the sight of an apartment door shutting. I heard shouting. Then gunshots that made me flinch and hesitate. The door was locked and inside there was yelling and the sounds of struggle. I rattled the knob and banged on the door to no avail. For what seemed a long time, but was likely less than two minutes, the door swung open and Luc bolted past me. He looked as terrified as I felt, his shirt bloodied. I could smell urine.

"When I looked back inside the apartment, I crossed myself. L'Anguille lay prone with Benoit atop him. There was a shaft of wood standing up from the shadow's chest. Seeing L'Anguille dead gave me no satisfaction. Since Marie had left the apartment, I think another piece of me died. I didn't have a passion for anything other than returning her to me. I ate, I slept, I showered, and moved through the day like a sleepwalker. I didn't hate L'Anguille. Seeing him lifeless on the floor roused some pity. Catholic schooling came back to me then, and I chose to forgive him.

"Roland and Benoit gave a holler of triumph. Though bruised, they were elated.

"I never learned what had got them into hunting and killing these shadows. They never spoke of their Maries to save or avenge. Looking back now, it was as though they saw themselves as playing a game. A real-life monster-slaying game.

"In that moment, I knew L'Anguille was correct. I am not like them. My cause is not theirs.

"I barely listened as they explained what had happened. An initiation rite to become a shadow required Luc killing them, while L'Anguille had come to have their hearts' blood. But Luc did not have a killer's instinct, nor one's aim. I was already leaving the apartment as they described how they triumphed. I no longer cared. No longer cared what they did with L'Anguille's body. No longer cared where Luc had gone.

"The next day, Benoit went missing. Roland could not contact him by phone and he was not at home. Fearing the worst, Roland came to my apartment to check on me. Taped to the hallway door was the envelope you saw yesterday. The one that read, 'Lex Talionis.' Roland was already opening it when he came inside. While I was brewing coffee, Roland examined its contents. They were photographs and with each one, Roland looked more and more stricken. He didn't finish, instead, letting them fall to the floor. He didn't say a word. He just went around the room collecting his belongings. I picked the pictures up and understood immediately what so troubled him. They were pictures of Benoit. He was strapped to a table, naked and screaming. Each picture drew closer to him, to his chest, then someone's hands appeared with a stake and mallet. The stake was pounded into his heart while he screamed.

"Only the slam of my front door took me out of my trance. Roland left for good. And I did the same. I packed up my car with the essential gear and never returned to my apartment. I swore off shadowing St. Croix or any of his followers. I simply kept tabs on Marie. Soon she made children of her own, starting with Eddie."

***

The slowest cab ride Lily has ever experienced is this one from Philadelphia International Airport to Reed's apartment. With daytime traffic thick on 95 North, each mile ahead is interminable and each mile behind a relief.

Lily takes what is at hand and hurries into the apartment building, leaving Aleron to haul the luggage from the cab inside. Using the key Reed had duplicated for her, she enters the apartment, shouting his name and running room to room. Just like the French suite, the apartment is empty.

In the bedroom, Aleron comments on the bed, "Looks slept in."

"It always does. He never makes the bed. I tried to get him to do it for the times I slept over. Still working on that." Cold water swamps her stomach. "We made a mistake, didn't we?" Aleron attempts to be reassuring. Lily had been so certain Reed would be here, waiting for her. She'd leap into his arms, kiss him over and over and never let him go. She feels sick with this, yet another, blow.

While she regains her composure, Aleron corrals the luggage in a corner where Reed had stacked packed moving boxes, then leaves to the living room. As far as her family is concerned, she is still in Paris, and she and Aleron have between now and nightfall to fill.

After a light lunch, they go to a nearby church for confession, reflection, and prayer. In the pew, Lily fingers her necklace and asks Aleron, "How does it work?"

Aleron quotes Psalms 27: "The Lord is my light and my salvation; whom shall I fear?"

"I fear," Lily says. "I fear for Reed."

Aleron stretches back, "You need to have faith. Roland never had it, even with all he had seen, he still scoffed at Benoit and myself for our superstitions and relied on practical weapons."

Lily frowns, "He lived. Benoit hadn't."

Aleron shrugs, "We each had our theories. Roland thought maybe it was a death cult that used powerful drugs to indoctrinate its followers and alter their chemistry. Make them aggressive, strong, insensitive to pain, with the side effects of a strange appetite for blood and a sunlight allergy. Benoit thought they were born of the Devil who fashioned horrific silhouettes of God's creation."

Lily cuts him off, "Please, Aleron, I want to hear there will be a happy ending for my husband." She thinks the man gets wrapped up in the story and neglects to answer what she is really asking. Like a doctor who will describe the minutiae of a disease, when all the patient wants is to be reassured that everything will be all right. "What happened to Reed and Marie, can it be undone?"

Aleron strokes his greying beard while considering his answer. "Yes. I think their souls have been misled into a dark maze and just need light to lead them out.

If there is a way in, there is a way out. Lily has heard Reed use that expression. "So they are still human, but soulless?"

"I shudder to consider Marie or Reed soulless. But..." He shrugs once more.

Lily wonders too. What would such a person be like? Someone incapable of feeling love? Someone callous and cruel? She cannot imagine Reed as anything but loving and compassionate.

It could be all nonsense too. There is nothing supernal about cruelty and violence—such things arise from human choices. Aleron might just be coping with circumstances with an elaborate story—perhaps Benoit gave him the idea in the first place. But Lily has seen much of it herself and she is at a loss about what to believe.

Exhaling and crossing her arms, she says, "It is difficult to take this all in." Her eyes take in the spiritual iconography and the whispering candles surrounding them, then she continues, "I believe in God and accept His only Son as my savior... But I have moments... moments when I feel like a curiosity to others who do not understand. And while we sit here, speculating about the Devil and whether my husband and your fiancée are human any longer, I can hear myself through their ears, how I sound to someone who doesn't have faith. Are we crazy?"

Aleron says, "Maybe that's the shadows' advantage. That is how they hide. Not believed to exist, they are overlooked or rationalized away. To speak of demons you may as well be committed to a sanatorium."

With shame, Lily recalls thinking so of Aleron.

"These past months, I have had time to spend at libraries and consult with clergy at St. Denis. The priests I have spoken to either dismissed me as unsound or assumed I was speaking metaphorically of modern demons, such as addiction, abuse, or profane popular culture. I did meet Father Lambert, who is now my confessor. I do not know if he is simply humoring me or if he truly believes what I have described to him, but he has given me limited access to texts kept on the premises and references to others elsewhere.

Lily asks, "Are shadows something the Church knows and has kept secret? I never learned about them in Catholic school."

"Whatever they know, I cannot say whether I have read all of it or only a small portion. The older texts are in languages of Eastern Europe and from antiquity, so I cannot read them. From what I did understand, the legends are not definitive. Numerous, yes, but few that accord with one another. In my discussions with Father Lambert, we agree that one cure that often turns up is to destroy the one who cast the victim into the shadows."

"So that means…"

"By destroying Claude St. Croix, we free Marie. And if we free Marie, we free Reed. An evil chain severed."

"Killing. Murder. Why does it have to be that way?"

"It doesn't matter. St. Croix is impregnable. Until he makes a mistake or someone else does my job, there isn't anything to be done."

***

Lily takes a nap in Reed's bed. In the afternoon, she does his laundry, folds clothes, and remakes his bed. At one point, she finds Aleron has brought a chair from the kitchen into the living room. By his feet are pieces of wood. He helped himself to her husband's bins of project material and now works on shaping a piece in his hands.

"Is that a chair leg?"

"It's good to be prepared."

"You are making stakes?"

"If there are shadows in Paris, it stands to reason there are shadows in Philadelphia. When we visited the church, I made a donation and got some holy water. It can be effective as well. Drops of it will burn a shadow's skin."

It is as though he told her that he has a degenerative illness. She is anguished by his burden and pities him. This has become his world. There is a shadow in every corner. It is all he thinks about.

She bends to give him a hug, trying to impart reassurance. "I'm going to make you dinner."

She has time to walk to the market and get fresh ingredients and be back before sundown.

Groceries in hand, and the sky deepening in color, Lily considers what Aleron had said. If there are shadows here, where would they live? Who might have they hurt? Dear God, isn't there enough evil in the world as it is? She looks around herself, wondering how many times she has walked at night and passed one of them and never known it. Might one be in Reed's apartment building? She thinks she may do well to get mace or a taser.

She quickens her pace, hurries inside the building and jabs the CLOSE DOORS button of the elevator.

Aleron is thumbing through a trade magazine when she returns. Before preparing dinner, she decides to find something to keep him entertained, or at least, help distract him from his cares.

Looking through Reed's movie collection, Lily narrows her choices to comedies, though what she selects, she hardly finds funny. But Reed does. And it has the virtue of the viewer not needing to understand English to be watchable.

With a DVD of the *Three Stooges* playing, she busies herself in the kitchen. Aware that the sun is down, she steals glances at the unlocked front door hoping Reed will enter.

By the time she has the meal ready, Aleron is bruised from laughing. He thanks her and sits with her to dine. They share a bottle of wine, Asian-style salad, salmon fillets, and steamed veggies.

She is glad Aleron came. She could not sit here alone, waiting for Reed to return. They chat about little things and better times. But with each passing minute and hour, Lily knows Reed is not here. With every faint ding of the elevator, Lily's breath catches as she strains to hear solitary footfalls advance in their direction. Occasionally she hurries to the door, opens it and peers out. Only neighbors, visitors, kids running down the hall.

As midnight nears, Lily fears Reed will not come at all. Then what? She has no options to pursue. And what will she tell her in-laws? How can she explain to the Williamses their son is missing? Missing being the least of it.

Past midnight, Lily puts on coffee to remain awake while Aleron looks through the cabinets for a snack for them both. He finds toaster pastries and pops them in. Lily puts out creamer and sugar. Absorbed in their conversation as they are, the ding of the elevator hasn't been heard. The approaching footfalls go unnoticed. So the sound of the front door opening surprises them both.

Peering from the kitchen entryway, Marie says, "This is unexpected."

part
IV

twenty-one

Alive

R eed, Kyle, Michael, Malcolm, and Aleron peer into the apartment's utility closet.

"That's a hell of a splinter," Michael quips to work in some levity in the otherwise grave sight.

No one hears him. The attention of the other four men are fixed to the view beyond the door. Beneath the circuit breaker panel, slumped to the rear wall, head tipped back, is the body of a man.

Death. Michael is decidedly not a fan. Though he cannot recall the reason or reasons he had left his human life behind, if he would guess, he believes it was to avoid looking like a corpse one day. A lover, not a fighter, he has used charm or misdirection to get out of tight spots, keeping his entanglements with corpses to a minimum.

Obvious to all is the manner in which the man met his death. Buried in the man's chest is a shaft of wood, perhaps from a table leg.

Michael looks away.

"Let's get him up," Kyle speaks with a blend of calmness and authority. And a casualness that gives Michael cause to wonder if Kyle is an old hand at body disposal. Michael thinks about Kyle's gun and how he had joked earlier about Kyle being a contract killer, and that perhaps it was not funny after all.

"Michael, get his feet. Reed find some duct tape. Malcolm bring that chair over here."

When Michael hesitates, Kyle snaps his fingers three times in front of his face. "Now."

Michael pinches the cuffs of the man's slacks rather than grip the man's legs. Kyle hauls the man out by his arms. Together they get the body seated in the chair Malcolm uprights and brings toward them. In better light, Michael can see the body is of a young man, well dressed but for the torn shirt. Goofish hairstyle: tight cap of hair slick with gel and long sideburns.

Ron.

Reed recognizes Ron. And as Michael and Kyle remove him from the closet, he finds small satisfaction in seeing him dead. He wishes he could have been the one to do it. All this time he has been itching to release his rage on someone who deserved it. Someone has to take the heat.

As Michael and Kyle sit the corpse of Ron on the chair, Reed turns on the Frenchman. He grabs up the collar of the man's trench coat, walking him hurriedly backwards till he's up against the wall dividing the kitchen from the living room. The man's head jars against the wall. A picture frame falls to the floor.

"Who are you? Where's Lily?"

Pain and panic run over the man's face while a lot of French words sputter from his mouth. He appears older than everyone in the room by at least twenty years. Reed doesn't recognize him and wonders how the man got into his apartment.

Three pairs of arms yank on Reed, failing to budge him.

"Let him go! Reed, you're going to burn him."

The heat of Reed's chest surges to his grasping hands singeing the stitching, smoldering the polyester. His vision changes and his teeth sharpen. Now the Frenchman is grey while sharp flickering blue envelopes his body with a human vitality.

"*Mon dieu!*" Aleron gasps.

The thought occurs to Reed that this man had wanted to ambush Reed and killed Ron by mistake. Reed vows he won't be taken again.

"You won't learn anything about your wife if you kill him." Kyle gets himself between them.

"Lily," Reed says. In a moment, he returns to himself.

To the recovering Frenchman, Kyle commands, "Explain."

Malcolm spends the ensuing stretch of time translating Aleron's account. He plumps up some of the telling. It's a thrilling tale. The lengths Lily had gone for her husband. That needed no exaggeration. But he can't help himself. The daring rescue, the pursuits, the close calls, all culminating in a scene that had played out right here, perhaps just minutes before they all arrived in the apartment.

Lily and Aleron had been discussing the topic of redemption when the apartment door opened. Instead of being greeted by the absent Reed, they found Marie, Eddie, and Ron standing at the threshold of the kitchen.

Too slow to react, Aleron witnessed Eddie snatch Lily from her seat. Ron snapped the crucifix from her neck and tossed it down the hall. "Won't repeat that trick."

"Where's my dear one?" Marie asked in a mixture of concern and impatience.

Aleron mistook her meaning for himself. She meant Reed.

At this turn in the story, Reed bristles, pacing behind the others. He glares at Ron's body. "Did he hurt her?"

Malcolm continues: Ron lunged for Aleron who was now ready with his effulgent crucifix. Its brightness was intensified by the kitchen's white walls, tile flooring, and confined space. Blinded, Ron misstepped, giving Aleron a moment to take one of the stakes and use Ron's momentum to nail it, angled, through his shirt, through his flesh, into his heart, till Aleron's thumb pokes through the torn skin.

By then, Marie and Eddie retreated with their hostage to the front door.

"Let her go."

Eddie caused Lily to cry in pain when Aleron came too close. "When Reed gets here, tell him to come find us."

Reed breaks his silence, "What are you saying? Lily's at their mercy again? Fine. Marie can have me then."

"Don't work yourself up, Reed." Kyle says while picking up the roll of duct tape and standing beside the body. Tearing long pieces off, Kyle secures the man's wrists and legs to the chair. This is for psychological rather than practical effect. Getting free from duct tape is actually kids' play for any kind of person not overcome with panic.

"Why are you tying him up? He's dead," Michael says.

Kyle explains, "The ichor collects in the heart. A stake of wood in the heart will immobilize us, not kill us. Hadn't Zelda taught you that?"

Having fought the Rotters years ago, he has made extensive use of them. The right length matters—too short or too long is impractical. Fourteen inches or so, and slender, however not so slender as to snap before hitting home. And always solid wood, preferably ash.

Kyle puts a hand on Ron's chest, bracing as he pulls the stake out with the other. The man's eyes snap open, black. Meant to be intimidating, but failing. Ron tests the restraints, but Kyle places the tip of the stake by the edge of the wound. "You're going to sit right there and answer our questions. Or this goes back in. Then we put you under a Jersey landfill. Understand? How many are in your entourage?"

Ron attempts to look around, assess, but Kyle will not have that. He cracks Ron on the head with the stake's blunt end, bringing Ron's attention back to himself.

"Five all together," Ron answers via Malcolm.

"What was the plan, Ron? Take Reed back to Paris? Then what? What do you need him for?"

"It was Marie's idea, not that I have a choice. I would have killed them both. She's after St. Croix."

"The one who made her?" Aleron asks.

"Yes. Marie's building a force of numbers to destroy him."

"Are you certain?" Aleron asks, incredulous.

"She despises him. But he's powerful. She's crazy—"

"Don't speak of her like that," Aleron shakes.

"I'm not waiting anymore," Reed storms for the door.

Kyle cuffs Reed's bicep, "You're not going."

Reed pulls away, "We're wasting time here."

Kyle weighs the stake in his hand, rolling it in his enclosing fingers. "You heard Ron. She controls him, likely all of them. And you, if you get close."

"I won't let her, Kyle. Lily's my wife, and I'm not going to forget that."

Kyle considers Reed's words, his thumb itching at the shaft of wood in his hand. This has gotten to be more of a mess than he anticipated.

Looking to each man in turn, Kyle grasps an idea of a compromise. "Fine. You'll come along." He puts his free arm around Reed's shoulders, drawing him close. "Remember one thing though."

"What's—"

In a swift arc, Kyle cuts Reed off, plunging the wood deep into Reed's chest. "I need you to remember that this is for her." The sharp pain causes Reed to puff out before collapsing in Kyle's arms.

"Kyle—what—what the hell?!" Michael gasps.

"I echo and amplify Michael's exclamation," Malcolm says.

"I thought the plan was to save the damsel, not kill the knight," Michael says.

Kyle reminds them, "He's not dead. No one has to die if we do this right."

"He's in no condition to do anything now. And how do you think he will react—a pissed-off erif—when you pull that stake out of him?" Michael asks.

"If the plan goes as I hope it does he'll be busy reuniting with his bride. You'll be helping. Right?"

"You made your point with Reed. I'm a quick learner," Michael says.

"Can you speak French?" Kyle asks.

"I'm fluent in the language of love." Michael grins wide. He does that, Kyle has learned of Michael. He goes from one emotion to the next in an instant. Panic to braggadocio.

Malcolm says, "French *is* a Romance language, however the word refers to its lingual wellspring, not—"

"Never mind. Malcolm you're in. Now here's what we'll do."

twenty-two

Plan C

T he Whitpain Hotel is one of the city's tallest structures and most luxurious. Lily has been to the Whitpain for family functions, though never as a roomer. From the top-most stories guests have a beautiful view of the Schuylkill River and the Franklin Parkway lit up under the velvet darkness.

If she survives this night, she plans never to return.

While coming here, Eddie held onto her for nearly the entire way, bending her arm behind her back like a chicken wing. Solid as concrete, Eddie could snap her arm as if it were hollow as a bird's, she had no doubt. He promised that for her cooperation, she'd be free. As soon as they have Reed.

Lily would sooner believe the Devil as Eddie. Maybe they are one and the same.

Her back is to the floor-to-ceiling windows and her wrists and ankles are lashed with nylon cord from the drapes to a Queen Anne chair. The elegance of the suite—as well appointed as Le Hervey's, its walls decorated with bright watercolors of local landmarks—has been turned into a murder scene.

Her face wet with tears, Lily watches Jean-Paul put the woman's body in the adjoining room with that of her husband's. This had been the couple's suite until Jean-Paul and Clarice had secured it. From what Lily can surmise, while Marie, Eddie, and Ron were in Reed's apartment, these two gained access to the suite, perhaps with a Room Service knock. The husband was dead by the time Lily had been dragged in here. The poor woman sobbed around her gag. She had been saved as a feast for Marie and Eddie. Their fangs slashed the woman's trembling flesh, neck, wrists, taking the spurting blood into their demonic mouths. The muffled screams faded just before the light from her eyes dimmed empty.

Lily hadn't imagined their frightening features that night of her rescue. This had been the death they intended for Lily—frightened, drained, and discarded. Aleron had been right.

Lily prays to speed the woman's soul to heaven to be reunited with her husband. Then she vomits up the remnants of her Pop-Tarts.

Amidst the bloodletting, there was heated discussion amongst the four. Where was Ron? How could they leave him? What is *she* doing alive? Why didn't they tell her? Where was Reed? Why did we come here?

Marie is livid. She yells obscenities at the others, pacing in anger in front of them like a drill sergeant dressing down fresh recruits.

Jean-Paul breaks from the group, stamping toward Lily. She's trussed up and helpless on the chair singing her hymns in whispers. Kneeling before her, Jean-Paul eyes her with contemptuous daggers. With great will, she keeps her gaze while continuing her chants.

She says, "I know not, oh, I know not, what joys await us there…"

His hand seizes her throat. Squeezes.

She hacks, "what… radiancy of glory…"

"Don't touch her," Marie says, wiping blood from her face with a hand towel.

"She pays for Ron's life with her own," Jean-Paul says.

"Not yet," Marie says.

"Your Reed will not come."

Lily can smell the husband's gore when he speaks.

Marie says with assurance, "Yes, he will. That's why I chose him. He will always do the right thing."

Jean-Paul lets her go with a snarl of disgust.

They make a small effort to straighten the room as though nothing had occurred. Watching them move about, Lily notices by the lamplight that she is the only one throwing a shadow.

Then at the door, there comes a knock.

***

A man fitting Eddie's description opens the suite door, and Michael notes how unalike are their attire. Michael still wears his choice dinner jacket, pressed slacks, polished shoes, and pomade coiffed hair; Eddie wears a jean jacket, frayed jeans, hard boots, and hair that looks lathered with motor oil. He smells of blood. Michael hopes it isn't Mrs. Williams's.

"Where do I know you from?" Eddie asks.

Though dressed the same since leaving Sylvia in the Kimmel Center, Michael is someone new: Eduardo Vega.

"Eduardo?" Kyle had been skeptical back in Reed's apartment where Michael worked on the details of this role tailored to the information Aleron supplied.

Michael said, "Eduardo is a man of mystery, wealth, and sophistication. A dilettante who loves art and fashion. Marie will swoon." The character draws from bits of soap operas and some real people such as Fred "The Hussle" Russell, whom Michael knew from Las Vegas. A smooth real estate salesman, the man could sell the imitation Eiffel Tower standing at the hotel Paris Las Vegas to the French government.

In Reed's bathroom, Michael straightened his suit, combed back his hair, rinsed his mouth. He dabbed some of Reed's cologne at his neck and had thought to compliment Reed on his taste in quality fragrance, but the man was indisposed.

Kyle said, "Just don't forget you're going there to talk Marie into freeing Reed's wife. Eduardo."

In fact, Michael appreciated the challenge. He never applied his talents to hostage negotiation; a test of his charm he is certain to pass.

Answering Eddie's question, Michael says, "Are you a subscriber of *Union Jack Yachting* magazine? There was a cover story about me last month. My first mate," he nods toward Malcolm, whose body screens Eddie's view of the extended hallway, "I have much to discuss with your Lady Marie."

In the room, Michael notes everyone's eyes are on him, wondering who this suave, handsome man is. He spares a look at Mrs. Williams. Though bound, trembling, and tear-stained, she doesn't seem abused.

"A great pleasure to meet you, Marie de Telfour," he says in a cultured voice. Malcolm interprets as Michael continues, "I am Eduardo Vega, a great admirer of Parisian fashion. I have followed your work for some time and it is an honor to behold your beauty in person."

As though the man himself, Michael plays his part with confidence that already dials down the tension in everyone's wound up body language.

With gentleness, he takes Marie's hand in his own and raises it to his lips. Hovering over her hand and meeting her eyes, he says, "I remember you had once modeled for Yushchenko at the Jardin du Palais-Royal. I believe that shoot most captured your spirit. I would say that you were fortunate to work with him, but," he pauses to kiss her hand, then places his other hand atop of hers as though sealing his impression into her, "I believe he was more enriched by his time with you. Do you agree?"

Marie's smile confirms for Michael that his opening gambit is a success.

She says, "I do not recall, and I regret to say that I have not heard of you."

Michael steps closer to her, returning to her brown eyes. "All the better that our paths should cross here in America. We can start fresh, get to know one another."

"That would be delightful, Mr. Vega."

"Eduardo, please."

"What do you want?" Eddie asks, less charmed and too protective. Michael considers that the man might be jealous.

"To welcome you here, of course. All of you. You have had a long flight and chose to secure lodgings, refresh, and relax before calling on my master, Lord Elias Devlin. No doubt you are unfamiliar with our customs in the New World, so he does not begrudge this breach of etiquette."

Michael takes the temperature of the room and finds Eddie still to be cool. Like a bodyguard to a pop star, he is all business. "I also know that you are not here for a fashion show." He motions with one hand toward Mrs. Williams, while stepping closer to Marie and slipping his hand to rest at her back.

He lowers his voice, "You are here for a certain man in our domain. Am I correct, beautiful mademoiselle?"

She stiffens at bit, "How do you know this?"

"Do not be alarmed. Lord Devlin has many eyes and ears. We will, of course, assist you in any way we can. We respect the bond here. We are certain you will be reunited in short order. Do not trouble yourselves with seeking sustenance during your stay. We have ample supply."

Eddie says, "She is not food," referring to Mrs. Williams. "Yet."

Michael wonders who popped Eddie's balloon. The little man grates, but Michael does not show it. He says, "She is security. I understand.

Fortunately for you, you will need her for neither purpose. I will take Mrs. Lily Williams off your hands, while I will ensure your every need is met."

He looks to Mrs. Williams once more and his hand is now at Marie's shoulder. "Yes, I know you, Mrs. Williams. I regret not being able to attend your wedding. I understand it was grand. I trust my gift will be a sufficient recompense."

To Marie, "Mrs. Williams is an extraordinary human. My master will approve your taking such good care of her." His fingers brush Marie's hair back, then caress the nape of her neck.

Marie's eyes drift closed at his touch. Then they open, mesmerized. She says, somewhat abashed, "She will stay here," She seems reluctant to contradict Michael, which tells him that he is close.

He says, "I'm not surprised you do not know her value. You do not follow Philadelphian politics. She is a member of a prestigious family and thus useful to my master."

Eddie says, "All thanks for your welcoming us like we're all old chums, but we will do well ourselves."

"Eddie," Marie admonishes, embarrassed. She leans into Michael, "As Eduardo has said, we are his guests and should appreciate his and his master's generosity."

Michael looks down at Eddie, "I do not mean to question your resourcefulness. I am sure we can come to an amicable agreement."

The kids, Clarice and Jean-Paul, look around themselves, bored, offering no input and leaving the conversation to the grown-ups.

Eddie sweeps an arm in Lily's general direction, saying to Marie, "Remember why we're here. Why we need her."

Marie turns to Michael, sighing, "Eddie is correct. I must decline, dear Eduardo."

Michael makes an exaggerated nod. "Very well. Nothing for nothing. A trade then." He cues Malcolm who then goes to the suite door. "A trade, Mademoiselle de Telfour, to demonstrate our hospitality and generosity."

***

Kyle glances at his wristwatch. Michael has to work fast and time is growing short. If Michael's alter ego can convince Marie to release Mrs. Williams, then all to the good. Michael can be convincing, but Marie is volatile; and her determination to retrieve Reed likely will win out.

Ron must be uncomfortable on the floor, nose to the carpet and his arms extended toward Kyle, palms down. They occupy the end of the hallway. While Kyle listens, he keeps his Colt, its suppressor still attached, aimed at Ron's head, standing five feet from him.

Now it has been ten minutes. The longer Michael is in there, the more doubtful Kyle becomes. Ron is Plan B. It seems to always come down to Plan Bs, causing Kyle to wonder why even bother formulating Plan As. Foolish hope, he answers himself.

Malcolm's opening of the suite door prompts Kyle to get ready. So the first plan—Mrs. Williams gratis—has failed; Kyle hopes that Mrs. Williams in exchange for Ron will turn out differently. He makes a noise for Ron to get on his feet.

In his bottomless shoulder holster, Kyle secures the Colt before clapping a firm hand on Ron's shoulder as they move through the open door. He surreptitiously leaves the door ajar with the security latch, should things get spectacularly dicey.

The gasps in the room upon seeing Ron alive demonstrates they don't know any more than Michael about the effect of stakes to the heart. Kids today.

Yes, Ron is alive, Kyle thinks. Hallelujeh. Let's parlay that into goodwill and get Mrs. Williams out of here.

While Michael resumes negotiations, Kyle barely listens. His eyes work the room, tracking everyone to gauge body language, divining hostile intent the moment it may arise, so that he can act in a swift, decisive, and deterrent manner. Eddie stands by Marie, his attention divided by Michael and Ron; Jean-Paul and Clarice are farther back in the room, their half attention on the conversation.

They are all young, Aleron informed Kyle. Each less than a year old. Except for Eddie, Aleron wasn't certain the others had any more choice in their situation than Reed. Kyle wonders if loved ones are missing them. And how much control has Marie exerted over them? How often? Some sires abuse their bonds. Some can strip their child's will, reducing them to automatons.

Kyle notes Malcolm, still interpreting, moving near Mrs. Williams who looks confused that more strangers are piling into this room and not one of them her husband.

"No trade," Eddie says.

When Ron turns livid, Kyle returns his hand firmly to the man's shoulder, reining in any strike that might come. Instead, Ron spits an insult. It must sting to be so unwanted.

"I ask you to reconsider," Michael presses. "You will have Reed quicker with our mutual cooperation."

Eddie consults with Marie. "We keep the bird in our cage till we have Reed safely aboard our flight home. The sooner we have Reed, the more blood she gets to keep in her body."

Kyle lets out a controlled breath. "Be reasonable. You are guests in our domain. You will respect our terms in the spirit they are given." Need to stretch this out.

Drawing her from the others with his arm about her, Michael says, "My beauty, let us not squabble. Put all this aside for now. With Paris east of here, you cannot return home tonight. These evenings are not sufficiently long enough for a journey that ends before sunrise. So you will be our guests longer than you expected."

Michael straightens up, allowing a moment to reframe his approach. "Let's you and I get acquainted. Alone. I propose that I give you a personal tour of the art museum tomorrow night. It is world class. I believe there is a special exhibit of the Impressionists: Degas, Cézanne, Monet…"

Marie says, enlivened, "Monet?"

"Why yes. Do you like Monet?" Michael asks while knowing the answer.

"Yes. Yes, I do."

"*Parfait*. I am certain we have much more in common. You are a French woman. I love French women…"

***

For Malcolm, this is real adventure. He watches Kyle escort Ron inside. The next stage of the plan Kyle had formulated in the moments following Reed's incapacitation via wood to the heart. When Kyle explained Malcolm's role—interpret and don't move—Malcolm was delighted to be asked to participate. The plan and its contingencies were superb—though Malcolm really has no frame of reference in his personal experience. Still, he is part of the plan to save Mrs. Williams. A Sancho Panza to Don Quixote de la Mancha in their quest to rescue Dulcinea del Toboso.

The others congregate around the social center of gravity that is Marie and Michael's conversation, while Malcolm steps toward the less occupied area of the suite. Nearer Mrs. Williams.

The mechanical task of exchanging French for English and vice versa is simple enough, and as ever, Malcolm takes care in choosing his words, especially considering that this is a delicate contest; one that is not going well for the home team.

"You repay our goodwill with ingratitude," Kyle says.

"*Vous rembourser notre bonne volonté avec ingratitude,*" Malcolm interprets.

While interpreting occupies one track of his facile mind, Malcolm's other track regards Mrs. Williams strapped to the chair. What an ordeal for love. And what's this? Her lips move, expressing something in gold wisps. Prayer. Catholic prayer for salvation. Ms. Situ—Grace—could be seated there and if she were, would Malcolm come to her rescue? But Grace had made her choice. No, that is not true. She never had one because he did not act. Too careful, too clinical. Heartless. He is missing his heart. There it is on the chair. For once, for once he has to shut out reason and just listen. Really listen to the words. The spirit that threads through them. Their soul. Words have soul.

Bird that soars with my heart.

That's what he sees. He must set his free, if just for a moment. He can do it. Free her.

Malcolm comes behind the chair and tugs at the nylon cords. Lily's fingers are red and swollen. "I am going to untie you," he slips in quietly between the others' conversation. "This is quite the Gordian knot." He isn't nimble enough to make much headway. "You wouldn't have a blade on your person—even a file—for fingernails, not woodworking."

"*Hé!*" Clarice shouts.

"Hey!" Malcolm interprets.

***

Kyle need not listen to the conversation to understand they are not willing to hand over Mrs. Williams.

And time is nearly up.

Kyle turns to look and look again. Malcolm is working to free Lily of her bonds. Kyle hadn't counted on Malcolm taking the initiative. Interpret and don't move. Wasn't that clear?

"Hold it, Malcolm!"

Too late. Clarice is already advancing on Malcolm, who turns around in time to catch her punch with his jaw. Staggering back, his legs wobble and collapse underneath him.

The situation is deteriorating rapidly.

Before Kyle can say another word of protest, Michael is off to aid his friend. And soon everyone is on different trajectories. Keeping a level head, Kyle draws his gun. Marie is key, but his target is blocked by a charging Eddie. With a step to the side for better aim, Kyle fires just before Eddie barrels into him. The shot goes wide, hitting Ron in the chest. Well, that was something. Pain seizes Kyle; his whole body vibrates as though he is a bell and Eddie is a mallet.

***

The blackbirds are gone. The field is gone. The world is gone.

Reed is himself: skin and muscle, not flannel and straw.

Is he dead? It's darkness all around. His vision went out like someone flipped a switch. It had to have been Kyle. He remembers Kyle talking to him, perhaps still talking to him. Reed can hear voices far away. Kyle had put his arm around him, there was a crack of pain, then lights out.

Did Kyle put that stake through his heart?

There is an ache there, in the center of his chest as though a heavy object is pressing down, slowly, continuously. The fire is out. His chest is no longer warm.

He tries to lift his arms, to move his hands and explore his front and pull the stake out. He cannot see them. Are his arms moving?

Reed must be lying down. In a coffin? Is he dead? He is dead. He's in a casket on a bier at a firefighter's funeral.

Suddenly claustrophobic, Reed tries to scream. Fails. Nothing is working. Nothing obeys.

I'm alive! Don't bury me!

Movement. Reed thinks his body is being moved.

The voices. Kyle perhaps. And Michael and Malcolm. And someone French. They're talking about him.

Reed cannot move. He cannot see. He is trapped within himself. Is this what Ron experienced in his utility closet? Have they switched places? Who will save Lily?

He had come so close. If only Reed had demanded Mr. Ashton or Kyle take him straight home earlier tonight he would have beat Marie home and reunited with Lily. He could say I love you and hold her and kiss her. He'd go to church with her, he'd help with the soup kitchen, join the choir, singing of the Father, the Son, and the Holy Ghost. He truly believes. Just for one more moment with her.

The lights are back. Reed lets out a loud gasp as though he had been underwater for far too long. The pressure disappears and he sees the underside of the upturned trunk lid of Celestine.

The Frenchman peers over him, a scrap of paper in one hand, the stake in the other. He hands Reed the note, "Lily."

"Lily," Reed echoes after reading the room number. He vaults out of the trunk and dashes for the elevator and stairwell area, leaving Aleron to catch up.

Inside the elevator car, Reed paces like a hungry bear in a cage, waiting for the moment to claw his way out and tear into something.

Marie. She's near. Up in the suite. That splinter of her thoughts needles his own.

Aleron presses into a corner.

Kyle had stabbed Reed and left him out of the plan. Kyle was right: Reed is too emotional, too hot-headed, but Reed likes that fine. The furnace within his chest reignites, having cooled too long. The power is back and once more he feels he can demolish any obstacle.

Ding!

Reed shoves himself through the too-slow-to-open metal doors. Marie's itching sharpens as he races down the floor and bangs through the suite door left open. Kyle had been right once again: he didn't need Reed to screw things up—he did fine all on his own.

Objects career, people collide and Reed will not even bother to sort it out. Only Lily matters, and there she is, fastened to a chair in the eye of a hurricane. Her eyes are fixed shut, head down, mouth trembling.

The sight of her—it's miraculous.

"Lily," he moves to embrace her, but he misses the bus that rams him into a wall with such force that he nearly loses consciousness. He gets the number though: Eddie.

"Eddie!" Marie shouts in part concern, part reproach.

Reed's pained expression changes to a savage smile while his world turns black-and-white. This new part of him delights in the opportunity to finally cut loose. He makes a fist Popeye could be proud of and wallops Eddie. Though Eddie falters, he isn't as injured as Reed hoped.

"Reed? Reed!" Lily can't believe he's really here. Locked together, he and Eddie battle behind her and on to another part of the room. She cranes her head, trying to follow.

"*Ne bouge pas*," Aleron says pulling a utility knife from his pocket. In seconds, he frees Lily and returns to her her grandmother's crucifix.

Marie shouts, "Eddie, *non!*"

Eddie is tough. His punch detonates a shower of pain within Reed's body. He dodges Eddie's next haymaker, but only just. Reed has greater reach, but his tags are ineffectual and he can do nothing as Eddie boxes him into a corner.

Reed had wrestled in high school, damn it, but his grappling is barely effective. Eddie breaks his holds. No room for kicks either. He attempts to punch Eddie's smirking face—it's like the asshole is enjoying this—but Eddie throws himself into Reed knocking him into the wall again, pinning him. Reed grunts. Wooziness spins his mind and fresh pain tells Reed that he has snapped ribs.

Before either can help, Lily and Aleron run into Jean-Paul and Clarice. Aleron puts a vial into Lily's hand. Appearing determined to finish what he had started, Jean-Paul reaches for Lily. Panicked, Lily uncaps the bottle of holy water and flicks it several times. Each drop that lands on his skin splashes with light—the same light of the crucifix. Jean-Paul falls to his knees in a howl of pain and he covers his eyes with his hands, frightening Lily back several steps.

Clarice breaks off from Aleron when she hears her lover scream. Lily raises the vial, expecting the woman to attack her as well. Instead Clarice takes Jean-Paul up by the shoulders and ushers him away.

The crows call for Reed. He's almost gone—mere tatters of a human silhouette.

You're the shadow now.

Yes, he is. He's not human anymore. Maybe never again. He had died two nights ago, his body just didn't get the message. Time to face up to it. Right now. Let him snap apart, just collapse in on himself like the husk of a burned up house. Let's burn it down, Eddie. Fuck the blackbirds. Fuck Marie's head games. Fuck you, Eddie; let's kill each other.

Feeling pinned, Reed digs within himself. He takes Eddie's spite, Marie's scheming, and adds his own anger, channeling all of it back into Eddie.

Reed's long teeth cut his lower lip when he snarls. His fury churns and lashes. He roars aloud, pouring all his molten rage into Eddie and melting that sadistic grin off his face. Holding onto the man's thrashing body, Reed can see black veins run up Eddie's neck and smell the cooked flesh, till at last Eddie falls dead.

Aleron runs over to Marie. "Stop this!"

Marie shoves Aleron aside, causing him to trip over Kyle who is only now regaining consciousness.

"Reed, *mon cher. Mon lion.*"

Reed's eyes snap to her own as though magnetized.

"Kill her. Then we can go home."

When Reed turns on Lily, her breath catches. His inhuman eyes and sharp teeth are just like those of the others. He appears utterly different, like he lost himself. Whatever tenderness, compassion, empathy he had, has been swallowed up, absorbed by those lightless eyes. She can't take her gaze away from those merciless eyes. Please be in there. She prays, pleads for him to find his way out of the maze and into the light, "Reed, it's me!"

He grabs her by the wrists, hurting them till they bruise, and pulls her close. His hands are hot like blacktop on an August day. She feebly resists, her folded arms crushed between the two of them. Tears spill down her cheeks.

Aleron, on his knees, says, "You must stop this. It's me, Aleron. There is a cure, Marie. We'll find it back home."

Not looking at him, Marie says, "St. Croix has to pay. We will punish him!"

Reed's scarecrow form hesitates. He scratches at the hollow of his chest. Something is in there after all. Emerging from the straw, fingers of white petals appear. Reed grimaces. He reaches in and digs out the flower—a lily. The birds dive for it. Maybe it was what they had been after all this time. He should surrender it. Let it all end. He's tired of running in these endless fields, falling over himself, coming apart.

Aleron asks in French, "Who did he take from you? Who?"

Marie's angry demeanor falters, "I don't remember. It all drowned."

"This isn't you, Marie. You are kind, not cruel. Remember all the young women you protected." Aleron rises and circles to Marie's right. "We can cure you."

"Cure what?" She refocuses on Reed, moving closer.

Aleron, keeping at arm's length, gets between them, "You want to kill St. Croix? Then come back to me, and we'll do it together. Don't make any more people suffer what St. Croix did to us."

"I don't know you, old man, and I already have everything I need." She flanks Aleron, saying to Reed in English, "Kill her, now."

Lily shakes. Has Reed forgotten her too? She sobs in his arms, the ones that carried her from the fire, carried her over the threshold, now will carry her into death.

Marie grins in triumph as Reed brings Lily closer, opening his fanged mouth. He leans down to bite.

Lily trembles, "I forgive you." Better that she die by him than the others. "I love you."

But it was you. Lily had said that it could have been anyone who saved her, but it was him.

Reed's gloved fingers close around the lily. He won't let birds have it. He won't let them take the best part of himself.

Color returns to his life. "Lily," he says and kisses her.

"*Non, non, non!*" Marie wrenches them apart, then sweeps Lily around, grabbing her by the collar of her shirt. Marie's sharp teeth aim to stab.

The color around him evaporates once more as Reed moves to stop the evil witch once and for all. But Aleron has already stepped behind Marie. His arm goes out, gripping a stake, then the arm swoops underhanded between the two women.

Marie's cry is cut short. She rolls to the ground and Aleron scrambles to her side. Kneeling over her, he weeps.

twenty-three

Trust

K yle recovers from Eddie's drubbing and peels himself off the floor. The ringing in his head dulls and his vision focuses as he tallies the score. His side: all are alive. Other side: Eddie is dead, Marie is staked, and the other three have slunk away into the night. A less than ideal outcome, but acceptable, Kyle assures himself.

He notes a tearful Lily clings to Reed, her attention on Aleron, who sobs over Marie's prone form. Lily doesn't notice Reed's hungry features. His dull black eyes fix on Lily, perhaps her white throat. Fangs appear, daggers ready to tear the gentleness there. Reed's an addict ready to give away the best of himself for one more hit.

Kyle cleaves the pair before either realize what he is doing. He claps his hand on the back of Reed's neck, grabbing the collar of his shirt. Without a word, he pulls Reed into the bedroom and throws the door shut behind them.

Inside the bedroom each man is slapped with the smell of congealing blood and death. The corpses of a husband and a wife spoil Kyle's victory. They are lain on the bed, tucked under the bedspread, positioned so that their hands clasp each others' atop the cover. Kyle sneers at the tender repose in the violent scene, no doubt meant to horrify an unsuspecting

227

maid all the more. How foolish and rash of Marie and her crew. The risk the murders would have put them in had this night turned out different.

Reed can see the macabre spectacle, but it doesn't touch his conscience. He can only think of wanting Lily and needing blood. He returns to the door. When Kyle bars the way, Reed shoves him, but his strength is gone. The fire is gone. "I need to see her!" They are so close now. Not oceans, not cities, but only yards apart. Her faith, his faith, pulled them together.

Kyle says, "I saw the way you were looking at her. You can't be in there now." He feels the weight of his gun near his shoulder, hoping he will not need to use it again. Ever again.

Reed's pride needs to prove Kyle wrong. He can control himself. For Lily's sake, he can do it. He is not weak. He is not a coward. Just some blood, is all. Just a bit. Kyle had said he didn't need to kill. Lily would be okay.

His back to the door, Kyle snaps his fingers in Reed's face, "Think, Reed."

"You stabbed me," Reed says.

"It worked. Lily, your *wife*, is safe." Kyle emphasizes, "As long as you stay in *here*."

Blood. Blood. Blood. Urgency swells inside Reed's mind. He rubs his hands, this time not for nicotine. He's so close to Lily. She's in the next room. Alive. If he doesn't live another moment, he can die satisfied he did that much. But he is alive, such as he is, and that means more moments with her. He just needs to get through this and he can have his colorful world back.

He just needs blood.

Reed takes a small step back. Kyle is right. He was right about Marie—the control she had on Reed's thoughts. She almost succeeded in making him kill Lily. And Kyle's right that he can't be with Lily now. "What do I do?"

Kyle believes he is getting through, but remains watchful. "Take a breath." He guides Reed away from the door, passing the bed, toward a writing desk near the curtained windows. "Let's think this through. Lily is out."

"Yes," Reed says, his words almost atop Kyle's.

Kyle straightens his tie, adjusts his holster, and buttons his suit jacket. With dismay, he wiggles a finger in the tear on the seam of his slacks. Checking his watch, he says "The hotel staff is light and the guests are asleep. In any case, this hotel has seen enough violence." He peeks through the curtains, "Anyone out on the street at this hour is likely more trouble than you can handle."

"Then what?" Reed asks, his voice plaintiff and thin. He's having difficulty thinking. Nicotine cravings never had him by the balls like this. He wonders if the bodies on the bed have drops of blood left. Reed refuses to even look at them. No, he will not defile the dead. Well, maybe. Maybe a few drops still could be found by their wounds.

Kyle wrestles with an imperfect solution. In truth, it is one he had considered an eventuality when he formulated his plans. Now with the possibility in his face, Kyle hesitates. The risk lies in his misjudging of Reed and thereby jeopardizing his ascendancy and more.

But he thinks of Mrs. Whittaker and the evasive feeling he has had since waking. He feels on the cusp of clarity.

Rubbing his chin, he says, "There is another option. We will need to trust each other."

Reed looks hopeful.

Kyle had been wrong to believe money alone made things right—that the money had been for the sakes of the Mrs. Whittakers in his life, rather than for his own. Indulgences to assuage his pain. But by speaking to the widow, by sharing just a little of the truth, he alleviated her suffering, if just a little, if just for a little while. Enough for him to change. It was a breakthrough. His feeling is one of a burden lightened. As though all this time he had been Jacob Marley in chains, and one shackle fell away.

Is he prepared to share more?

"Remember what I had told you earlier back at the Wawa? About sharing ichor?"

"Yes. What are you saying?"

"I'm going to give you some of mine. Only enough to take the edge off. You'll feed properly tomorrow night."

Reed shakes his head.

Kyle says, "I'm not certain about it either, but this—this is easy. Come tomorrow, you're going to have to learn to do things less pleasant."

"I remember how it went with Marie. I still have her in my head, her memories."

"And you will have me in there."

"Controlling me."

"That's the trust part, Reed. I will have, limited, control. For a time. It fades."

"How long?"

"Depends on the person and the amount. Days, weeks, even months, sometimes. The trust goes both ways. You get a bit of me for a time. I don't know what you'll experience. Sometimes it's just emotions, other times its memories or a glimpse of their essence. Keep in mind, you may not like what you see. I would appreciate your considering whatever my past, you think of what I did tonight. And keep it to yourself."

Kyle slips off his brown jacket and folds it over the back of a chair. Rolling up his sleeve, he says "You've come so far, just this last mile." He holds out his arm, pale and strong, with red hairs glinting in the lamp light.

Guided by Kyle to sit in the chair, Reed hesitates when taking hold of Kyle's bare arm. He did this before. He started this new life drinking the substance from Marie. But the context is different. Now he has to bite his—keeper? ally? friend?—Kyle's wrist.

"No time to be squeamish, Reed."

"I'm not."

Goaded, Reed bites. His fangs puncture the cold red-haired skin, lips seal around the wound, and his tongue laps the oily ichor.

The ichor affects Reed immediately. Perhaps because he is prepared this time, willing even, and perhaps more likely, his deep need for it, the taste, the experience is almost euphoric. It isn't like food. A thick ribeye, flavorful, marbled morsels of fat that crank up the deliciousness, doesn't sate, doesn't satisfy in way this ichor does. It zaps away the mental fog. Thinking sharper, the feeling of aliveness, and also power. It is a feeling to hold onto.

"That's enough," Kyle says firmly, twisting his arm.

Reed let's Kyle's arm go and turns away. Life's colors return and his fangs recede. He feels nearly as potent as the previous night. So much like a drug, perhaps a shot of cocaine or heroin? He's buzzed with energy. And as with Marie, alien memories rush into his mind that Reed barely comprehends. He would have continued drinking if Kyle hadn't stopped him.

Kyle flexes his hand. The twin wounds close up. He watches Reed. "Remember what I said. I'm different now."

Reed doesn't look at him. Instead he opens the door.

***

"Word of advice, Mal: when someone swings at you, you duck," Michael says while helping Malcolm up from his spot on an overturned couch. Distracting himself from the grim scene—the dead and the griev-ing—Michael tries to unsee what he just witnessed moments before. He had glimpsed Reed and Eddie tear at each other, reared up like evenly matched grizzlies. You don't get in the middle of that fight. Then some-thing happened. The Brit, the one who cramped Michael's style earlier, screamed in ultimate pain. He looked as though he was being barbecued from the inside. A portion of neck and lower cheek blistered like cheese in a fondue pot. The stuff that disturbs one's sleep.

Michael supposes he can understand why Reed had done what he did. He's inexperienced and fighting for his wife as much as himself. Even so, Michael feels unsettled and will be careful around Reed in the future.

Seeing Malcolm steady on his feet, he says, "Too bad we don't keep scars."

"How so?" Malcolm asks while brushing his brown hair from his eyes.

"War wound. Badge of courage."

"*Schmisse*. A bragging scar resulting from a duel," Malcolm nods. Though he did little to adequately defend himself or Mrs. Williams, he feels a rush. An exhilaration of a different kind. The skirmish smashed his shell, leaving him exposed and vulnerable, but he has survived. He feels as though he plunged into the very stories that entertain him. His well-ordered life spun around for a moment.

"A conversation piece. Many women like that. Could have shown yours to Gracie."

"Grace," Malcolm corrects. "She is under no illusion of my pugilis-tic proficiency." Malcolm takes his friend's point. Having a visible sign of tonight would have added to their triumph. Perhaps a line over his right eye—no, his eyeglasses would detract—maybe a crooked nose, or a wide rude gash on the cheek.

"She's not the only one. Sylvia would have been more helpful than you." Michael draws his friend close. "You know, if you had done as Kyle told you to, I could have convinced Marie." He holds up his fingers just spaced apart, "This close."

"I am as surprised as you are. In the moment, I did what seemed right."

"Did you see what Reed did to Eddie? I mean as it happened?"

"I did not."

"Lucky you."

The slam of the communicating door draws their attention across the room.

***

The door slam causes Lily to reconsider following Reed and the other man into the bedroom. With an eye to the door, she kneels beside Aleron, hugging him as he sobs over Marie's body. *Reed will be fine, we both will be, now that Marie is dead.*

A scowl creases Lily's face for a moment. She finds it difficult for her to imagine the woman was ever the loving fiancée Aleron described. While tied to a chair, Lily had seen Marie slash into the flesh of the poor woman, exulting in her blood as though it was rain come to a parched land. An unconscionable act. What madness had driven her all this time? She truly forgot Aleron, her faith, her love, her very humanity. Is Aleron correct, that her soul got lost in a dark maze? So lost that she was no longer aware of her circumstances, blindly lashing out at the darkness.

And just a moment ago, Reed had been there with Marie. His pitiless eyes were windows to that darkness. Oh, if they had not found Reed tonight, how many days would he have been able to hold on to himself? Would she have the strength to put a stake into Reed as Aleron has done to Marie? Thank God, and thank Aleron, the question is now moot. Her admiration for Aleron swells and she feels a sudden shame for not only doubting him, but misjudging his character when they first met. She kisses his temple, "I am very sorry."

Sorry for him, but not Marie. Lily never would have believed she, in her deepest heart, would wish someone dead, but here she is. Not a Christian attitude. Lily's grandmother would admonish her to forgive Marie. Lily would counter that Marie doesn't deserve it. Grandmother would say, such people are those who need forgiveness the most. Maybe Lily will pray for Marie's soul. But not now.

Aleron grows quiet and nods softly as though answering unheard questions.

Lily's nose catches Reed's scent and she hurries to her feet to greet him. Only it's Eduardo Vega, the Latin man who seems to know Lily and her family. He's handsome in that sharp suit of his. The interpreter beside him puts on his tortoiseshell eyeglasses.

"I thought you were my husband," Lily says to Mr. Vega, "You wear the same cologne."

"He is a man of superior taste, as evidenced by you," Mr. Vega says in a cultured voice. Despite having been in a fist fight, the man seems collected, as though Lily and he are at a dinner party and he had to step out for a phone call and now just returned. She smiles at the compliment.

He asks her, "Are you injured?"

She had forgotten about her wrists and fingers and flexes them. Shaking her head, she says, "Excuse me, but who are you?"

"Excuse us for not properly introducing ourselves. I am Michael. And this is my friend, Malcolm."

"Professor Malcolm Gold," the other man says. "A pleasure to see you out of those bonds."

"Michael?" Lily says. Did she mishear his name?

Ignoring her confusion, Michael Vega says, "The one in there with your husband is Kyle Dowd."

"But how? Why are you here?" Though she heard the entire conversation before the fight, she didn't understand what they were talking about.

"We met your husband, and Aleron here, some hours before. Kyle designed this rescue plan."

"But you know of my family? I'm embarrassed to say that I think I remember you, but not from where or when."

"Don't trouble yourself. Important thing is that you are alive."

Lily trips over her words. So many questions to get out at once. Pointing to the door, she says, "Will they be in there—" The door opens. "—long?"

Lily and Reed rush toward each other. She hugs her husband tightly, squeezing out fresh tears. Reed holds on, trembling as well. Mute, they embrace, simply relieved and happy and bewildered and tired.

Lily is in these arms again. Like home. Shelter from bitter winds that have battered her these days and nights. As though blind, Lily uses her hands to recollect the map of his body; she feels the iron strong shoulders, solid back, sinewy arms, the topography that is uniquely his. He's solid and warm. The slight dark stubble around his mouth, along the jaw. The arms that held her atop the Eiffel Tower and lifted her in the suite.

Kyle stalks out of the bedroom, all business, saying to the room, "Don't go in there. And don't touch anything here." He points to the couple, "You have one minute." He waves Michael, Malcolm, and Aleron into the hall while getting out his phone. Malcolm translates Aleron's questions for Kyle as they leave.

"I'm so sorry, Lil," Reed whispers.

She shushes him. "I knew you'd come, Reed. You save people. It's what you do."

Reed's hands hold Lily's face, "They told me you were dead. I shouldn't have believed them, but I didn't know what to do. I'm so sorry to have left you. You must have been so scared."

She can hear anger rising in his voice. "Reed, we're here now. Together. That's all that matters. I love you."

But Reed can't shake the feeling that the flaw remains. Though justified, he can't help but recall a part of him relished the violence. Can she love that part of him?

Reading his mind, she says, "I know you're different now. But not where it matters most to me. And we can fix the rest."

***

"What the hell went on here?" Mr. Webb bends over the corpse of Eddie, wrinkling his piebald mustache.

Mr. Ashton emerges from the adjoining room, having seen the blood-drained bodies of the wife and husband.

"This is unacceptable, Brother Kyle," Mr. Ashton says, not in a tone of reprimand, but of weariness. "We have enough with one body. Now you give us four more."

Kyle describes what occurred in the suite and the events that led to it becoming an abattoir. "We made every effort to come to an accord."

After the fighting ceased, Kyle directed those left standing to leave discreetly. Meanwhile, he reached out to Mr. Ashton and made sure to hang the DO NOT DISTURB sign on the door knob.

Mr. Ashton says, "I had been quite mistaken. I should have destroyed Mr. Williams from the start."

Kyle responds, "Frankly, I wouldn't have cared if you had. But now, now I know different." The man impressed Kyle with his ramrod integrity, indefatigable will, and undying love for his wife. "He's a good man, Brother Alcott. I trust him. He came through when it mattered. And now that he knows his wife is alive and safe, he has every incentive to learn from us. From me."

With dawn coming in a few hours, Mr. Ashton soon will have to leave matters to Mr. Webb. They check on the identities of the renters and debate on cover stories. That this is a luxury suite indicates the couple had money. Money will be missed.

"You have three suspects." Kyle suggests pinning the crime on those who fled: Ron, Clarice, and Jean-Paul. "Make sure to clean the security tapes of everyone else who came here." He says to Mr. Webb, "Do what you want with Eddie, but make preparations to ship Marie back home."

***

"He put a stake in your heart?" Lily asks over a yawn. She pauses from sweeping shards of glass into a dust pan. "How are you okay?"

Reed unbuttons his shirt for both of them to see his unmarked chest. "I just am." He picks up a pair of scissors. Cutting heavy black garbage bags into rectangles, he says, "One minute, I thought I was dead. Then I woke in the trunk of a classic car."

"And Marie…" Lily's lips twist realizing now that she had been mistaken to believe Marie died. In the penthouse floor hallway, Kyle explained that he would remain to clean up, and assured Aleron that he would take care of Marie. He spoke with authority that Lily didn't question. She was relieved to leave the horror scene.

Malcolm drove everyone home. During the ride, Aleron remained silent, his wet red eyes fixed on the back of the seat before him. Words failed Lily as well. She wanted to be of comfort to him, but she dared not touch him, afraid he would shatter under her fingers. Or snarl, leveling a furious gaze on her. After all, the idea of pursuing Reed to America had been hers and she convinced him to follow. Maybe he regretted involving himself, regretted rescuing her in the park. At her door, Aleron hugged her in one great sigh before taking his travel bag into the apartment.

The embrace caught her off guard. She held tight, trembling while feeling relief.

Soon after, in the quiet of the car, her grandmother's voice came to her. "You cannot hold grudges Lily-love," she would often tell Lily when she was cross with Charlie and his torments. "They call it holding a grudge because it is a very heavy stone that you must carry everywhere. You only wear yourself out. You have to put it down, and the way to do that is to forgive. You may not feel like it, but Charlie needs it. You both do. Forgive your brother."

Lily's fingers worried the hem of her blouse and her heart struggled to heed her grandmother's admonition. This wasn't a case of hair shorn off a beloved doll—Marie's actions had done real, devastating harm.

Lily breathed out, breathed in, out and in.

But Aleron had been right: Marie was a victim too. Marie hadn't escaped the dark maze.

Reed had.

With Reed beside her, alive, she searched her husband's face, his square set jaw, the stubble on the chin. She wondered what he was thinking, but not enough to break the silence. As she stroked the back of his hand, feeling the solidity of him, her breathing steadied.

Reed flipped his hand over, catching her fingers. He gave a reassuring squeeze. She squeezed back.

And so, Lily offered her grandmother a compromise. She would pray on forgiving Marie.

In his bedroom, Reed says, "I hate this shirt." With a glance he finds the crushed cigarette pack still in the breast pocket. He removes the shirt and tosses it all into the waste bin.

Lily assists him in stapling the trimmed bags over the broken window, blocking out the view and the sunlight that will come. They add a second layer just to be sure. Then a third.

Come morning, I'd kill myself, Mr. Webb had said.

Not going to happen. He can't take his eyes off Lily, feeling close and distant at the same time. She saved his life.

Lily's yawns deepen. He feels wide awake.

"You need to sleep," he says.

"I can now that you'll be with me."

Reed strips off his slacks and tosses it in after the shirt. Socks and underwear too. Need to incinerate that shit.

He gets his own briefs from a drawer then slips into his own bed and reaches for Lily.

Under the warm covers, she scoots close, tucking her head into his shoulder. Another yawn or two. Weird thoughts. Then she shakes, tittering.

"What's funny?"

"I'm just thinking on how Aleron saved me." Giggles now. "And how you hated the taxi rides."

Reed smirks, though not fully getting it. By the time Lily finishes describing Aleron's hell-for-leather driving in the park and along the Seine, they're both in fits.

After the laughter passes, Reed says, "What do we do now?" Now meaning their future.

"As far as anyone knows, we are still in France. For the time being, you will stick with Kyle and learn all you can so you won't hurt anyone, especially yourself."

"And you?" Reed asks.

Lily says, "You're sick. I'm going to find a way to make you well again."

Reed doesn't feel sick. To believe Marie and Eddie, they're gods. Or according to Alcott and Kyle, they're members of an elite society. But he doesn't say this aloud. And here he goes again, holding back, not sharing with Lily. How can he express what he is feeling without frightening her? He feels steady, strong, vital. But also apart. He has glimpsed a shadow world that few human beings know exists. And he is in that world now. He is not human and he is not sick. A shaft of wood was embedded in his chest, its tip punctured his heart, but here he lays, not strained in the least.

Lily says, "I don't understand everything, but we promised to be there for each other. Tomorrow will take care of itself."

Reed chooses to believe her. Her resolve dwarfs his doubts. He bats them away along with regret and thoughts of blood. All that matters is holding Lily and knowing she is safe. He listens to Lily yawn into slumber and feels her human signs grow drowsy. He curls around her as the scarecrow huddles over the flower, protecting the best of himself and watchful of the circling darkness.

Acknowledgments

I am deeply grateful to God for the wonderful, remarkable people in my life. First, to Monica, my best friend, my wife, my beloved. Thank you for sharing me with this crazy project and believing in me all the way through it. I'm in awe of you. To our family: Bubbe Sandy; Carole and David; Lynn and Gary; Zachary, Lauren, and Curt; Michelle, Seth, Harrison, and Mikey; Lauren, Andy, Samantha, and Lily; friends: Alan, Steve, and Rich; and those alive in our hearts: Zayde David, Zayde Herman, and Bubbe Esther.

To members of my critique group for their well-considered, thorough, and spot-on feedback draft after draft. Tom Fuhrman, Libby Hall, Andrea Tatjana, and Mary Miley Theobald, I couldn't have done this without you.

Also cheers to my fellow scribblers of James River Writers who celebrate each other's success as their own.

To Erica Orloff, who not only is a phenomenal editor, but now my dear friend. I am deeply in your debt for your discerning advice that was humbling and heartening. Your exclamation marks were treasures!!

To my beta readers and technical advisers, much appreciation for Rishonda Anthony, Bill Blume, Karen Chase, Lindsay Chudzik, Eugene Pogue, Captain J.R. Powers, Robert Toms, and Chris Williams. Any inaccuracies are entirely my own.

Thank you to the super Silver Diner staff for the good coffee and great company.

And thank you, the reader.

Author's Note

I hope you have enjoyed your introduction to the world of *The Shadowless*, a series set in Philadelphia. My plan is that *Shadows Within* begins this core set of novels interspersed with short stories, which may offer different points-of-view that deepen the larger plot, spotlight a character in a stand-alone tale, or experiment with style, setting, and genre.

Writing Book Two is underway, which picks up where we left off a few pages ago. After all, Reed's ordeal has only begun. At the threshold, he must now step forward into the larger world that is the Society of Brandywine, filled with its colorful members, as well as its fractious outsiders, such as the Rotters and Roxy Marchetti.

Still coming to grips with his inhuman nature, Reed has much to learn. Is there a way to restore his humanity? Lily is determined to find one. And Kyle, Malcolm, and Michael still have Reed's back, right?

To keep up with the latest, visit TheShadowless.com.

Also, subscribe to my monthly newsletter, The Scrapple, at jpcane.com/newsletter.

And if you liked what you just read, please share your thoughts on social media, in reviews, and with me at jpcane.com.

Thank you, kindly!

J.P. Cane
September 2017

About the Author

J.P. Cane is a long-time reader and first-time writer of vampire stories. His debut novel, *Shadows Within*, begins *The Shadowless* series, mostly set in his hometown of Philadelphia. He hosts a podcast on writing and enjoys supporting fellow writers. He and his wife live in Virginia.

Contact him at jpcane.com.

www.ingramcontent.com/pod-product-compliance
Lightning Source LLC
Chambersburg PA
CBHW021008120726
47905CB00009B/2917